DEATH IN THE MIST

JO ALLEN

AUTHOR'S NOTE

All of the characters in this book are figments of my imagination and bear no resemblance to anyone alive or dead.

The same can't be said for the locations. Many are real but others are not. As always, I've taken several liberties with geography, mainly because I have a superstitious dread of setting a murder in a real building without the express permission of the homeowner, but also because I didn't want to accidentally refer to a real character in a real place or property. So, for example, you won't find either Jude's home village of Wasby or the village of Blacksty on the map and while Bowscale Fell and the tarn are very much real, Mosedale Barn is not.

Although I've taken these liberties with the details I've tried to remain true to the overwhelming and inspiring beauty of the Cumbrian landscape. I hope the many fans of the Lake District will understand, and can find it in their hearts to forgive me for these deliberate mistakes.

ONE

It was an hour before dawn and the edgeland between the fells and the dale sagged under a blanket of freezing fog. As Jude Satterthwaite drove through Mungrisdale, on his way home after a long, and only partly fruitful, night the headlights of his Mercedes bounced off the twisting wraiths of fog and back into the car. Other, oncoming, lights reflected off the moist air like those of an alien spaceship, and gave him warning of an advancing vehicle. He pulled over to let it pass.

Jude was a detective and gave everything a second look. He couldn't help it, though sometimes this urge to look more closely was a curse as much as a blessing. The car coming towards him was a ten-year-old silver Renault, with a dented side panel and its number plate almost obscured by mud, though still (he noted) just about legal. The driver was a woman, with a knitted hat pulled down over her hair, and she was clutching the steering wheel and peering into the fog as he had done. As she eased the Renault past him, squeezing it dangerously close to the dry stone wall that bounded the road, she gave him a furtive glance, exactly

1

like the ones his ex-girlfriend would give him when they met, unable to ignore him but not keen to engage. He allowed himself a wry smile at the thought, touched the accelerator and pulled away.

Barely thirty seconds after he'd moved on, more lights warned him to pull over — a tractor, this time, but fortunately he'd moved beyond the section of narrow road where the walls had forced him so close to the Renault. Sighing, he pulled into the lay-by where, in better weather, walkers parked to head up to Carrock or Bowscale Fells. As the tractor rumbled past, bouncing a trailer of animal feed behind it, he finally acknowledged the futility of this slow crawl through the countryside. From here it would be stop-start all the way from Mungrisdale to Penrith as the agricultural community woke up and went about its business.

He reached across to the passenger seat to retrieve the flask of coffee he'd not had time to drink, unscrewed the lid and slopped a sad quantity of thick black liquid into it. Then he picked up his phone and dialled. 'Doddsy. Enjoyed a good night's sleep down in the big city, I hope? It's more than I did. You owe me, pal. Big style.'

At the other end of the phone his long-term colleague and best friend laughed. 'Aye, I know. Thanks. And yes, I slept like a baby. Did you have good hunting?'

Jude reviewed the night's work, rapidly and clinically, before he answered. 'Mixed. Two in custody, possession with intent.' Further charges would surely follow. 'They're just the small fry, though.'

'Any drugs?'

'As expected. We found several kilos of what looks like crack cocaine. It was worth losing a night's sleep to get that lot off the streets, but the main men never showed.' A frown formed on his brow. He hated a job left incomplete; if the significant actors in the drug-running lines were happy to leave their subordinates to walk into a police trap and take the rap, it was either because the couriers knew nothing or their bosses were confident they were too scared to tell.

Still, it wasn't his problem. The lead came from the Merseyside force, where the drugs had originated, and his part in the operation was limited to spending a cold winter night staking out a barn in the bleakness of Mungrisdale. He'd been better prepared for it than his city-based colleagues, that was for sure.

'They must have seen something and steered clear.' At the other end of the line Doddsy's fractious sigh echoed Jude's own mood. 'We'll get them in the end.'

'Let's hope so.' Jude suppressed a yawn as another tractor went by. Caught in its headlights on the other side of the road, a lone sheep stared at him with the same kind of baffled fascination the woman in the Renault had shown him. It was seven a.m. and the place felt busier than on a Bank Holiday Sunday. 'Thank God it's your problem and I'm just the hired help.'

'No worries, son. You can leave it with me, now. I'll be back in the office by noon.' Doddsy, the junior officer of the two, was the man on the job but a court case in London had kept him out of town for the crucial moments. The rattle of trains in the background to the call and the blaring of a station announcer at Euston gave away his location. It would have been a late night and an early start for him, too.

'I always did like spending a January night in a ditch at the back end of the Lakes.' Jude swirled the tepid coffee round in the top of the flask and swigged it down. 'You'll have my report on your desk as soon as I've had some sleep. Sir.'

Doddsy laughed. A day down in London must have

seemed like a holiday, even if it had involved a court case and an evening of paperwork. 'Take the rest of the day off, lad.'

The next day — this day — was a rest day. If the lead officers on the case hadn't held out for hours in the vain hope of hauling in the main targets, Jude might have been back in his bed in time to save his day off. 'I'll see you tomorrow, then.'

With seven o'clock, the first flush of dawn crept up over the wooded hills of the Greystoke estate away to his left. Ending the call, Jude waited a moment before heading home. The glow of dawn behind a hillside was always alluring, even in this shifting, grey fog. With the higher slopes in the clutch of the cloud, it was a day to stick to the low fells; on another day he might have been tempted to linger and take a brisk hike up to Bowscale Tarn or along Grainsgill Beck to blow the cobwebs away. Discretion — or age, or exhaustion, or just plain world-weariness — got the better of him and he screwed the lid back on the flask, though he waited a while before starting the engine. It had been a long night.

'I'm not as young as I was,' he said, aloud. He wasn't a dozen miles from home, but the narrow lanes of the valley floor were as twisted and tricky as a baited trap in the half light, with a gloss of ice lying like a void in their shadowed bends. It would be wise to wait for the caffeine to kick in before he negotiated them and took the slow road round the bare shoulder of Berrier Hill.

The windscreen misted up in the weak heat of the coffee. On a whim he got out and stretched, turning to see what he could see while it cleared. Maybe the main men hadn't gone. Maybe they'd hung around to see what had happened, who'd been caught. There were only two in custody. Others must have made their escape.

4

An eerie silence saturated the land. Further down the road, red brake lights showed a car — maybe the Renault — parked in a scrape at the roadside that passed for a lay-by, a hundred yards or so behind him. Jude allowed himself a wry smile. He might be in the habit of looking twice at everything, and anyone would have had reason to look twice at him, too, parked up by the side of the road looking as furtive as the criminals who'd escaped him, but something about the woman had caught his attention. It had been the wariness with which she'd looked at him, not even raising a hand to acknowledge him in a community where most folk gave even strangers a cheery wave.

His mind sharpened by caffeine and a top-up of fresh air, he got back into the Mercedes. As he pulled out from the parking space he passed another figure — a walker this time, with a small rucksack on his back, muffled in scarf, hat and gloves. It was a man, checking his phone as he walked so the light from the screen briefly illuminated his face.

Jude took that habitual second look, because you never knew and either of these two strangers might be the criminal mastermind behind the drugs gang, waiting for the daylight to check out what was left of this rural outpost of their operation. More likely they were just hillwalking enthusiasts, snatching at every hour of daylight to feed their obsession, bent on ticking another Wainwright off their list.

He understood the lure of the fells. He'd been like that himself one day, before time and duty had overridden him. He sighed and turned the car towards home.

TWO

'Okay, Emmy?'

'Fine. Just fine.'

The mist that plagued Mosedale was as thick as it had been on the day when Luke hadn't come home, but the well-trodden path led Emmy and Tino faithfully onwards through the approaching dawn. Even if it hadn't, even if she'd been blindfolded or sleepwalking, Emmy knew her steps would have taken her there. Every year on this day, for fifteen painful years, she'd taken this path in good weather and in bad, one day famously running just ahead of a blizzard. She took it on many more nights, in her dreams.

In her dreams, Luke always came back. In her dreams she rounded the corner below the outflow, just as she was about to do, and he was sitting on the rock where the beck tumbled down from the tarn, waiting for her with his sweet, childlike grin.

Dreams lied, so often and at so many levels. Latterly her son had shown her very little of that open, boyish smile, and a teenage scowl had been permanently in evidence. After his disappearance, she chose to forget those things. Fifteen years on, she remembered only the joy of his presence and the aching pain of his absence.

They scaled the last few yards. A tall lip of rock hid Bowscale Tarn from view; above them, Bowscale Fell crouched like a predator in ambush. Leaving Tino behind, Emmy forged forwards, pushing to be there before him, and as he always did he hung back and let her reach the spot first. Despite herself, the sombreness of the occasion, the gloom of the weather, she couldn't suppress an affectionate smile. Each year cost her a little more in effort but Tino was youthful in his outlook, barely changed since the day they'd married, bar a few grey hairs.

On the lip of the scooped-out dip of rock, she paused. The crag that sheltered the tarn from sun and wind was patched with snow, streaked brown with thin soil washed down from above. The surface of the water below it was still and menacing, black with the absence of light.

They said the sun never reached it. They said its depths were occupied by two immortal fishes. It was fifty feet deep and even in good weather it looked as if it went down for ever, to the very centre of the Earth. It was cold and it was dangerous. She swallowed back a tear.

In a scattering of small stones, Tino jumped along the last few yards to stand beside her. 'All right?'

She nodded. He'd recognise the lie but she didn't think he was asking her, only seeking reassurance. Like Emmy herself, he was sure everything would be all right. One day the great load of guilt she'd borne during every moment since they'd come to tell her they'd found her son's bicycle by the side of the road would fall away, and she would find redemption and salvation.

And forgiveness. Of all of those, forgiveness was the

most important and the most elusive. 'And you? Are you all right?'

'Of course.'

That was a lie, too. Tino was a positive, bubbly character, as light of heart and word as he was of step, but whatever he pretended, the optimism that carried him through the world always abandoned him on the anniversary of Luke's disappearance. *Tino and I share so many lies*, she thought.

'Here.' He held out the half a dozen daffodils she'd brought with her and which he had carried for the last half a mile or so to allow her an easier scramble up the final stretch.

She took them. This pathetic gesture was all they had left, a sad pantomime that mimicked all they'd never be able to do for their son. It was no wonder they came in secret; their neighbours would only mock them. She advanced the few steps to the shore of the tarn. There was a frill of ice at the edge of it. She shivered and drew back.

'Wait. I brought something to put them in.' He took off his rucksack, dug around in it and fished out a jam jar, which he dipped into the still water. As he turned back to her, the ripples rolled out from the edge and broke over a drowned object, fanning out across the dead water. For a moment they stared at its mesmerising pattern and he seemed to sense her hesitancy. 'Shall I?'

'I'll do it.' She peeled off her gloves, dropped them on the wet grass and rammed the stems of the barely-budded flowers into the jar. 'These were the best I could manage. It's early for them yet.'

'You should have said. I could have got some at the garage.'

Garage daffodils, false yellow, flown in from the Isles of Scilly. Emmy turned her nose up at the thought. She liked to bring them from the garden, forcing them under cloches so they were ready in time, but it had been a harsh winter. 'These were the best I could find.' She'd set the bulbs in a sheltered corner of the orchard, where they could capture the low sun in the middle of the day, the spot where Luke and his friends had built summer dens, before they grew too old for it and he stopped bringing his friends home. She'd thought of that when the police had come, and had told them. *He likes to hide.* And they'd looked at her, knowing as well as she'd done that hope was wasted on a teenager as wayward as Luke.

Tino waited while she placed the jam jar on the water's edge but he leaned down to wedge it in place and their ungloved hands, red with the cold, touched and somehow stayed together as they straightened up.

'Shall we pray?' he asked, as he always did.

'You do it.' Truth be told, Emmy's relationship with God always stilled on this day. He never came to Bowscale Tarn and when she stood there only the human, flawed Tino offered her a crumb of comfort. Nevertheless, they played out this charade. She closed her eyes while he intoned a prayer, thinking of the last time she'd seen Luke, watched him swinging a long thin leg over the crossbar of his bike and pedalling down the hill without a word of where he was going or why, or who he was going to see, or when he planned to be back.

The police had gently suggested he might not have intended to come back. Emmy shook her head at the memory, then pulled herself back together, as she always did. Without her faith she'd never have made it through the pain and the guilt and the loss, but faith was the rock to which she clung and it would see her through. When she left this place that God had forsaken she'd find Him again and He would help her.

'Amen!' she said, firmly, when Tino had finished, and then he was looking at her and the little smile hovering on his lips showed that he knew what was in her head.

'I pray for Luke all the time,' she said, by way of explanation. 'But it's strange. Today I so desperately wanted to believe he was here.' Though he wasn't. The police had sent divers down into those black depths and there had been nothing in there, not even the immortal fishes.

'Yes. I know.'

Luke had been his child, too. It wasn't that she forgot that, though time had moved on and Emmy and Tino's marriage had been wrecked on its trauma and uncertainty. She was married again, now. Her second husband was determined to carry the burden for her but only made it increasingly hard for her to remember that other people had loved Luke and lost him, too. Not only Tino, who shared her feelings with discretion and never-ending patience, but her parents, and even Chloe. She stopped to think of Luke's teenage sweetheart and the smile was a bitter one. Their relationship might have lasted but the chances were that it would have foundered, in its own time. In the end what Chloe had acquired from it was a father-less child and a victimhood earned by timing, like a child at a birthday party, left holding the parcel when the music stopped. It hadn't been love.

Or had it? Who knew what love was? The only thing she could be sure of was that it was complicated and it tied you more tightly than you thought possible to people you were better off without. She turned back to Tino. 'Should we go?'

'Best to,' he said, still staring at the water. The faintest breeze slid down the steep headwall, rolling over the crags, sending a pitter-patter of light over the surface of the tarn, lifting a lock of his greying hair. 'You probably want to be away from here before anyone wonders where you've got to.'

'Rob's away to Manchester for the day,' she said, almost breathless with emotion. 'I took him to the station first thing, so it was easier than it usually is.'

You could come back to the house, she wanted to say, *or I could come to yours*. The second would be a better option, because he lived a little out of the village and they were less likely to be seen. For a moment she hoped, but he was already shaking his head. 'Best not.'

He was right, of course, but she could tell by looking at him that he wanted her as much as she wanted him. If it wasn't so cold they could have come together there — not beside the tarn itself where there was always a risk of being interrupted by a passing stranger, but beyond the shoulder of the hill where no-one ever came. 'I know. Someone will see us and we can't risk that.'

'If he's away all day, we don't have to hurry back. Maybe we could go somewhere for a coffee, at the very least. Let me think. I have client meetings. I could shift them.' He moved closer to her.

Her breath came out in a long sigh, crystals on the air that only merged into the mist. She should never have left him. She should never have married Rob. Her life was one mistake after another, and when she had what she wanted she hadn't realised, and had ended by throwing it all away. If only she had the courage to put things right.

'Em,' he said, and kissed her.

She kept her lips closed to begin with, but only because she loved the way he pressed on them, the sense of urgency and desire. After a second she gave in, a long, slow surrender all the sweeter for knowing the moment would come. The first few pilgrimages to the tarn had been made in the awkward silence of divorce and shared loss, but over the years they'd settled into a comfortable partnership in Luke's absence. She and Tino understood one another far better than she and Rob ever would, and this kiss was part of their mourning ritual.

'We'll go, then,' he said, releasing her. And, turning back, he cast a final look over the glassy water. 'Does Rob know you're here?'

'I don't know. He knows I go out by myself on the anniversary.' For the first few years he'd tried to insist on looking after her but latterly it seemed to dawn on him that she preferred to spend it without him. His trip to Manchester wasn't, as far she she could gather, entirely necessary. 'I think he made himself scarce.' For the first time she realised that Rob might have things to feel guilty about, too. Throughout their marriage he'd come across as a man with a glossy confidence in God and in the right thing to do, and that left him no room for a troubled conscience. Maybe, after all, he was getting older and thinking, as she was, about the mistakes he'd made.

Driven by some impulse she didn't understand, she bent and picked up a chunk of soft grey stone, sharp-edged and freshly-fallen from the rocks that buttressed the path and held back the water. From somewhere in the cloud a harsh cry of a bird — a crow of some kind — was the only sign of any living creature apart from their two selves.

'What are you doing, Emmy? Come away. We've probably hung around here too long already.'

The cloud broke and a Jacob's ladder of sunlight spilled down like a spotlight onto the jar of daffodils, before the bird broke the weak sunbeam and its shadow fluttered over her soul. With a sudden chill, Emmy tossed the rock as far as she could into the centre of the tarn. It broke the surface and went under, though not as she'd expected. There was a strange disturbance just under the water, as though something was there. 'Tino, what's that?'

'It doesn't matter. Let's get back down.'

'But there's something in the water. How can there be? It's supposed to be deep.' But maybe it was deep only in the centre. Who knew if there were shallows? Fifteen years earlier she hadn't paid attention to the details, caring only about what the tarn had turned out not to hold. 'Look. That's really odd. And what's that? Surely it can't be a goldfish?'

He'd been back at the lip of the tarn, impatient to be away, but at that he turned back and looked where she pointed, at a curl of orange just below the surface, blurred by the water. On second glance it was far too big to be a fish. 'It's a guy rope.'

'But what's it doing in there?'

'Some vandal couldn't be bothered to take it home, I suppose.'

Emmy stepped to the edge of the water and out on to a flat stone that stood like an island a few inches from solid ground, then bent down and reached out for the curl of orange.

'Just leave it. We can't take it back down with us.'

'Why not, if it's only a bit of rope?' She closed her fingers on it, tightened up and tugged. There was a weight at the end of it, playing on her fingers like an angler's line. 'Do you think I've caught one of the immortal fishes?' she asked, and laughed.

'Em. Just leave it.'

She couldn't leave it now. She tugged again and whatever it was broke away and jerked towards her. Jumping back from the rock to the path, she dropped the nylon rope and it splashed back into the water, but what it was attached to kept coming, drifting serenely towards them under its own momentum. Olive green nylon. She reached out again and got a grip of it, gave an impatient tug. It was heavy, far too heavy to be an abandoned tent.

Now, at last, she understood why he'd been so alarmed. 'Oh God. Tino. There's something in it.' She couldn't bring herself to say *someone*, but that was what she thought. He was thinking it, too; his face had gone cold and graven like the crags above them. And they shared the thought, that this was what might have happened to Luke all those years before. Now it had happened to someone else and they, through the cruellest, most spiteful twist of fate, were the ones to discover it.

Oh God, Emmy said to her absent saviour, with more than a little irritation, *why did You have to do this? Haven't I suffered enough?* 'Should we call the police?'

'No. Let's just go.' He took her arm.

'But we can't leave—'

'Someone else will come up here and find it. A walker. A birdwatcher. Leave it for them.'

No-one in their right minds would go walking up such a dreary path on a day like this. And there were no birds, other than that single, ill-omened crow. 'We can't just walk away and leave it.'

'Of course we can. I don't want to, either. But if we call the police we'll have to explain what we're doing here, and that could get complicated.'

'Why? We aren't doing anything wrong.'

'No. But it won't stop with the police, will it? If they want to talk to us you're going to have to explain yourself to Rob.'

She was silent. She loved Rob, but it was hardly surprising that her second husband's one blind spot was in relation to his predecessor. She could understand it. 'Perhaps just one of us…'

For a moment she stood there, watching him and waiting for him to offer to stay or be the one who'd call the police, deflecting the attention of the village from who he might have been with up at Bowscale Tarn, but he didn't. Instead, he took another shuffling step along the path, already dropping a foot or so below her on the beginning of the descent to Mosedale. 'You do it, then. If you think you need to.'

'I will.' Her cold, wet fingers closed on the phone in her pocket. She had signal. Thank goodness.

'At least give me time to get away,' he said, with anxiety in his voice.

She regarded him for the very first time with disappointment. She didn't want people to know she was out with Tino without Rob's knowledge, and the damage would be huge if the village gossips got hold of it, but she wasn't like the rest of them. She knew what had to be done. If there was a risk she'd have to be the one to take it. If she was right, and some poor soul had come to grief in the icy water, as a human being she had an obligation to restore them to their loved ones as soon as possible. 'How long do you need?'

'Half an hour will get me most of the way down.'

Half an hour with her own thoughts, with the body of a stranger. If it was the only way to balance the right thing and the convenient thing, to help a fellow human and yet save her reputation, then she would do it. But she knew she'd spend the half hour bitterly disappointed with his abandonment of her, rather than in quiet communication with their lost son.

It was bright, now, and the daylight was strong and firm, but the mist still blanketed the fell top and hung around the water like smoke. Emmy focussed her attention on the daffodils and tried to pray, but all she could think about was Luke and what might have happened to him that last day.

Her dream would be different tonight. Tonight she would dream it was Luke's body that she discovered under the shadow of the crags.

THREE

By the time Ashleigh O'Halloran had managed to hike her way up the fellside, the mist had thinned enough for a helicopter to land on the elevated area of flat land adjacent to Bowscale Tarn. Before long it would remove the man's body which the tent had turned out to contain, and be barely a hum in the sky on its way to the mortuary in Carlisle. Ashleigh's route, from the dead-end road through Mosedale and straight up the hill, was shorter than the one Emmy Leach had taken, but much steeper. Though she was reasonably fit and, these days, a regular hillwalker, it was a tough climb and she took a moment to catch her breath as she reached the top.

A funny one, this, and no mistake, DI Chris Dodd had said when he sent her off to Mosedale to see how the land lay. The local mountain rescue team, who had been first on the scene, reckoned it was a freak accident, but they weren't as naturally suspicious as their emergency service colleagues in the police. Doddsy was never one for overstatement and this was, indeed, a funny one.

Standing on the approach to the tarn, she turned her

back on the uniformed policeman who was politely turning back a pair of middle-aged walkers a couple of hundred yards back along the path, and took stock. A teardrop-shaped glacial lake stretched away under a steep headwall. The slope was concave rather than sheer, and its exposed rock glistened with January ice. Anyone — or anything — falling would have had nowhere to come to rest, even if they'd had their hands free to try and snatch at safety.

There had been wind the previous night but not, Ashleigh thought, anything exceptional, even at the higher levels; the morning had brought that still, heavy fog that had only recently lifted in favour of dull, high cloud. Had the tent been badly-secured and poorly-sited? Had the wild camper, waking confused in the night, somehow managed to catapult himself and his belongings over the edge of the abyss? Or had he been camped on the edge of the tarn, stumbled and drowned without a preceding fall?

She jumped down from her vantage point and strode along the path to where several white-suited crime scene investigators were at work, one of them photographing the mess the mountain rescue team had left on the thin grass of the shore. The body lay beside the water, where the mountain rescue had hauled it out, and Ashleigh was glad that the olive green canvas covered the man's body and concealed his face.

Thank God she didn't need to look too closely with the CSIs on site. Doddsy was obviously in belt-and-braces mode if he thought there was much to be gained from sending a detective to visit a scene so comprehensively trampled it lent itself temptingly to a conclusion of accident, and the constable had everything already as much under control as it could be. She stepped a little closer and addressed the figure with the camera. 'Hi, Tammy. How's it going?'

'Bloody cold,' said the woman, from behind her mask. 'I don't know what I did in a former life to get sent out on this job, but whatever it is, I'm sorry for it. I'm way too old to go lugging my kit up to places like this.'

'Have you found anything interesting?'

'Not yet. We only got here about fifteen minutes ago, and the mountain rescue lads left us a hell of a mess to sort out. But I don't suppose they had much of a choice. They had to get him out of the water, just in case.'

'Can I walk around the tarn?' asked Ashleigh, intrigued.

'No. Everyone tells me it looks like an accident but I always work on the basis that it isn't. I want my team to have a look round and see what's going on and who's been where, before you clodhoppers leave your bootmarks over it.'

Behind the mask, Ashleigh sensed a grin. 'If you won't let me look for myself, you can earn your keep by telling me what's happened. Where do you reckon the tent came from?'

'Up there.' Tammy jerked a gloved finger towards the monochrome crags. A small patch of sunshine had tiptoed across the base of the dale and part of the way up the opposite hill, but the scooped-out bowl of Bowscale Tarn remained in deep shadow. 'You can see where it must have come down the slope. When we're done down here we'll go up and see what there is to see on top, but I'll be surprised if we find anything. There's a path of sorts, but the surface looks pretty loose. There were a couple of fell-runners up it before I got here, I'm told, so if there was anything there they'll have destroyed it.'

Ashleigh made a mental note to check if someone had taken their names. 'There's no other way up there? I'd like a look.'

'Oh, sure, if you want to go a hell of a long way round. It's a bit of a wasted journey for you.' Beneath the mask, Ashleigh again sensed that the smile was friendly. 'At least you got a jolly out of it. You plain clothes lot spend far too much time indoors. It's not good for you.'

Ashleigh looked again, from a secure distance. On the edge of the water, a jam jar of daffodils stood tilted towards the lake. 'What are those? Were they there when you came? They look fresh.'

'Picked this morning, by the look of them. They're hardly out and they haven't had time to wilt.'

Emmy Leach must have brought them, then, unless the deceased had left them there for reasons of his own. 'Is that a note with them?'

'Yep.' Tammy held out her camera and enlarged a photograph she'd taken. 'Here. It's a bit messy.'

The ink on the card had curdled in the damp atmosphere, but it was clear enough. *To darling Luke. Always in our thoughts.* 'I don't think I'll be here long, though, Ash. Whatever happened, there won't be a lot to see. But feel free to come up here on your next rest day if you feel like losing yourself in the wilderness.'

It was hardly worth the effort, Ashleigh told herself, thinking of all the other things she could have done if Doddsy hadn't been so determined she should come up there. She knew what that was. Jude was out of the office and Doddsy, acting in his place, knew as well as the rest of them that their boss always looked for the sinister explana-tion before the simple one. No matter how often they might put out the bland explanation of *cause of death unknown* Jude, more than any of them, began with the assumption of foul play.

Doddsy couldn't have been up to Bowscale recently. If he had he'd have known just how little there would be to see. 'I'll leave you to it, then' she said to Tammy, and headed out past the policeman on watch, without so much as a gnarled tree stump on which to tie his forbidding blue and white plastic tape, and headed down to her main port of call — an interview with Emmy Leach.

Emmy and her husband lived in the village of Blacksty, a cluster of dwellings at the northern end of the Greystoke estate, a bare five miles away from the tarn. As her car crawled up along the road behind a tractor, Ashleigh could clearly see the dark block of Bowscale Fell looming in her wing mirror. Hopefully Emmy wasn't too emotionally fragile; every time she came out of her front door she'd find the stark reminder of what must surely have been a traumatic discovery, confronting her.

She pulled the car up on the verge outside Blacksty Farmhouse, the Leaches' home, and took a moment to look it over. It might once have been a farmhouse in the truest sense but time and modern living had rapidly overtaken it. The square, grey stone frontage of the main building still looked as it might have done a couple of centuries earlier, but what must have been the attached barn now sported picture windows looking out over the fells. In front of the house was a neat garden with a white-painted fence between it and the road. A short, grassy lane at one side led to a cobbled courtyard, where bright planters and pots swathed in horticultural fleece stood around a picnic table and chairs. In the courtyard an old silver Renault and a new black Audi were parked side by side in front of well-kept outbuildings. Beyond them, a wintry garden unrolled up into the shrouded forms of trees in the near distance and disappeared into the mist.

21

After a moment's contemplation of this well-kept, affluent setup, Ashleigh got out of the car and went up the path. The door opened before she got there and a woman, holding back as if to keep in the shadow, stepped aside to wave her in. 'You're the police? About this morning? I'm Emmy Leach.'

'Detective Sergeant O'Halloran.' Ashleigh flashed her warrant card but Emmy Leach barely gave it a glance. Instead she turned and led the way into the kitchen, where she waved Ashleigh to a seat at the breakfast bar.

'Do have a seat, Sergeant. The kettle's just boiled.' Her words were confident and her bearing disciplined, but her eyes were wary. 'I suppose you want me to go over what happened.'

'Yes, though hopefully it won't take long.' Ashleigh settled herself on a tall, uncomfortable bar stool. 'It must have been very traumatic for you.'

'Yes, it was, although I didn't see…well, the body. But you have to be brave, don't you? You always have to be brave.'

While Emmy turned away and busied herself with the kettle and a jar of instant coffee (obviously not deeming a mere detective important enough to benefit from the sparkling coffee machine on the granite worktop) Ashleigh took stock of her surroundings. Emmy was a tall, good-looking woman, probably in her late forties. She wore no make-up and her skin had the pink freshness of a woman who spent a lot of time outdoors, an impression reinforced by the spattering of mud on the calves of her jeans. Her hair was long, loose and dark and her movements, initially hesitant, grew in confidence as she made coffee.

As Emmy turned to the fridge for milk, Ashleigh cast a glance around the room. There was a full-height bookcase on the wall, filled with items of local interest — everything from Melvyn Bragg to William Wordsworth, via a host of local guides and cookery books. On the opposite wall was a framed photograph of Emmy, in a dove-grey suit and holding a bouquet of flowers, standing beside a tall, dark man, whippet-thin and gazing at her intently. A curling palm cross was tucked in behind it. Half of the back wall consisted of patio doors which gave out onto a sad-looking terrace, beyond which was a bed full of hard-pruned roses. A greenhouse hovered still further beyond it and the bonnets of the cars were just visible in the courtyard to the left.

It was a nice little setup. The Leaches must be well-off.

'Here you are.' Emmy set the coffee down on the table and nudged a packet of biscuits over, but Ashleigh waved it away. 'I'll tell you all I can. But I don't think I know where to start.'

'At the beginning,' Ashleigh suggested, a slightly flippant approach that usually induced a smile from a nervous interviewee.

On this occasion, it failed. Emmy's brow creased into an expression of slight concern. 'The thing is, I don't know where the beginning is. But I'll begin with today. I took my husband to the station for the twenty to seven train. He's in Manchester today, on business. He goes down every couple of weeks. Then I drove from the station up to Mosedale and parked there to walk up to the tarn. I was by myself.' She licked her lips.

'Do you walk up there a lot?' asked Ashleigh.

'Yes, I do, on my own. It's a pilgrimage I make.' Emmy folded her fingers on the table and stuck her chin out a little. 'Today is just the wrong day for it to happen. It's fifteen years ago today that I lost my son. Luke. He was sixteen.'

'I'm so sorry to hear that. Was it an accident?'

Ashleigh's eyes left Emmy's face for just a second and did a quick skim of the room. There was no picture of a teenage boy and she was sure there had been none in the hall — only a photograph of the man in the wedding picture, on the wall as she'd come in to the house.

'We don't know.' Emmy's voice was cool and controlled. 'He went out one morning on his bicycle and he never came back. They found the bike up at Mosedale, at the start of the walk to the tarn. It was somewhere he used to go, often. It made sense that that's where he would have gone, but they never found him. They searched for days, in case he'd had a fall and got injured, or had hit his head and wandered off and got lost. Dogs. Helicopters. Volunteers.' She sipped her coffee, waved aside Ashleigh's repeated condolence, and pressed on. 'In the end I gave up hope. My heart told me he was gone. But that's why I was there. Every year on this day I go up to the tarn and I leave flowers for him. You'll have seen them.'

That unhappy bunch of daffodils, with their sad little note. 'Yes. I wondered.'

'Did you leave them there?' asked Emmy, forlornly.

'I don't think there's any reason to move them.'

'If someone does, let me know. I'll take more.' Abruptly, Emmy turned her head towards the window at the front. A taxi drew up and a man jumped out, seized his briefcase, handed a note to the driver and strode purposefully up the path.

'My husband,' said Emmy, suddenly breathless. 'Rob. I wasn't expecting him back so soon.'

A key turned in the lock, the front door opened, and Rob Leach swung through the hallway and into the kitchen. 'Emmy. I know you said not to, but I couldn't leave you on your own. Not today, of all days. I cancelled my afternoon meeting and came back as soon as I got your message. Are you all right, my darling?'

'Yes, only very shaken. Because of…you know.' She dipped her head. 'Rob, let me introduce you. This is Sergeant O'Halloran. She's a detective.'

'A detective?' His sharp eyes looked Ashleigh up and down.

'It's just routine, Mr Leach,' said Ashleigh, as cheerfully as she could. 'We have to investigate every unexplained death.'

'There was someone in the tent, then?' asked Rob, suddenly alert. 'Emmy said—'

'I suppose I knew there must be,' said Emmy, and at last her self-discipline wavered. 'It was why I called for help. But I didn't look and no-one told me for sure.'

'Yes. I'm afraid there was.' Both Ashleigh and Emmy had risen to their feet when Rob had entered, and now they resumed their seats. He crossed the room to stand beside his wife and laid a hand on her shoulder. 'I'm sorry. I didn't realise you didn't know. It was a man.'

Emmy flinched. 'Oh.'

'Em, sweetheart. It's okay. Does the sergeant know about—?'

'Your wife was just telling me about the loss of your son, Mr Leach.'

His eyebrows flicked upwards. 'Oh, Luke wasn't my son, though naturally I took him on without any reservations when I married Em. He was part of the package.'

'I hadn't got that far,' protested Emmy. 'And anyway, this isn't about Luke.'

'The police need to understand why you were up there without me.' He addressed himself directly to Ashleigh. 'If he'd been my boy we'd have done that together. Of course, if Emmy had wanted me to go with her I would have done. Never think otherwise.'

It was a challenge. Rob Leach might care for his wife's welfare but he was equally concerned about how his own part — or lack of — in the drama might appear. 'Of course.'

He nodded, as if satisfied. 'At the time your people suggested he might have run away rather than had an accident, sergeant. But that's quite another story.'

He massaged Emmy's shoulder, very gently, and she lifted her hand to touch his fingers before picking up her story again. 'As I was saying. I go up there every year on the anniversary — lots of other times, too, but always on the day he died. This morning I was up there early because I'd dropped Rob off. If he's away I usually spend a lot of the time in my studio. I'm a potter. Craft shows, mainly. Anyway. I thought I'd get something done so I wanted to go up to the tarn early. I took some daffodils from the orchard and went up there and I put them in a jar and wedged it in at the edge of the tarn, just by the rock he used to sit at when he was fishing. As I was standing there looking out over the water I saw something.'

She picked up her coffee and sipped.

'I wasn't sure what it was at first,' she said. 'Then I realised it was the end of a piece of rope, that thin plastic rope you get as guy ropes with tents. And it was a long piece of rope. I picked it up and I pulled it and this huge thing came towards me, like a monster. It was a tent. And it was heavy. So heavy, I knew at once what it must be and immediately I thought of Luke. I didn't try to get it out myself. I didn't know if I could, or how long it had been there, and I didn't want to…well.' She shook her head nervously. 'You know.'

'I can imagine.'

26

'And of course I just…well.' Emmy stuttered to a halt. Her eyes flicked to the clock. 'I must have sat there for a few minutes. I wasn't sure what to do. I had no phone signal. I walked about a bit up there until I could get signal and then I dialled 999 and asked for the police and the mountain rescue, but the mountain rescue got there first. I've no idea how long it took. I lost track of time. I cried.'

'Oh Em!' said Rob, all compassion, and she gave him a grateful smile.

'Then they told me I could go home, and a lovely gentleman walked me down to make sure I was okay, and offered to drive me home, but I managed.'

'Did you see anyone when you were up there?'

'No, but it was so early. Barely light. I mean, I normally wouldn't have gone up so early but I'd dropped Rob off at the station. This day is always so hard for me. I wanted to get it over with as soon as possible. And that's it, really.'

There had been slender pickings up on the fellside, even more so down at Blacksty Farmhouse. That was all Ashleigh had expected. 'Thanks, Mrs Leach. I'm sorry it was so distressing for you.'

'It won't just be distressing just for me, Sergeant.' Emmy's bottom lip quivered. 'This poor man. He must have a family. Maybe he has a wife. Children.' She paused. 'Parents,' she mumbled.

Poor Emmy, thought Ashleigh, as she closed her note-book. This death would be bad enough even if she hadn't her own traumas, and now she was layering someone else's grief upon her own.

'You're done then?' asked Rob Leach. In real life he was even more handsome than in the photograph, but the quirky smile of his wedding day was a sneer in the January light of his own kitchen, as chilly as the white granite work-tops and ash wood cabinets. 'Thank you so much for stopping by. I pray you find out what happened and some poor family can lay their son to rest just as Emmy was never able to do.' He turned back to his wife as she sat immobile at the breakfast bar. 'I'll see the sergeant out. You just sit here. I'll get you another coffee and then we can talk.'

For a moment, Ashleigh lingered. There was nothing untoward about his arrival or his behaviour, but she had a sixth sense that there might have been something more to come from Emmy if he hadn't arrived. It wouldn't necessarily be relevant to the case, but she'd been involved in dozens of interviews where witnesses poured out their own stories to a sympathetic ear when what they had to say was, they thought, irrelevant. And sometimes — just sometimes — they offered a clue, some trivial thing they hadn't known was important and sometimes ended in solving a crime.

Rob's appearance had put a stop to any such confidence. When he'd seen her off the premises, politely but firmly and watching her from the doorstep until she was safely in the car and out of sight, she drove only as far as a forest gate some half a mile out of the village, where she pulled off the road and called in to the office.

'I don't want to risk you having me up for insubordination, Doddsy.' He was a cheerful character and could take a joke. 'But that was a bit of a waste of my valuable time.'

'No joy, then?'

'Tammy wouldn't let me anywhere near the scene, and our witness was about to pour out the story of her lost son when her husband came home and she dried up.'

'Emmy Leach, was it?' She could imagine him rubbing his chin, thoughtfully. 'I can't say I'm surprised.'

Nor was Ashleigh. 'There's something about her husband, isn't there?'

'You think so? I'm not so sure. It's more likely she

didn't want to unload her grief on him. The boy being another man's son.'

'You know the story, then?'

'Of young Luke? Aye, I remember it clearly. The Leaches were of interest to us at the time.'

The parents and step-parents always were. 'Do you reckon that's why he went so cold about it?' Luke hadn't been Rob's child. That might matter more to him than he wanted his wife to know.

'It wouldn't surprise me. We can talk it through later, when I've rounded up anything else they can tell me.'

'And found out who he is.'

'Aye, that as well. He's a youngish bloke, I'm told, and not in good nick. Not from the water — he hadn't been long enough for that to do any damage — but life in general.'

'Do we know he was?'

'Nope. He'd no ID on him.'

It wasn't unreasonable not to take ID if you went camping and travelled light, Ashleigh thought as she hung up and drove sedately round the twisting, forested lanes along the edge of the Greystoke estate and back down towards the A66 and the police HQ at Penrith, but even this simple answer to a not-so-difficult question puzzled her. She was reluctant to say it to Doddsy, who was far too practical a detective to take it on board, but there was something about Rob Leach which had stopped Emmy in her tracks.

She'd seen that sort of thing before. She'd been through it herself, in a doomed marriage, when the arrival in any situation of the man she thought she'd loved — no, she must be honest, the man she had loved and probably still did — had sucked all the joy and spontaneity out of her, and a fear of disappointing him had filled the void and altered the way she interacted with others. Emmy might or might not love her husband, or he her, but there had been something unhealthy about the change in mood.

She couldn't have explained it without referencing her own failed marriage and Doddsy, settled in a relationship with a young man half his age and revelling in what seemed a partnership of equals, couldn't have comprehended it. Jude, who was her former lover as well as her boss, might have done, but these days they tended to avoid one another. It was unlikely she'd find the chance to tell him and she wasn't going to seek him out for that purpose.

It was as well. When she was thinking of Scott, Jude always knew, and that was why what passed for their romance had faltered and failed.

FOUR

When the detective sergeant had gone, Emmy succumbed to a huge wave of relief. Guilt troubled her too much and too often, and although the lie she'd told had been the most innocent imaginable, she felt its weight keenly on top of all the other responsibility she'd laid up for herself. In her mind her mother's exasperation rang clear. *If I'd known you were going to take every little sin to heart, Emmeline, I'd have kept you well away from the church.*

On another day she might have smiled at that, because her mother was anything but a perfect human being and picked and chose her religion as and when it suited her. Perhaps as a result, guilt never seemed to trouble her. Today, though her mother wasn't there to chide her, Emmy's own heart did the job far better than any other human could. The discovery of this innocent's body was a punishment for the way she'd failed to protect Luke. She would carry it along with the rest, and suffer, because that was what she deserved.

The lie, that small lie, nagged at her. Not because it was

bad, in itself, but because she was never a good liar and throughout the interview she'd been sure the policewoman could see it in her face. Rob's intervention had saved her from any further questioning and for that, if nothing else, she was grateful to him, but just then she needed her own company.

'Do you want to talk?' he was saying as he made coffee from the machine and she sat at the breakfast bar with her head in her hands, eyes closed but still seeing the image of that huge nylon shroud, bloated with trapped air, drifting towards her with the inevitability of a submarine mine.

'Emmy. I said, do you want to talk? Or not?' He set the coffee down opposite her and stared at her as keenly as the sergeant had done. 'Whatever you want. It's up to you.'

She wasn't sure what she wanted, though she was sure he'd be happier if she did confide. At least then he'd be able to offer her some comfort and she could pretend it was helping and make him feel good. She picked up the mug and curled her hands around it. The cold air that had blown in when the sergeant left still swirled around her feet. She shivered. 'I do want to talk about it.' Her courage failed her. 'Just, not now. It's too soon.'

'Whenever. You know I'm always here if you need me.'

He'd cancelled his meetings and come straight back to look after her even though she'd told him she wanted to be alone, so she owed him gratitude. With gratitude came submission. 'Perhaps later. I'm sorry. I suppose I knew the minute I saw it that there must be someone inside and I must have known they had to be dead. But I hadn't actually admitted it to myself. When she spelt it out like that…'

'I should put in a complaint. She should have been gentler with you after everything you've been through.'

Ashleigh O'Halloran had, Emmy thought, been properly diplomatic. 'She doesn't know how I feel about Luke. How could she?'

'We've had this conversation before. I will not have you beating yourself up over what happened to him. And anyway, remember. We don't know what happened.'

Rob was tender and loving most of the time, but on the subject of Luke their views diverged. Stepfather and stepson hadn't got on, though that hadn't been Rob's fault, but she sometimes wondered if Rob had been a little relieved at Luke's disappearance. Rob was a glass-half-full man, one of nature's optimists with an expectation that everything would be all right. It was the one thing he had in common with Tino. But the thought that he might see a silver lining in Luke's death — even if that silver lining was flattering to Emmy herself because it meant that the two of them could be together without the trials and tribulations and sheer black-hearted resentment that Luke bore towards his stepfather — would always come between them.

'No. We don't.' Poor Luke. Drowned, or lost in the cold and the wind, overwhelmed by the soft suffocation of hypothermia? It didn't matter. Somewhere out in the hills her child must lie, his bones picked clean by the crows and the buzzards or nibbled by wide-eyed, wary fish, subsumed into silt at the bottom of a tarn or sinking into the soft bog somewhere among the heather and bracken over on the Caldbeck fells.

'In your own time,' he said, reminding her too much of the policewoman whose questions had been bland and whose look sharp.

But not just then. She couldn't put Rob off for ever — he was way too persistent for that — but she could delay. 'I'll take my coffee outside. Is that all right? I might just go down to the studio for ten minutes or so. Then I can come back and rustle us up some lunch. We can talk then.'

'I'll do lunch. After that you should probably go and sleep for a bit.'

Sleep was never her friend on the anniversary, but it was easier to take his advice. 'Thank you.'

Picking up the mug of coffee and her phone, she scrambled to her feet and stepped back through the hall and out through the side door. She took no coat and it was chilly, but the cold left her unmoved. With half a nervous eye on the kitchen windows to be sure Rob wasn't coming after her, she walked down the damp garden path to her pottery studio and opened the door.

This was her space — the kiln in the corner, the long workbench with pots and cups and ornaments placed ready for baking, the smaller table under the window where she sat to decorate the pots — and its familiarity both overwhelmed and comforted her. Rob never came in there, and she never went into his study. Maybe he drew the same sense of relief from isolation there as she did in the studio. She breathed deeply, but didn't switch the light on, standing by the window instead and looking out across the grey-green grass at the bird feeder, where a blue tit swung acrobatically from an empty half coconut. Then she set the mug down on the wooden table top and took out her phone. 'Tino. It's me.' As if he wouldn't know.

'Are you all right?' he demanded. 'I've been worried half to death. Do you want me to come round? I can cancel my afternoon calls.'

'Rob's back home. He cancelled his meetings. He said he thought I sounded distressed on the phone and he couldn't leave me on my own.'

'And are you distressed? Any more than you were this morning, I mean.'

If it had been any other day, without this weight upon her soul, Emmy might have coped. 'No, not really.' She drew a heart in the thick clay dust on the worktop. She hadn't been in the studio since before Christmas and her sanctuary, always slightly disorganised, had quickly acquired a neglected look. 'But the police came and interviewed me. Well, sort of. It was very soft, really.'

'I should hope so. You're just an innocent passer-by. A witness, that's all.'

She supposed that was the difference. When the police had interviewed her and Rob after Luke's disappearance they'd been icily courteous, but their questions had been persistent and penetrating. She was sure they'd thought her responsible, and they'd spared her nothing in extracting the whole painful story of her marriage to Tino and its ending, of how she'd met and married Rob, of how her son had strained against the bonds of family life and kicked them over, and how the story had ended in tragedy. The records would be in the archives, part of an old, cold case. 'Yes. So I suppose they'll be much kinder. But it still reminded me of how awful it was.'

'They should have known better. You should complain.'

'Oh, Tino,' she said, amused. 'The poor girl they sent will barely have been out of school when it happened and she isn't even local. She won't have known anything about it. And most of the people who worked on the case will have retired by now. Be kind.'

She heard the chuckle and it warmed her heart. 'Yes, okay. You're right. I'll be a bit more charitable, But I was only thinking of you.'

She was so blessed to be surrounded by people who cared about her. Blessed to be materially well-off, too. These would have to do duty for the blessing she was missing, the love of her son. 'Anyway. I just wanted to tell you.' Because she worried about Tino, too, more than was appropriate. 'It's okay. I never mentioned you. I told her I went up there alone. And I got away with it.

'Good girl,' he said. 'And thank you. I appreciate it.'

They lingered, in silence, both reluctant to end the call. Eventually she took the lead. 'I'd better go. Rob's doing lunch.'

'Any time you need me, my dear,' he said, and she imagined his smile. 'You know where I am.'

FIVE

etective Superintendent Faye Scanlon was standing by the door, her arms folded and a neutral look on her face, when Jude arrived at the meeting room where Doddsy had set up camp to consider the mystery of the body discovered up at Bowscale Tarn. Jude's relationship with Faye was fraught with discomfort, for a range of reasons both personal and professional, and he nodded her a respectful good morning as he passed. Cardboard cup of coffee in one hand and notebook and iPad clutched together in the other, he reviewed the situation as he crossed the room. The case of the dead man had landed, initially, on Doddsy's desk but Faye had sent him a message the previous afternoon communicating her desire that he should take over.

That suggested there was more to it than met the eye, or she thought there might be. Her presence, cool and at a distance, carefully positioned where she could listen in to the meeting without being part of it, indicated an extra degree of concern and therefore a degree of press interest.

Faye was notoriously touchy about the press. Even the

local media, looking for the slightest story to fill column inches and never too keen to interrogate it in any detail, filled her with a deep distrust unjustified by any of their actions.

He slid into the seat beside Doddsy. In the day since Emmy Leach had discovered the submerged tent, the case had acquired a dedicated (though small) incident room and a whiteboard crowded with maps and photographs. Knowing the area as well as he did, he had little need for the maps, which did little other than show paths he could navigate blind, but the photographs intrigued him.

Rest day or not, he'd spent an hour or so the previous day filling himself in on the outline of the case and knew what to expect, but he kept his powder dry until Doddsy had taken a seat beside him and the other two members of the team had shuffled in. The core team assembling in the room was exactly the one Jude himself would have chosen — hardly surprising, since he and Doddsy had been working together for years — but nevertheless he'd shaken his head when he saw Ashleigh O'Halloran's name. There was no reason not to include her; no-one in the department had anything approaching her instinctive understanding of a witness and her nose for a lie, and when that was allied with her uncanny knack for getting people to talk she was someone you wouldn't want to leave out. But he and Ashleigh had made the mistake of letting their personal and professional lives intertwine. It had ended cordially but it made things complicated.

It was Ashleigh who'd called time on the relationship. Women always did, in Jude's limited experience, but when the love of his life had dumped him years before he'd suffered a whole lot more than when Ashleigh had confided she couldn't get her errant ex-husband out of her head, and that what had existed between them was over.

'Ash,' he said, with his best, affable smile as she came through the door. 'Have a seat. This looks an interesting one.'

'It certainly does.' She gave him her coolest, most professional smile in return. In the few months since they'd split they'd seen little of each other and he had scrupulously avoided seeking out information about how she was getting on without him. Everyone in the department had been aware of their relationship and they'd given no-one any grounds to criticise them for it. Jude had always prided himself on his professionalism and self-discipline, to a fault. It had cost him the relationship that really mattered, with Becca Reid, and continued to strain his commitment to his family to the point at which it was a heavy grievance for his much younger brother to hold against him, but Becca was outside work and Ashleigh was inside it. It mattered.

'You can tell us what you made of Emmy Leach in a moment.' Doddsy cleared his throat and the final member of the team, Chris Marshall, bounded in and rattled into his seat. 'I'll round up what we've got, Jude, though I'm pretty sure you're on top of it already, and then you can take over. There's more work for me to do on the county lines job.'

Doddsy was affable, capable and knew his limitations but Jude nevertheless suspected that being bumped off charge of a job like this wasn't going to be good for his ego. That was fairly typical of Faye. At some point she'd decided to move the job up a grade and she wasn't interested in the impact on other people's feelings. People management wasn't her strong suit. 'Right.'

'Shall we start?' asked Faye, still keeping her distance. 'I want to listen in for a bit but I have a meeting in a few minutes.'

'Right.' Doddsy glanced at the clock. 'You all know

what happened. I've got the results of the post mortem, I've had a chat with the mountain rescue lads and Tammy's given me a full report on the situation as she sees it. It makes an interesting whole.' He waved a hand towards the board. 'We'll start with the body.'

'Did he drown?' Chris, who was nearest the white-board and always the most enthusiastic of them, turned his keen eyes on the board and its photographs. 'If he wasn't dead before he went in then he must have done.'

'Yes. He drowned. But he had injuries consistent with a bad fall.' Doddsy reeled off a list of bumps and bruises, a litany that told of a rolling, sliding descent over loose scree and exposed rock, rather than a long drop to instant death. 'He was still in his sleeping bag so there was some cushioning. He sustained a blow to the head but nothing serious, maybe enough to cause slight concussion. He had no broken bones. And, as you say, the cause of death was drowning. But let's discuss him, first. Male, five feet eleven. Caucasian. Hair short back and sides, dark. Brown eyes. Age — difficult to say but late twenties or early thirties. Puncture marks on the veins suggest he was a heavy intra-venous drug user but we're waiting for the results of the toxicology tests before we can confirm that. Distinguishing marks — a scar on the back of his hand that looks like some kind of crush injury. Plenty of tattoos, as well.'

Jude's thoughts went immediately to his previous night's work, and the missing men who'd never turned up for their stash of cocaine. Dealers were sometimes users. Couriers often were. Doddsy, he saw, had already made a note to that effect. 'How long had he been in the water?'

Doddsy spread his hands and shrugged. 'Matt Cork couldn't say. Some hours, at least. That's all he'd commit to. Something to do with the tent protecting him from the water.'

Matt Cork, the pathologist, was notoriously cagey about committing to a time of death. 'But we know he drowned, and before that he fell. So fill us in about where he fell from.' Though Jude could guess.

'What did the mountain rescue lads have to say?' asked Chris, turning again to look at the photographs of Bowscale Tarn and the deep shadow on the face of the crags behind it. They worked regularly with the mountain rescue teams and he, as a regular fell runner, came across them more often than most.

'This is where it gets interesting.' Doddsy nodded to Jude, a gesture that said *and this is why it's coming to Chief Inspector level.* 'The lads from the MRT say the tent was unzipped when they pulled it out. It's a good quality tent but both flysheet and the inside zip were fully open.

'He was trying to get out?' hazarded Chris.

'No. He was still in his sleeping bag. Neither arm was free.'

'If that's an accident,' Jude said, thinking aloud, 'it's a hell of a freakish one.' But it wouldn't be an accident. There might, conceivably, be a rational explanation for it but if there was it would take a lot of unravelling. Now he understood why Faye had escalated it. 'Let's think it through. It wasn't windy up in Mosedale that night. I grant you, it's always blowier on the tops, but you like to think your average camper would know how to secure a tent.'

'I'll come to that.' Doddsy crossed a bullet point off the list in front of him. 'But first I think it's important to look at what else was in the tent. Or rather, what wasn't. He'd no change of clothes, no camping stove or heavy gear, just enough food for his breakfast and even that was nothing more that a couple of fruit and oat bars and a can of Red Bull. So, unless he had them there and someone took them, there's nothing to suggest he was there for any kind of a long hike, or anything other than a quick overnighter.'

Faye looked at her watch, but she made no move to leave.

'Okay.' Doddsy had a sly expression on his face and Jude, who'd known him for years, read it. It meant there was more to it than the obvious. 'Was there anything else you expected to find that wasn't there?' he asked.

Doddsy grinned at him. 'Aye, I wondered if someone would think of that. Yes. There was. The other thing he had with him was a bag of camera stuff — lenses, tripod and so on. But the camera itself was missing.'

Jude thought about it. On the face of it it wasn't that unusual for a photographer to creep up for an all-nighter on the fells to photograph the stars or the sunrise or the Northern Lights. Bowscale Tarn itself offered views, though those on the fell top were broader, and it was the top where it appeared he'd been camping. 'Okay. So maybe he dropped the camera in the dark. Did you find it?'

'Oh, aye. It turned up in the tarn, but on the other side of it from where they hauled the body out.'

'Maybe we can get something from the camera card,' said Chris, searching away on his iPad for an answer to a question none of them had yet asked. 'If it's been in the water all night it's probably damaged, but it's worth a try.'

'Aye, well. Maybe. Except we don't have it. There was no card in the camera.'

Jude let out a long whistle. 'Right.'

'Yep. It might still be in the water. We're looking for it. We had to bring the divers down overnight but they're back up there right now. I'd like to find that card, even if we never find out what's on it.'

'Have the CSI team finished up there?' asked Faye. By

now she'd shuffled a little closer to the door. Her phone pinged with a message and she looked down at it in some irritation, though she ignored it. 'I need to go, but this is very interesting.'

'Aye. But we've got a team searching the top to see if we can find it up there.' Doddsy drew a photocopy of the OS sheet with Bowscale Tarn on it towards him and drew on it, a slashing arrow of black ink from the top of Tarn Crags to the water below. 'To answer your question about where he fell from, Jude. There are marks all the way down that slope. Snow and ice have fallen away. There's a fresh rockfall, clear as day. And there were tent pegs at the top of the crags, right where you'd expect them to be. Half a dozen of them, pulled out and thrown in the grass. The grass was flattened but Tammy reckons the tent wasn't there that long.'

Jude pulled the map towards him and stared at it, frowning. You didn't have to be a genius to work out exactly what might have happened, even without the clear signals on the map. The lone camper, up in his tent on the top of the crags. But why? Not photographing the night sky, for certain. The mist had been thick. Not watching, either, if he was in his tent and his sleeping bag. Hiding? Waiting? Had he left the tent unzipped? And if so, why?

However he'd come to be there, the end was clear. Someone must have pulled out the guy ropes, collapsed the tent, rolled their victim the few yards to the edge of the slope and then pushed him over. He'd have careered downwards, bouncing off the rocks and eventually plunged into the icy water of the tarn. And there, trapped, he'd have drowned. 'Okay. But there's one thing that doesn't make sense to me.'

'Only one?' asked Chris, and laughed.

'One obvious one. This is where he fell from.' He

tapped the map with his pen. 'And from the pictures you've got on the board, this is where they pulled him out. On the other side of the tarn.' It wasn't small; the distance in question wasn't far off a couple of hundred metres. 'I'm not an expert on this but we must know someone who can tell us whether something that size and weight could have got across that distance under its own momentum. I'll be surprised if it has.'

'Okay.' Chris was staring at the map, too. 'So let's think. Say the tent went into the water here.' He jabbed a finger on a likely-looking spot. 'Why isn't it still there?' And he answered his own question. 'Because whoever pushed him off there wanted something from it. The camera card, perhaps.'

'Or something else we don't have and don't know about.' Doddsy wrote the word *narcotics*, with a double question mark after it. 'Yes. Why not leave the tent it where it landed?'

It had been a while since Jude had been up to Bowscale and he tried to recall the details of the terrain. 'It's rough ground once you're away from the path, and it can be hellish boggy, even in summer. And there's every chance it was dark, unless the deed was done the day before. If we're dealing with one killer they must have come down the path from the top after they'd pushed our guy off. That brings you down a bit nearer the narrow end, where the main track comes in. They grab the tent, haul it to somewhere they can get at it more easily— which would probably be quite a bit further along — open it up, take what they need to take.'

'And hold the body under,' said Ashleigh, 'if the man wasn't dead.'

It was her first contribution. Everyone stared at her.

'Just a thought,' she said, waving the discussion on. 'Carry on. I'll say what I have to say in a moment.'

'Right.' Jude added his own arrows to Doddsy's sketch. 'Whatever our killer does, when they've done it they push the tent off into the water. I'm going to guess it's dark. Maybe they think moving the tent makes it less likely to be found. I don't know. But they're probably reasonably confident they've got away with it.'

'A hired killer,' said Chris, on cue.

'Maybe. And then they make their getaway. Whoever it is may have gone back the way they came. They may have headed off by a different route, but it seems they've made a clean getaway. And then in the morning, along comes Emmy Leach and finds the body.' Jude looked across the table at Ashleigh. 'What did you make of Emmy?'

'I'm not sure.'

'Does it matter?' asked Faye, still impatient, still lingering. Jude wasn't the only person to have had a relationship with Ashleigh, though the brief affair Faye and Ashleigh had shared had been a long time ago and had been a mistake for both of them. Faye, who regretted it more, was never good at concealing her discomfort and was always prickly when Ashleigh was around.

'I don't know.' Jude sat back and thought about Emmy Leach. 'I wouldn't say I know Mrs Leach but I certainly know of her. If you don't know the family tragedy, Faye, it's worth reading up on. Her teenage son vanished fifteen years ago and is still missing.'

'There was a suggestion he might have run away.' Doddsy was also looking at the whiteboard. 'He's never been traced. There have been no reported sightings of him. He just vanished.'

'He used to go up to Bowscale Tarn and go fishing, though God knows if he ever caught anything or if it was just an excuse to disappear and do some illicit drinking. The second, I think. They found plenty of cans up there when they were looking for him.'

'You're very well informed on a cold case.' Ashleigh flashed a smile at him, like a memory.

'It was my first week as a fully-fledged policeman. The details stuck in my memory. I was out in the team that scoured every inch of that fellside and the route back down to Mosedale. Under the supervision of DS Dodd as he then was.' He grinned at Doddsy.

'Cocky young lad you were, even then, as I remember.' Doddsy shook his head.

'Very interesting. If you two old soldiers are going to keep fighting past campaigns, you might want to do it in your own time.' Faye's interest in the case didn't appear to have waned but yet another notification on her phone finally drew her away. 'This is all very intriguing, but I must go.'

Faye had a reputation for being something of a micro-manager. Jude had learned early that there was never too much background for her to soak up. 'It isn't entirely irrelevant,' he said, as the door closed behind her. 'There's something a little too tidy about it being Emmy who found him, though, isn't it? I was looking over the case notes last night and thinking about it before the meeting this morning. There's a lot about this case that's odd and I just wanted to talk it through. I think I saw her, as it happens.'

'You saw her?' Doddsy sat forward.

'Yes. I was on my way back from doing your job for you the other night and I parked up to have a coffee and clear my head. It was about seven, I think. I saw a woman in a silver Renault coming along past Mosedale Bridge and I think that may have been Emmy.'

'There was a silver Renault parked outside her house,' Ashleigh confirmed.

'Right. What time did I call you yesterday, Doddsy? Sevenish?'

'Must have been about that.'

'It was immediately before then that I saw her. And that's what I can't work out. What time did Emmy dial 999?'

He leaned back and listened while Doddsy read out the timeline of the case. 'The first call came through at 8.47.'

Jude flicked up the call log on his phone. 'I called you at 7.06, which means I saw Emmy at the back of seven.' It was a mile and a half or thereabouts to the tarn, and a simple path, though increasingly steep. 'I'd expect to do that walk in about forty-five minutes, but I walk quite quickly.'

'Emmy said she went there straight after dropping her husband off at the station. It was the early train — twenty to seven, I think. So if she'd dropped him off at half six and gone straight there, that ties in with what you say.' Ashleigh looked down at her notes with a slight frown.

'We can always ask her,' said Doddsy, 'although I don't see that it matters.'

'It's the timing,' said Ashleigh, looking across at Jude.

He nodded, sat back and let her carry on. He wasn't sure whether it was comforting or faintly disturbing to find their thoughts still ran in tandem.

'She told me she was in a hurry to get it over with and get back. Let's say it took her an hour. But that still leaves a gap.'

'Forty-five minutes, let's say. Right. What was she doing for all that time? Did she say?'

'I got the impression Emmy has quite a strong religious

faith. She said she'd spent a few minutes thinking about Luke and saying a prayer, but that's all.'

'I'll struggle to believe she was standing in silent prayer all that time.' Chris's voice was scornful.

People could stand still and contemplate things for a long period of time, but Chris was right. There was a gap of half an hour, at least, on top of the most generous amount of time you might reasonably allow Emmy to seek peace and solace after a slow walk.

'I should also say,' Ashleigh observed, 'that I thought she was very uncomfortable with me and didn't like my line of questioning. Though as you'd expect, all I was doing was establishing what happened. It was a straightforward witness interview. She seemed to think she was being interrogated.'

Jude closed his eyes for a moment and played back the image of Emmy Leach, if it had been her, driving past with that anxious look at his car, pulled up to let her pass. And then the man walking past in the dark, looking at his phone, and the light that made Jude look twice because the face had seemed vaguely familiar.

He sat up and slammed the flat of his hand down on the desk. 'Tino Mortimer.' Then he looked at the three faces — Chris's full of expectation, Ashleigh's with interest and Doddsy's a dawning understanding. 'That's what it is.'

'Her first husband,' said Doddsy, by way of explanation.

'Yes. I saw someone walking past just after I saw Emmy and he looked vaguely familiar, though it wasn't light and I didn't get a good look at him. I never met Mortimer, but of course I know what he looked like. He was all over the papers as the grieving parent and he was a person of interest to the investigation. He's Luke's father. That's the explanation. I'll bet he and Emmy went up there together and she didn't want anyone to know. So when they found the tent, he must have scarpered and she stayed to report it.'

'Is that all?' said Doddsy, and laughed. 'That's the problem solved, then. Ours, at least. Someone can go down and see what Mortimer has to say for himself. If that's all it is, they can sort out their personal problems among themselves.'

SIX

Jude lingered by the whiteboard in the incident room for a few moments after Doddsy and Chris had left, staring at it. As a matter of course, Emmy had been a suspect in Luke's disappearance, though there had never been anything to suggest she'd had anything to do with it. Her discomfort at being visited by the police had a clear explanation. Nevertheless, he wondered about her.

'Ashleigh,' he said, as she gathered up her belongings, checked her phone and prepared to follow Doddsy and Chris back to her office, 'do you have a moment?'

'Sure.' She put her bag down on the table and crossed over to stand next to him in front of the board. 'It's a bit of a teaser this one, isn't it?'

'More than that.' He was still staring at the photographs of the tent, the makeshift shroud hauled up onto the grass beside the tarn. Under the dull skies beneath which the photographs had been taken the scene appeared monochrome, whereas a touch of sun would have brought out the blue of the water, rich bracken-brown, even the first green hints of spring. The landscape in the photo was fraught with secrets and silence, hidden even from the few dwellings scattered along the dale below. 'It's a pity sheep can't talk. They might have been able to tell us something.'

'There weren't even any sheep when I was up there.'

'You were in charge of the door-to-door inquiries in Mosedale yesterday, Doddsy said.'

'For what it was worth. Doddsy's Liverpudlian mates caught a few people's attention the other evening, though no-one picked them as cops. No-one saw anyone who can't be matched up to one or other of them, certainly not on the previous evening.'

He hadn't expected anything else. There were a dozen routes in to Bowscale Tarn, some straight and some circuitous, from every point of the compass. It would have been easy to get there without passing a house and there were few walkers in the heart of the Skiddaw massif in January. 'What about Emmy?'

'A couple of folk saw her. And one farmer was very excited to have seen a dodgy-looking bloke sitting in a Mercedes in a lay-by, talking on the phone and drinking coffee at 7am. He was convinced he'd seen a criminal.'

Jude laughed out loud. Ashleigh always had that effect on him, even now. There had never been any rancour as the relationship cooled; they'd parted as friends and still got on, though these days at a distance, but he had his pride. Even that was recovering a little now, and he was ready to make a bit more of an effort. 'I wanted to talk to you a bit more about Emmy Leach.'

She gave him a sidelong look, as if she knew what was coming. 'Right.'

'I wouldn't ask you in front of Faye, but I wondered what your gut instinct was.'

'Oh, I get it.' She curled her finger round the trailing end of her ponytail and frowned. Faye had no time for instinct and cared only for hard fact, and it hadn't taken Jude long to realise that anything that wasn't evidence-led was best not mentioned until there was something concrete to back it up. It was especially the case with Ashleigh, whose relationship with Faye was particularly fraught. 'I didn't think she was telling me the truth. It was just a feeling. She told me about three times that she'd been up there on her own and it struck me as odd. Because after the first time she offered the information I deliberately didn't ask her and she kept repeating it.'

'To make sure you knew.' Jude had come across that before. Guilty witnesses regularly committed the cardinal sin of answering questions they hadn't been asked. 'Interesting.'

'I thought so. But of course, people who lie to the police aren't necessarily hiding something criminal. If you're right and she was up there with her first husband, it seems perfectly reasonable she wouldn't want her current husband to know about it.'

'That's true, but she should have told the truth. I'm intrigued that our main witness — churchgoer, food bank volunteer, general do-gooder — looks as if she might be a liar.'

'I have some sympathy with her,' said Ashleigh, after a moment. 'It'll have been bad enough losing her son. I don't imagine whoever interviewed her back then was necessarily that sympathetic.'

Jude cast his mind back fifteen years, to a tough team of interviewers who pulled no punches and were happy to trample the innocent on the way to the guilty. In the case of Luke Mortimer, they'd failed. Maybe there had been no criminal to unmask. 'I'm sure that's right. But at the end of it, assuming she was lying about being with her former husband, why would that matter to us? It's not illegal.'

'It doesn't matter to us at all. But I'll bet it matters to her husband.'

Something in the way she framed the word *husband* alerted him. 'Did you meet him?'

'Yes, briefly. He arrived while I was there. I wouldn't say I disliked him, or that she seemed obviously afraid of him, but he was overly determined to look after her, and he made sure he saw me off the premises smartly enough. That's all.' She turned away.

When you spent time with someone as lovers you learned to read them. You learned to recognise when what they didn't say was as important as what they did. 'And?'

She hesitated. 'I'm projecting my own experience onto others. You should never do that in this job.'

Or any other. 'I think we know each other well enough that you know I'm not going to hold it against you.'

'Okay. So I think you know enough about this, but this is what I'm thinking right now. When I was married, Scott and I were very much in love. But it didn't work. It didn't work because we loved each other too much and I was always terrified of upsetting him.'

Jude had formed the impression that the marriage hadn't worked because Scott Kirby was a serial philanderer and Ashleigh naturally monogamous. Scott's expectation of his wife's forgiveness for his many affairs had far outstripped his capacity to forgive in his turn, and her one fling had driven the marriage onto the rocks. The fact that the fling had been with Faye Scanlon merely complicated an already murky situation, but there would be more to it than that. If, outside the office, he had the chance to ask her and the moment was right, he thought he might do so. 'Do you still see him?' Because when she'd ended her relationship with Jude it had been because Scott had reappeared, and all her determination to leave him behind had evaporated

She busied herself with wiping the screen of her phone. 'No. I lost my head over him for a couple of weeks and then I finally saw sense. He's gone back to Wilmslow and finally got himself a proper job. I'm not sure what it is and I don't need to know.'

Jude thought she tensed a little as she spoke, though her tone was even. This wasn't the time to ask further. 'Okay.'

'We'll need to talk to Tino Mortimer, obviously,' she said, repeating what they'd concluded, an obvious change of subject. 'Do you want me to do that?'

He considered. There was a lot to be said for it but also, in that last fragment of conversation, a strong argument against it. 'I think I'll do it myself. From what I remember he's an interesting guy. And it's piqued my interest. I'd forgotten about that case until now, and remember — it's still unsolved.'

She finished with the phone. 'It's good to be working with you again, at least.'

'Thought you were going to be stuck with dull old Doddsy, did you?' he joked, because Doddsy was steady but definitely not dull and was everybody's friend.

'No, but I do wonder why Faye took him off the case. It looks as if there might be a drugs connection and it's a bit too much of a coincidence for it to happen so close to Mosedale Barn, isn't it?'

Jude thought he knew the answer. Bowscale Tarn was no distance at all from Mosedale Barn, where he'd spent the night of the stranger's death in only partially fruitful watch. If it hadn't been so misty it would have been possible to see the barn from the fell top. There might be an explanation for the camera, there, too. Faye, who was territorial in the extreme, would be extremely keen not to have Doddsy working too closely on the one case when it could too easily be scooped up into one run by another force. 'She'll have her reasons.'

'She always does.' said Ashleigh with a shrug, and turned towards the door.

Jude watched her go, then headed back to his own office to read up on the old, cold case of Emmy Leach, Tino Mortimer, and a missing sixteen year old.

SEVEN

J ude went to speak to Tino Mortimer first, leaving Emmy until later in the afternoon. It was always better to be armed with the truth before you challenged someone on a lie and Tino was no liar in this matter, if only because no-one had had any cause to ask him a question. Blacksty was a small place, consisting of barely twenty permanently-occupied properties and as many again functioning as holiday homes, but it was big enough somehow to sustain both a pub and a shop and small enough for everyone to know everyone else's business. If Emmy had been sharing illicit liaisons with her first husband, sooner or later someone would find out and mention it to her second.

He stopped on the edge of the village to refresh his memory on the Luke Mortimer case, scrolling once more through the case notes he'd read over before he left the office and the key details relating to Tino that he'd scanned into his iPad. As a matter of course the man had been considered as a suspect in his son's disappearance, but as with Emmy there had been nothing to implicate him. He'd been living out of the county at the time, and his relationship with the boy — and with Emmy — had been so cordial it read like a template of how to maintain a civilised relationship after a breakdown.

Clearly some people found that easier than others. Jude allowed himself a wry smile. He'd had no chance to look up what Tino had been doing since then, other than to establish that he'd moved back to Blacksty three years earlier and settled down to become as impeccable a pillar of the community as Emmy herself.

It would be interesting to see how Mortimer responded to the interview. Closing the iPad, Jude slid it into the folder alongside his notebook, got out of the car and strolled the twenty yards or so towards Tino Mortimer's house. In the years since he'd left Blacksty, it seemed the man had done well for himself. He'd been a local manager in a car hire company and returned as senior manager in a company specialising in agricultural contracting across the north of England. There was a top-of-the-range red BMW parked outside the newly-converted barn in which he lived, and an open shed revealed a glimpse of a dirty four-by-four that looked as if it was used for rougher tracks. Although the property was compact and lacked the obvious trappings of wealth that characterised the Leaches' home, it had a look of comfortable affluence.

The doorbell jangled in the depths of the cottage and it was a few moments before Tino arrived. His eyebrows lifted in surprise when he saw his visitor, and even more so when Jude produced his warrant card and introduced himself.

'Police? Ah, okay. I knew you had people around here yesterday. I expect you want to talk about that nasty business up at the tarn.' He turned his back as he spoke, so Jude couldn't read his expression. 'Come through and have a seat. I expect you're talking to everyone, aren't you? Let me get you a coffee.'

It was unlikely that Mortimer was so naive he hadn't registered Jude's rank, even less likely that he thought a chief inspector routinely came out to do door-to-door inquiries. The offer of coffee was an obvious ploy to buy himself some time for thought. 'No coffee for me, thanks, Mr Mortimer. And yes, we are trying to establish who saw what. But I may as well come straight to the point and ask you where you were on Monday morning.'

The man barely blinked. 'Shall we sit down?' He led the way to the living room — small, functional but comfortable, and with a view to a plantation of skeletal beech trees at the end of a bleak, mist-filled winter garden. He waved Jude to a seat and sat himself.

Jude waited.

'About yesterday.' Tino ran his tongue around his lips, an obvious and uncertain liar, but one who seemed still trying to evaluate how much his visitor knew. 'Of course. Yes.'

'Where were you yesterday morning, Mr Mortimer?'

'Oh...I—'

He might as well go in all guns blazing. 'You'll know Emmy Leach called the police when she found a body at Bowscale Tarn. Mrs Leach didn't mention that anyone was with her when she went up to the tarn yesterday. In fact, she expressly told us she was alone. But someone matching your description was seen approaching the track heading towards the tarn at about seven o'clock yesterday morning.'

Tino Mortimer took a deep breath and placed both hands flat on the tops of his thighs. 'Ah. I see. Well. Actually.' Another deep breath and the truth came out. He looked for all the world like a man who hated to tell a lie.

'Yes. I went with Emmy yesterday. Of course you know why. It was the anniversary of our boy's death. It's difficult for both of us to go alone.' A fractional pause. 'Please don't be hard on Emmy. I don't want her to get into trouble.'

'It's not a question of being hard,' said Jude, taken a little aback by so sudden and complete a confession. 'And I'm not accusing anyone of anything — not you, not Mrs Leach. Right now I'm investigating a suspicious death and my role is to establish what happened.'

Tino digested this for a moment, and seemed reassured. 'Do we know yet who the poor man is?'

'Not yet. Why don't you talk me through your movements yesterday?'

'Yes. Of course. It's very straightforward. You know Emmy and I are divorced, and have been for years, but we're still on very good terms. We shared custody of Luke, although I was living down in Manchester at the time and saw him much less than she did.' Tino sighed. 'Every year on the anniversary of his disappearance she goes up to the tarn to pay her respects.' He paused for a moment.

'Why the tarn? Luke was last seen here in Blacksty.'

'Emmy's pretty sure that's where he was heading. They found his bike on the roadside by the track. And it would make sense. He and I used to walk up there, when he was a kid. I took him up there to go fishing sometimes. We never caught anything, of course. I don't think there's anything there to catch. But that wasn't the point of it. It was all about bonding.' Another pause. 'I tried to be the best father I could to him, despite everything.'

Jude endured a painful flash of memory. He, too, used to go fishing with his father as a teenager, but that harmonious relationship had frayed with time and betrayal and these days he struggled to maintain it in any form. 'So how come you went with her?'

'She asked me to, the first year I came back.' He gave a slight shrug. 'It obviously seems irregular to you, Chief Inspector, and I suppose it was, but I could understand why she didn't want to go alone and so I agreed. We've gone together every year since. Yesterday we met at Mosedale Bridge — which is where your witness must have seen me — and walked up to the tarn. We left flowers. Emmy was standing on the edge of the tarn and she spotted a rope in the water.'

Another pause. This time, quite clearly, he was deciding how much to say. 'She bent down and picked it up. I told her to leave it.'

'Why was that?'

'I could see from where I was standing there was something in the water. It was green. It looked obvious to me that it was a tent and I had a premonition there was something very bad about to happen. Or maybe not a premonition. Maybe it was just because I'd been thinking so much that morning about Luke and what might have happened to him all those years ago. It was almost as though I was expecting something terrible. If that was what it was, I didn't want Emmy to find it.' He twisted his hands together.

'And she still pulled it in?'

'Almost to the edge, yes. And then she realised what it must be and said we should call the police.'

'What did you think about that?'

He cleared his throat. 'It looks bad, Chief Inspector. I do appreciate that. But there is an explanation.'

'I'm interested in what happened before we have the explanation. How did you respond when she said you should dial 999?'

'I'm afraid I said we shouldn't. But that was because—'

'What did you suggest instead?'

'I said we should leave it.' Tino adopted a mournful expression, like a puppy in the wrong. 'Someone else was bound to come along and find it. They could have phoned.'

'It never occurred to you that whoever was in the tent might — just — be still alive?'

If anything, Tino's eyes widened still further, in pantomime shock. 'Really...oh, God, no. I never thought.'

'He wasn't, or so it appears. But I'm interested that Mrs Leach stayed with what you thought was a dead body and you left the scene.'

Tino was dressed for the office, even though he seemed to have been working from home. He ran a finger round his collar. 'I'm not proud of myself. She insisted on calling for help and so I left. Because I didn't want anyone to know we were up there together.'

Witnesses who came clean quite as easily as this were often liars. In this case, Jude had no sense of that. With this latter confession Mortimer's body language eased, as if he'd got a weight off his conscience. 'Why?'

'Emmy's married to someone else now, as you know. It wouldn't have been appropriate. Our relationship is entirely platonic, these days, but this is a small village. If people knew, there would have been talk and gossip and her husband would have heard it and maybe thought the worst. We didn't want that.'

He'd thought it sufficiently important to leave the scene where a crime had most probably been committed, and he'd left a man's body lying unretrieved. 'If your relationship is platonic, why not be open about it? She didn't think to explain it to her husband, I assume?'

'He doesn't know we go up there.' Tino almost rolled his eyes, as if at Jude's stupidity. 'He didn't know where she was. You think I'd be foolish enough to tell him?'

Beneath the gesture a tale lay untold, as sure and as sinister as the tent below the surface of the tarn. 'You've just told me you get on well with your ex-wife and everything is very civilised. I wouldn't have been surprised if you'd told me he knew.' But maybe he did.

'I'm not one to slander a fellow human being.' Tino turned sideways and looked down at the bleak, wet garden. He was tense. 'But yes, all right. Rob's the jealous type.'

'In what way?' Jude leaned forward, intrigued. 'Aggressive to you? Violent?'

'Oh God, no. He wouldn't dare. I'd give as good as I got if he tried anything, you can be sure of that. And I don't think he's violent with Emmy, either. But he's possessive. He doesn't like me being around. He doesn't like that there's still something she and I share and always will, and it's something he's excluded from. It's something neither of us would ever wish on anyone else, but he doesn't see it like that. So I have to be very careful when I see her. For her sake.'

This subterfuge might or might not be innocent; it would look anything but if Rob Leach were to stumble on it. Secret trysts, if only once a year; messages in secure WhatsApp groups, no doubt; secret calls, made and taken in corners. Emmy was Jude's next call and it was as well he'd had this heads up. He wouldn't be able to gauge the accuracy of Tino's fears until he'd spoken to her and now he knew he'd have to tread extremely carefully when he did so. 'Is Mrs Leach the reason you came back to the village?'

Tino spun back towards him. 'Not as such. At one level it would make a lot more sense for me to have stayed away.'

'You're originally from Carlisle, I believe. Is that right?'

Tino forced a smile. 'You've been reading over the old

case notes, I can see. Yes, you're correct. I met Emmy at school. We both attended the grammar school in Penrith. We married very young.'

'As soon as you left school. Is that right?'

'Yes. I'm sure you raised an eyebrow when you read that, but it wasn't a case of marrying in haste. I'd have stayed married to Emmy if it had been up to me, but she comes from a very strong religious family and she was fully on board with all that. Morality was everything to her — still is. There was never any question of sex before marriage and I wasn't prepared to wait, so we got married as soon as we decently could. Luke came along within the year.'

His gaze strayed to the mantelpiece. Jude had already spotted the photographs there and now he was able to pay closer attention to the image of a gap-toothed smiling young boy alongside a casual snap of an older teenager, failing to crack a smile. The curved bowl of Tarn Crags and the silver disc of Bowscale Tarn formed an ominous background to the second picture.

'Of course,' said Tino, after a moment's reflection, 'we were far too young.'

'Is that the reason the marriage broke up?'

Tino's attention had wandered to the pictures but he snapped back. 'What? Oh, no. Not at all. Emmy was determined to make a go of it and so was I. I adored her. I won't hide the fact that I still do. Except from Rob, of course.' A flash of a smile. Jude read that as an attempt to charm him: his suspicion, in consequence, sharpened further. 'No, it was my mother-in-law.'

'Right.'

'Yes. She did give her blessing to the marriage — rather reluctantly I may say — and almost certainly on the grounds that it was better for her daughter to marry than burn, as the Bible says. But she wasn't my greatest fan from the beginning and she put subtle pressure on Emmy. Emmy struggled with Luke. He was a difficult baby and an even more difficult toddler. I was working hard and not at home as much as I'd have liked.' His brow creased. 'My ma-in-law was always in her ear. It was inevitable Emmy cracked. She had a mini breakdown and went home to mother, taking Luke with her.'

'Interesting.'

The sideways smile again. 'Aren't you going to ask me why she disliked me, Chief Inspector? Or would you like to make a guess?'

The answer was in front of him, in the pigmentation of Tino's skin. 'No. I'd like you to tell me.'

'My father's family are from Jamaica and my mother is white. I was one of four children and we were the classic output of the old rhyme. One black, one white and two khaki. I'm one of the khaki ones.' He chuckled. 'I thought that would shock you.'

'It would shock me if someone other than you had said it,' Jude admitted, 'but yes. Go on.'

'I sometimes think if I'd been as lucky as my sister and been white, we might have made it work. I might have won Emmy's mother over. There's no reason why not. My parents were both professionals — a lawyer and a teacher. I'm as assimilated as I could possibly be. I have four good A levels and I turned down a university place to marry Emmy. I had a good job from the start and I've always worked hard. I've never been in trouble with the police. But I'm coffee coloured. My former in-laws aren't.' He sighed, almost apologetically. 'My former mother-in-law is a very nice woman at every other level and never overtly racist, I have to say. I sometimes wonder how she'd have been if Luke had taken after me in his skin colour, rather than Emmy. I imagine she was hugely relieved when she saw him and he was, to her eyes, normal.'

'You must have found that difficult.'

'I'm used to it. It was always there, underneath everything. I wasn't the man she wanted Emmy to marry. Once she got her home she was quick to move her away to the divorce courts on the grounds of irretrievable breakdown.'

'You didn't contest the divorce. Were you tempted? You didn't feel you wanted to give it another go?'

'Oh God, yes. But I misjudged. I thought if I let Emmy go, she'd come back to me in her own time.' He turned his back again, crossed to the window and stared out. 'I didn't foresee the eminently suitable, affluent boy next door rolling up and taking pity on her. But there you go. Maybe I should have fought a little harder for her.' He shrugged as he turned back. 'I didn't.' Bitterness flashed behind his eyes, but only briefly.

'You moved away after the divorce, though.' Jude cast his mind back to the files he'd just read. 'Why did you come back?'

'Why not? If I'm honest it's because I have some pride. Emmy probably thinks that's a sin, but it's who I am. I moved to get a decent job but I always liked it around here and when I changed jobs and could work from home a couple of days a week, it meant I had many more options.' He gestured across to an open door, which led to a home office. 'I like living in a village and after we lost Luke I came back up here regularly. Not that I thought we'd find him, but I felt closer to him, and the few happy years I had with him were here. The longer I was away the more I felt I was damned if I was going to let past mistakes keep me away. So I came back. To make a point to myself and my former mother-in-law.'

'And your ex-wife?'

Tino ran his hand through his hair. 'No. Not Emmy. I thought she might welcome my support where I could give it, and that's happened, as I explained, but I'm glad I made the decision. Luke's still out there, I know. When we find him, if we ever do, I want to be there on the spot with his body. In the meantime I have to put up with bumping into my ex and her husband every now and again and putting on a smile.'

And pretending he didn't care. Jude spared himself a wry smile at the way Tino Mortimer's past mirrored his own. He'd been with Becca Reid for eight years before she'd left him and she still lived in the same village as his mother, on the other side of the road. He, too, crossed paths with his former lover on a regular basis and forced himself to be civil and he, too, would have kept the relationship going if he could. It threw a light on Tino's motives. He seemed to take some pride in secret assignations with his old love and it sounded as if Rob Leach would put a stop to them straight away if he found out. 'Your ex-wife was quite traditional, then.'

Tino's expression reproached him. 'I loved Emmy very much, but if she did have one fault it's that she never had the capacity to be independent. Sometimes I felt she'd have been much happier in the 1950s, when she wouldn't even have to pretend to take a decision for herself.' He laughed. 'Anyway, that suits Rob. It means he can be in control and he likes that.'

'You don't get on with Rob Leach, then?'

'He doesn't like me. Why would he? I was Emmy's first love. I was the father of her child. Maybe I'm her only real love. Rob's a proud man, just like I am.'

'That's helpful, Mr Mortimer.' Jude could imagine the two men, each resentful of the other's love for Emmy. By all accounts she seemed oddly cast as a femme fatale. 'Thank you.'

'I never meant to inconvenience the police, you understand. I just wanted to protect Emmy's reputation.'

'I understand that. And now, if I may, more routine. Can I ask you where you were on Sunday night?'

'Here,' said Tino, with a shrug. 'I had a beer, watched *Match of the Day* and went to bed.' He waited for a moment, as if he expected to be challenged, but Jude let it pass. 'I suppose you're going to see Emmy now.'

'Yes.'

'Don't be too harsh on her.'

There should be no need to be harsh on Emmy Leach. Jude had a sense that she, like her former husband, would be only too relieved to come clean.

As he strolled from Tino's home at the edge of the village to the Leaches', in what passed for its centre, Jude fell back into an old habit and called Ashleigh.

'It seems pretty clear to me,' he said to her, mentally reviewing Tino's obvious nervousness. 'Awkward for them both, yes. Criminal, no. Tino Mortimer is clearly still in love with his ex, and I suspect he quite likes having her to himself. It puts one over on the new man.'

'You have to feel for him.' He imagined her tossing her head in frustration, the disappointed twist in her lips that came up whenever she thought of her former husband, as she surely must be doing. 'You try, you fail. At least you have to try. Though I must say I admire his patience.'

'Indeed.' Rob and Emmy had been married for a good twenty-five years, which made Tino's persistence all the more remarkable. Maybe, after all, Tino hadn't told him everything about his relationship with Emmy. He might think there was more on offer than just friendship. 'At least he was straightforward about it. Let's hope she will be, too.'

At the other end of the line, Ashleigh's sigh was more fractious. 'I very much doubt it, especially if her husband's there. You will be discreet, won't you?'

'What do you take me for?'

'I know, I know. I'm sorry. I don't mean to patronise you. I can't help it. I have a bad feeling about Emmy Leach.'

Jude checked his pace as he approached Blacksty Farmhouse. Feelings weren't enough. Ashleigh didn't need him to tell her that, any more than he'd needed her warning of discretion. On occasion, her emotions compromised her judgement. 'Mortimer says he doesn't think Rob Leach is violent.'

'He could be wrong. And you know yourself—'

'There are lots of different forms of coercion. Yes. I'll make sure I see her on her own.' He paused within sight of Blacksty Farmhouse. 'Are you okay?'

'Yes, I'm fine. I just have a bit of a sense for these things. She was really uncomfortable about something, and if she thought it was worth lying to me she must have had a reason.'

'That's a good point.' He left a decent few seconds, to see if she had anything to add, but she didn't. 'I'll be back in the office after I've spoken to Emmy.'

'I think Doddsy's hoping to have some ID on the body by then. If not then, we should have it by tomorrow morning.'

'Good. We can reconvene when that's in and see where we go from there. And obviously, if there's anything you need to talk to me about, you know I'll always listen. As a friend, as well as a colleague.'

'A friend is so much more useful than a lover,' she said, fractiously and hung up.

But, wondered Jude as he strolled up the path to engage with Emmy and her lies, would Tino Mortimer agree with that?

EIGHT

omeone saw me.

The message pinged in to the WhatsApp chat Emmy had made with Tino and called by her mother's name. Her mother never bothered with this kind of technology so Rob, who never bothered with her mother, hadn't asked questions about it. Emmy, who lied with the utmost reluctance and paid the price for it with a constant ache in her conscience, wasn't remotely surprised to see the notification.

A moment later her fears and Tino's warning were confirmed by the sight of a stranger, strolling up the road through the village with a sheen of rain on the shoulders of his Barbour jacket and talking on the phone. He was approaching on foot from the direction of Tino's house. That spelt one thing and one thing only: the woman detective had read her discomfort, and they knew.

Are we in trouble? she messaged back as the man lowered the phone, paused, looked and walked on, with an obvious whistle on his lips.

Doubt it. Tino's cheerful disposition even saturated

those two words and the thought lifted her. She waited a moment, drawing back from the window to watch as the man strolled along the road past the front of the house, casting a casual look at the courtyard and, she was sure, checking to see which cars were there.

Thank God Rob had gone into Carlisle on a site visit. She'd managed to reassure him that she was all right and he was sensitive enough to leave her be, but if the police knew about Tino she'd have to square it with Rob and hope for the best. Lying to the police to get them off your back was one thing, but Rob might reach the same conclusions as she feared the detective had.

She looked out of the window to see where Heather was, because she really didn't need anyone else knowing too much about her visitor. This was paranoia. Heather, who came once or twice a month to help with the garden, wasn't what you'd call a gossip, and she was at the bottom of the garden, clearing wet, black leaves from the furthest corner. It was none of her business who called to see her employer.

Out on the road, the man stopped by a gate and pulled out his phone again. A moment later Emmy's phone rang.

Her heart fluttered and she thought about ignoring it, but no. Tino's courage had deserted him up at the tarn — had it really only been the day before? — but Emmy was stronger than that. 'Hello.'

'Mrs Leach? My name's Satterthwaite. I'm a detective from Cumbria Police. I was passing and wondered if you had a moment to talk. In private, if that's possible.'

The day before they'd made an appointment for the sergeant to visit. This unannounced arrival smacked of a less empathetic approach. 'Yes, of course. My husband's away for the afternoon.'

'Excellent.' His voice was brisk and businesslike. 'I'm just outside. Perhaps you've seen me.'

She ended the call and was at the door before he'd made it up the path. 'You'd better come in.' Her heart fluttered again as she ushered him in to the kitchen and sat him at the breakfast bar where she'd seated the sergeant the day before. 'I know what it's about. Tino messaged me.'

'I see.'

This man was a very cool customer, she thought, impeccably polite and with an underlying charm, but the politeness was icy and the charm suppressed. She sensed hostility, even irritation. Which was fair enough. She was in the wrong and she knew it. 'Yes,' she said, to say something.

'I've just been to see Mr Mortimer, as you'll know.'

'Yes, and I—'

'Is there anything you'd like to add to your statement from yesterday?'

Emmy took a deep breath. She couldn't decide whether she liked this man or not. His manner was reassuring but his eyes were everywhere and she was terrified of what he might see. What would he learn, about her and about Rob? 'I'm sure Tino told you everything.'

'I'm interested in what you have to say.'

She perched on the edge of the stool and folded her hands in front of her. She was good at confessions; she rehearsed them often in her prayers, clipped and concise. 'Tino was there when I went up to the tarn. We went together. I didn't tell you because I don't want to upset my husband. We went so early because this is a small village and there's a lot of gossip. We wanted a reasonable chance of getting away unseen. That's all.' But they had been seen. She wondered which of her friends and acquaintances had spotted Tino and herself heading away, and had thought it important enough to mention to the police.

'Does your husband know?'

'No.' Unable to meet his gaze, she hung her head like a child in trouble, as Luke had done when he'd been small and biddable.

'Is he likely to be upset?'

'Well, of course.' Emmy looked out in the garden. The first crocuses were poking up beneath the ornamental cherry tree. 'I know he feels guilty because he let Luke down, just as I do. But Luke isn't his child and he hates that he can't help me. So yes. He'll be hurt. Rightly so.' And angry, with that repressed but obvious fury she was never quite able to appease.

Satterthwaite took a pad and pen out of his pocket and jotted down a few notes. Though Emmy's eyesight was good she couldn't read it and didn't dare be too obvious in trying. 'I just wanted to cross-check that. Which of the two of you suggested calling for help?'

'I did. It seemed the obvious thing to do.' Indeed, it had been the only thing to do, the right thing. Saying that seemed a betrayal of Tino, made it look as if he'd gone scuttling away from scandal and the law.

'You were quite right. You waited, though.'

'Just half an hour. Just to give him a chance to get away.'

'That's fine. Thank you, Mrs Leach. I understand your concerns.' He smiled, and the tension in Emmy's shoulders relaxed, as if she'd negotiated a difficult moment. 'But in future, you can make our lives much easier by telling the truth. It helps.'

'Yes, I know. But I didn't want any unpleasantness.'

He paused for a moment, looked at the wedding photograph on the wall as if he was reading Rob's character from that moment frozen in time. 'You'll forgive me for being forward, Mrs Leach, but if you ever feel threatened, in any way, please remember the police are here to help.'

'Thank you, Chief Inspector. Of course, you have to say that, but I can promise you. Things between Rob and myself are just fine.' She felt her face flush scarlet and he had the grace to look away as if he'd spoken out of turn. 'Naturally he'll be upset to know about what happened but of course I'll tell him.' If she didn't someone else would, and there was value in occupying the moral high ground.

'Just bear it in mind. Crime, violence and abuse don't only happen nine to five. You can call our domestic violence unit any time, in the strictest confidence, or the Council social work department. I'll give you some numbers.'

'Really. There's no need. Thank you and I'll bear the offer in mind. Now, if there's anything else…'

'Nothing else, thank you.' He slid a card across the table and she was relieved to see that it was his business card, not some number that would send Rob's suspicious mind into overdrive. 'Call me if you think of something else. I expect you'll see us around in the area for a little longer. Not necessarily myself, but certainly some uniformed colleagues. But that's routine.' Yet another pause. The man dealt freely in them and every one gave her space for a further confession. 'Obviously I understand how difficult this is for you. Because of your son.'

'Thank you.' She slid off her seat to ease him out of the door when she would normally have waited for him to end the interview, and she was relieved to see that he took it calmly enough and didn't linger with any more questions.

What other questions were there? She'd told most of the truth to the sergeant and the rest of it to him. She had no more answers. Whatever had happened to the poor young man in the tarn — and though she was naturally curious about it she couldn't bring herself to ask — she was completely innocent of his death.

When DCI Satterthwaite had gone she waited for long enough to realise that the pounding headache which had begun the moment she'd seen Tino's message wasn't going to go away, took two paracetamol and returned to her phone. Emmy wasn't always decisive — indeed, she hated being forced into a decision — but when she made her mind up, she got on with it. She called Rob's number, hoping he wasn't driving or in a meeting, and struck lucky. 'Rob. Is this a good time?'

'Hi, Em.' He sounded cheerful. 'I was just going to call you. Meeting's done. Do you want me to pick up anything for dinner?'

'There's a casserole in the fridge. That'll do.' She stopped, breathed deeply. Rob would be fine. He always was. She couldn't blame the detective for seeing things that weren't there: it was the man's job to look for crimes, even when there was nothing to see. 'I'm afraid I have a confession.'

The line crackled. 'A what?'

'The police were round again. I'm sorry. I wasn't entirely straight with you about yesterday.' She rushed on, before he could interrupt her with questions. 'I didn't go up to the tarn on my own. I went with Tino. Because I couldn't bear to go alone and I didn't think it was fair to ask you.'

'Em—'

'We go every year.' There: the secret was properly out. 'But I swear it's completely innocent. It's all it is. It's just to remember Luke and to leave him some flowers.'

'Em. Why didn't—?'

'And I may as well say, I wouldn't have told you because I didn't want to hurt your feelings but someone must have seen us and the police were asking about it and now people will be talking about it in the village, and I don't want you to hear a garbled version from someone else instead of the truth from me.' At last she stopped and waited. Her headache intensified, like a mad wife screaming in the attic. 'Rob?'

'Let me get in out of the rain.' A car door shut. 'Okay. Well, I'll admit it doesn't surprise me. Everything I do is to help you, but I can only understand some of what you went through. I know you didn't like me being with you on that day, and I get that, too. So I never asked. I even get that you wanted to go up with him. But keeping it a secret? We've been together a hell of a long time, Emmy. Haven't we?'

It was twenty-six years since Rob had first shown a romantic interest in her. She and Tino hadn't even rustled up five together. Strange how those five had increased in value. 'Yes.'

'I just wish you'd told me.'

'I was afraid.' It was out, and she hadn't intended it. She squeezed her eyes shut.

'Afraid of me? For God's sake, Emmy!'

'Not like that.' The chief inspector had jumped to the same conclusion. 'Not afraid you'd hurt me. I wasn't even afraid you'd be angry. But I thought you might be upset and I didn't want you to be. So it was easier to say nothing.' Now she saw what huge folly that had been. 'I didn't want you getting the wrong idea. That's all.'

'I wouldn't have liked it, I admit. But I'd have understood.'

Tears rose in Emmy's eyes. It was the stress of losing Luke and remembering him, the illicit kiss with Tino now corrupted by the knowledge that some poor soul had been lying dead just feet away. The questions from the two detectives had awakened the searing grief of Luke's disappearance, and now she realised that she had, after all, got everything out of proportion and not only given the wrong idea to the police but to Rob as well. 'I'm so sorry.'

'I just wish you'd told me. Okay, I wouldn't have invited the guy in for a cup of tea and a biscuit when he brought you home but at least you could have gone with my blessing.'

She dug out a tissue and dabbed at the tears. It was always the same. She constantly made mistakes and never learned from the cycle of confession, repentance and forgiveness. At the end of it, she only felt foolish. 'Can you forgive me?'

'Don't be daft. There's no need. But if it makes you feel better then yes, of course.' And a pause. 'I'll nip into M&S and see if I can find a nice cake or something, shall I?'

'That would be nice.'

'I'll see you later.'

She was astonished it had been that easy to make things right. If only the same could be said for every problem, every situation. If only she could free herself from guilt at her failure as a mother.

If only Luke could come home.

It was still daylight, but gloom was already gathering in the east and the light was retreating behind the high rampart of Carrock Fell. In the garden, Heather was reaching the end of her short day's work, bundling the last of the sodden, heavy plants she'd been clearing into canvas bags and wheeling them to her van to take them to the tip, or back to her smallholding for burning.

Emmy fetched boots and jacket from the utility room,

slipped them on and squelched her way across the wet lawn. Some fresh air would do her good, even if only for a few minutes. 'Do you want a hand?'

'I'm all but done.' Heather gestured at the last of the bags with a gauntleted hand. 'But thanks anyway.'

'You know I don't mind helping.' In the summer Emmy enjoyed pottering about at the edges of the garden and trying her luck with a few flowers while Rob turned his hand to the heavy stuff and the vegetable patch. Heather, who'd come to them via some contact of Rob's, helped out with the clearing and the cutting and kept the large garden manageable. In the winter, when the weather was less conducive, she gave a day a month to clearing the sodden overgrowth at the wilder edges, trimming the thick beech hedge that separated the vegetable garden from the orchard and pruning the apple trees in the spring.

'This'll see you through February,' she said. 'You want to think about plants for the summer.'

Looking beyond her to the orchard, where the emerging daffodils glowed like rising stars in the grey grass, Emmy wrapped her coat around her against the cold wind. Heather was ex-army and never seemed bothered by the weather, down to her shirt sleeves in all temperatures when it was dry and ploughing on through the rain when it was wet. She was brisk and to the point and latterly Emmy sensed that some kind of tension had arisen between her and Rob. These days he manifested his gift for being elsewhere whenever necessary and managed to be absent when Heather came. 'You've done a grand job. And you work so hard.'

'I wouldn't do anything else. I love the outdoors. The army was fine to start with, but I was spending too long behind a desk. It was time to move on.' She hoisted the last sack onto the wheelbarrow as she spoke and carted it along the path towards her van.

Emmy followed in her wake, past the rows of parsnips with their wilted tops, the regiment of green-uniformed leeks marching along a raised bed, and the steel-grey froth of kale that rippled in the breeze. 'You're invaluable to us.'

At the van, Heather turned her back to shift the bags from the barrow. 'I saw you had a visitor.'

'Yes. It was the police again. Just checking up on details about yesterday.' Picking at a strand of hair, Emmy wondered how long it would be before the world and his wife knew about Tino. That was what worried her about it. She didn't want Rob to feel she'd humiliated him among his peers, which was almost certainly how he'd see it, but she reassured herself. Heather, who lived alone, was one for asking questions but it seemed to be for her own satisfaction. Emmy always found time to chat with her, almost as a matter of charity, and on the rare occasions when she'd let slip something she shouldn't, it had never surfaced elsewhere.

'Sharp-looking lad. That was an expensive suit, by the look of it. They must pay their boys a lot these days.'

'He's quite senior,' said Emmy, and then realised she might make it sound more serious than she wanted it to. 'I mean, it wasn't important. He was just passing.'

'Found out who it was, have they?'

'I don't think so. If they have, he didn't say.'

'Harry down at the Gate Inn says the lad was murdered, but quite why anyone would confide in him I don't know. Not that I'd believe anything he says. It's gossip at best. Lies, some of it.' Into the van went the last bag, and Heather slammed it shut. 'It must have been a rare shock for you.'

Emmy downplayed the understatement. 'I'm sure it

wasn't as bad as anything you would have seen in the army. I never saw the body. The mountain rescue people hustled me away before they got him out.' Thank God for that. The whole thing was a bit of a haze for her, now.

'That's not good. And where's old Rob? He should be at home looking after you.' Heather bent to unlace her boots.

Heather might have arrived at Blacksty Farmhouse via a contact of Rob's, but it wasn't so surprising there was no love lost between them. He disliked any kind of confrontation, with man or woman, and she was just the type to put his back up. Sometimes Emmy thought her own submissiveness was probably a little too old-fashioned and she was occasionally, secretly, ashamed of it, but there was no denying it made life easier than dealing with her husband's hurt feelings. When she'd been married to Tino there had been debates and discussion about everything and their frequent but short-lived rows had always ended in laughter — and sometimes, to her surprise, with her getting her own way — but Rob always had to have the last word. 'He's only out on a site visit. And he came back from Manchester to look after me.' A more spirited woman would have answered differently. *I don't need looking after.*

'I don't know how any woman puts up with what you had to put up with, losing that poor lad. I've seen some things in my life, yes, but I always found closure.'

Naturally it would be easier for Heather to find closure when the tragedies she'd dealt with had been other people's. Emmy suppressed a sigh. Everyone always wanted to talk about Luke and she just wanted to keep his perfect memory where it belonged, a secret cherished only by Tino and herself. 'He and Rob didn't get on terribly well, you know. It was the old stepfather-teenager thing. I think that's the worst of it. Eventually he'd have grown out of it and they'd have turned into good friends.' This tragedy — this punishment — was that they hadn't.

'You poor soul. Well, if you ever want a chat with someone who doesn't live in the village, you can always call me.'

Heather made this offer of friendship on a regular basis, and sometimes Emmy was tempted to take her up on it. It would have been good to have someone else to talk to rather than her neighbours, with whom she felt obliged to guard every word. It was a shame Rob wouldn't approve; he wouldn't have said anything, but he'd have made it clear in other ways.

'Maybe I will,' she said as she said every time, and then stepped back as Heather got into the van and drove away from the house with a cheery wave.

NINE

'Wait until you hear this one.' Doddsy had been sitting frowning at his iPad and now looked up. His face was a mask of innocence.

There had been a hiatus of a couple of days, in which the pace of inquiry into the body at Bowscale Tarn had slowed and been overtaken by others. Jude had drifted into the incident room to catch up and to spare a few more moments to check on the fruitless results of the inquiries. Faye was there, too, following him down the corridor when, he thought, she hadn't really intended to but was unable to leave the case to anyone else. She perched on the edge of the desk, staring at the whiteboard with a fixed frown and she and Jude both turned to their colleague.

'It had better be good.' Faye was in an increasingly bad mood these day, and not just because of the proximity of Bowscale Tarn to the location of the partly-failed drugs bust. The case had attracted a lot of press interest and she was caught between her hatred of dealing directly with the media and an inability to delegate it to anyone else.

'Oh, God,' Doddsy said, shaking his head at them. 'It's

good all right. It took them long enough, but we've got an ID on the body.'

Ashleigh had been at the next desk and she, too, looked up inquiringly. 'Go on. Surprise us.'

'I might, at that.' Doddsy sat back, looked at each of them and tapped his fingers on the desk. 'They found a DNA match. We already had him on file. It's Luke Mortimer.'

'Whoa!' Ashleigh's face registered shock.

Faye merely narrowed her eyes. Jude froze and thought about it. His mind went back fifteen years to the television images of Emmy, appealing to a horrified local community for help, and to those fruitless hours he and a hundred others had spent combing the heather in Mungrisdale. Fruitless, because Luke hadn't been there at all.

'All right.' Faye dropped into a seat at the table with a jangle of her chunky copper necklace. Their casually-connected activity and shared interest became a meeting. 'I'm shocked, yes, but are any of us really surprised? With hindsight, wasn't there always a possibility something like this might happen? Because suddenly it all seems a little too neat to me. Doesn't it?'

Did it? It might have been more feasible if it had been an accident. 'I think I'm surprised,' said Jude. 'Not with hindsight, perhaps. You're right about that. It all looks pretty neat, now. I'll even hazard a guess at what he was doing there.'

'Waiting for his parents of course.' Ashleigh joined them and sat with her elbows on the table, chin on her hands. 'Emmy goes there every year. Tino's been with her for the last few. It's entirely plausible he knew they'd be coming. It would be one way to surprise them. Maybe in a pleasant way. Maybe not.'

Jude was shaking his head, still processing the information. Yes; it was all too neat. 'Okay. That gives him a reason for being there, but it's the rest that bothers me. Where has he been for the last fifteen years? Why did he leave? How did he turn from a wayward kid from a loving home into a murdered drug addict? Why did he come back? And who killed him?'

'All right,' said Faye, again. 'Maybe I should have paid more attention to your reminiscing the other day. Talk me through Luke Mortimer. Talk me through what we know of him. Tell me anything we have that gives us a clue as to what he might have been and what might have brought him back here now.' She looked to Doddsy. 'You worked on the case, I think.'

'Aye, but not at the coal face, so to speak. I was managing the door-to-door interviews mainly. The Ashleigh O'Halloran of my day.' He grinned across at her.

'The file's here.' Jude had it on the desk and he tapped at it.

Faye's look was sharp. 'Then you clearly aren't surprised after all.'

'It never occurred to me that it might be Luke. I dug out the file to give me a feel about whether Emmy Leach was telling the truth about what she was doing up there.'

'And it turned out she wasn't. So—'

'It was a lie of convenience, I think, rather than one intended to obstruct us. But yes. It's still a lie. Also, I was reading it out of interest.'

'Nothing better to do, eh?' said Doddsy, with a grim half-smile and a wry acknowledgement of their collective workload.

Jude opened the file. The unsolved case notes of Luke's disappearance, inches thick, told a long, repetitive and ulti- mately inconclusive tale. No-one had seen him, or even a shady figure in the distance that might have been him.

Abduction or a teenage runaway: whatever the answer, Luke's cold case was very much live again, all its old questions unanswered and a long list of new ones to boot. 'I don't know how much you know about it.'

'Only the bones, so to speak. Youth reported missing, never found, case still open. There are plenty like it.'

'Yes. Luke was a bit of a lad, by all the accounts in here. His parents married young — far too young, by the sound of it — and the marriage broke up fairly quickly, but not with any kind of aggression. It seems Luke was too small to register what happened. His mother moved back in with her parents, in Blacksty. They were devoted and affluent. He wasn't short of anything. After a couple of years Emmy remarried, a local man. He was also very well off. That's Rob Leach. And that's when the problems started.'

Faye nodded.

'By all accounts the Leaches were — still are — model citizens,' Jude went on. 'That doesn't always count for much in families. In this case there was the natural tension of Luke competing with his stepfather for his mother's attention, but there was the added problem that his parents were fairly strait-laced about life in general and about religion in particular. They were pillars of the church. They attend every Sunday, they don't drink, they do good work. Luke was kept on a pretty tight rein and the resentment he already had towards his parents, and his stepfather in particular, blew up when he reached his teens. His father, who everyone said he idolised, wasn't around much at that time.'

He shook his head for a moment. When his own parents had divorced, his much younger brother, Mikey, had gone off the rails almost as spectacularly as Luke had, though Mikey had cherished no devotion for his absent father. But then, there had been no stepfather either — only Jude himself, already an independent adult and cast in the role of the male role model Mikey needed. As he still was, and it was no easier, even though Mikey was twenty-one and, hopefully, through the worst of it.

'Drink? Drugs?' prompted Faye.

'Pretty much everything, I think. He wasn't exactly what you'd call feral — the village is too small for that. There was always someone who knew where he was and what he was up to, but in a way that made it worse. He put two fingers up at them, literally and metaphorically. He drank. He smoked weed.' The toxicology reports showed Luke had moved on to harder drugs, at a dangerously high level. 'He ran with a rough crowd, some of them much older than him. He was at the Community College. My dad taught him, I think. There was a young woman who gave birth to his child at the age of seventeen, a few months before he vanished.'

He heard Ashleigh's sigh, even though he wasn't looking at her. 'That's an old story, isn't it? Poor kid.'

'Did you consider the child as a possible reason for his disappearance?' asked Faye of Jude and Doddsy, as if either of them had opinions that had carried weight at the time.

'They considered it, but I don't think there was anything in it. Neither Luke nor the girl — her name is Chloe Ferris — seemed perturbed about it one way or another. She certainly seemed to have no inkling he was bothered about it. In fact he seemed pretty content with the life he was living, apart from the tension with his step-father. Her parents were laid back about it. It was the Leaches who were scandalised.'

'Some young people enjoy kicking over the traces, of

course,' said Faye, thoughtfully. 'What did Tino Mortimer think of his unexpected grandchild?'

Jude shrugged. '*Boys will be boys* is the quote.'

'Interesting. The case was left open, obviously, but the investigating team must have come to a view.'

'Yes. The parents were convinced he'd got lost and come to grief up in the hills but I think the general view of the investigating team was that Luke had upped and left.' Jude closed the file and tapped his fingers on it. 'It looks like they were right.'

In the short silence, he thought of the photo of Luke that he'd seen in Tino Mortimer's living room. The relationship between that and the image on the whiteboard was anything but obvious. 'And now, here he is. He must have decided it was time to come back.'

It seemed an unnecessarily theatrical way about it, but perhaps that was the only way Luke could be sure of seeing his birth parents together without alerting them beforehand. Jude withdrew a photograph of the young Luke Mortimer from the folder — a school portrait, with a fake smile — and pinned it on the whiteboard next to the one that had recently materialised there, the same face but fifteen years older, bloated and waxy from its watery end. 'But the camera. That's what gets me. Someone killed him and someone stole the card from the camera. Why?'

Faye stared at the folder in silent perplexity. He could tell her mind was racing as fast as his, turning all sorts of possibilities inside out. 'He must have kept out of trouble for the last fifteen years. Or we'd have known he was alive. Fingerprints. Forensics. Whatever.'

'Kept out or been kept out,' mused Ashleigh.

'What do you mean?' Faye turned cool eyes on her.

'Only that Luke obviously moved in some kind of criminal circles, if only to source his drugs. Maybe it was more than that. It might sometimes be useful to have someone around who isn't in trouble with the law. I don't know. I was thinking aloud.' She twined a finger through the end of her pony tail.

'Or else he just didn't want to be found and was careful to keep his nose clean.'

'Those poor parents.' Ashleigh shook her head and Jude could tell she was thinking of Emmy. 'Someone will have to go and tell them their son's dead. Again. I suppose we should tell the former girlfriend, too, given that there's a child there, but I think that can be done discreetly by telephone. But Mrs Leach and Mr Mortimer will have to be told in person.'

Jude sat back. Would it be easier for them to hear such dreadful news a second time? There would be no sudden sense of loss, but any hope either Tino or Emmy might have had of seeing their son again had been snuffed out. 'I should do it.' It was the worst part of the job, and one no-one could enjoy, but it wasn't something he could shirk. 'I'll get one of the family liaison officers to come with me, if we can find one at this notice.'

'I could do it.' Ashleigh lifted her head from the folder. She'd been looking at photographs of Emmy, and reading back over the transcript of her statement.

Doddsy cleared his throat, a warning Jude didn't need. Ashleigh was a talented investigator and an empathetic questioner, and her compassion for victims and witnesses was beyond dispute, but you could be empathetic and compassionate to a fault. There was no doubt at all in Jude's mind that she'd handle the matter impeccably as far as Emmy, in particular, was concerned, but he had to consider Ashleigh's own welfare. He had grave doubts about how far she could keep herself sufficiently detached.

'I'll see who's available. I need you to deal with other things.'

'I don't know there's anyone free right now.' Faye, who could be tone-deaf to emotional undercurrents, scowled at him. 'I was reviewing our available resources earlier on today. And it's not as if the parents haven't been through the process before.'

Ashleigh drew in an outraged breath and Jude, who normally got on reasonably well with Faye, immediately understood why his respect for her was never as complete as it ought to be. She might have a sharp brain and a manager's mind but the empathy and the compassion were missing. 'It's preferable to have someone with up-to-date training. What about Mandy Phillips? I worked with her on a couple of cases recently.'

Faye's laser mind whirred behind her eyes. 'Mandy is on leave this week. Ashleigh has the appropriate training.'

He recognised the signs. Faye was in the mood to pick a fight. Someone, somewhere had taken her on and won a small victory — probably something to do with the drugs bust she was so keen to keep separate from anything else that happened on her patch — and she was asserting her authority on the next available person. 'Technically, yes.' Faye would know, as well as he did, that Ashleigh's decision to follow the liaison route had been a mistake and had been swiftly reversed. 'But—'

Doddsy looked down at his iPad. Ashleigh, troubled, looked from one to the other. Belatedly, Faye seemed to realise that it wasn't an appropriate conversation for a briefing meeting. 'Someone needs to go and see them, sooner or later. The two of you can go down there and break the news.' She got up and turned to the door.

Jude followed her, as casually as possible, catching up

with her in the corridor. 'Faye, can you spare me a minute?'

'I'm very busy.'

'I think you know why I'd prefer not to take Ashleigh with me down to Blacksty.'

She kept walking, though more slowly. 'And I think you know I don't have the luxury of taking your preferences on board. We're light on personnel.'

'I'm not sure she's the right officer for this job.'

'I understand you rate her very highly as interviewer.'

But she wasn't interviewing. That was the problem. Ashleigh had an emotional history not just with Jude but with Faye herself. It was between them again, the thing they both knew and neither would acknowledge. 'I've learned in the past that taking on a full FLO role isn't necessarily the best use for her skills.' Especially not if Ashleigh was emotionally vulnerable. That was what he couldn't say, in so public a place. He sensed it because he'd slept with her, but Faye, who had slept with her too and somehow missed it, was in no mood for compromise. Usually he was properly respectful of her authority and content to let things slide. Not today. 'I can't spare her from this case.'

Hesitation preceded concession. Faye backed down, at least in part. 'Leave it with me. I'll get Mandy onto it when she's back from leave. Or I'll find someone else to work with the family over the duration of this case. Ashleigh can go down to Blacksty with you today. ' She stopped and looked at her watch. 'I have to go. I have a meeting. Let me know how you get on. I confess, I'm intrigued to see what comes out of this.'

TEN

Faye's barely-suppressed hostility to Ashleigh was nothing new. It was a hazard of the job, a by-product of a rebound relationship with a superior officer, whose prickly sensitivity manifested itself in an inability to let an old relationship die. Every professional disagreement was a slight, every submission a point scored, every interaction an unnecessary tussle. Thank God, thought Ashleigh as the low shoulder of Greystoke Forest slouched away to her left, that Jude was so much more phlegmatic, both as a colleague and as a lover. It had made it much easier to move on from him. After the initial period of silence, generated by embarrassment on her side and (she thought) injured dignity on his, they'd slipped with surprising ease into the relaxed working relationship that had preceded their romance.

It meant Ashleigh felt comfortable challenging him, though she waited until they were on the long, straight road that bumped downhill into Blacksty before she broached the subject. 'You weren't keen on me coming along, were you?'

Jude cursed, silently. She saw his lips move. 'You heard what I said to Faye. I can use you better elsewhere.'

She smiled. She wasn't the only one to struggle with Faye's managerial limitations. 'She was in a mood. There's no point in picking a fight with her when she's like that.'

'No, but I don't want you to get the wrong idea. It wasn't because I think you aren't capable.'

'It's okay. I know my own shortcomings. But I'll have to do it, if she insists.'

His fingers loosened a little on the steering wheel. 'She won't. She's going to get Mandy Phillips in after all.'

Ashleigh spared Mandy a moment's thought — hard-headed and professionally competent, a woman of lists and boxes ticked in order. She might be the wrong person to handle frail, guilt-ridden Emmy, but she was emotionally unreachable and that, in its own way, was a good thing.

'Don't worry about me,' she reassured him. 'It's all good. I admit it. I do feel sorry for Emmy and I under-stand exactly why she didn't tell us the truth. And I can see why she might be especially jumpy with the police if she associates us with the loss of her son and with her being questioned about it.' They wouldn't have been kind to her. 'I think I might be better attuned to that than anyone else, just because I've already spoken to her. That's all. The public good. It's right that I should be here now.'

'That's fine, but you'll forgive me for being personal.' He half-turned to smile at her. 'I know what you're like. I don't want you getting too emotionally involved.'

'That'll hardly happen if I'm not involved in the ongoing family liaison process. Let Faye have her victory. It does no-one any harm and it might make things easier.'

He slowed further as they entered the long, thin village. 'We'll see Emmy first, I think. She'll be in. I called Tino

Mortimer and he'll be around, too. I didn't tell either of them why we were coming.'

Blacksty unrolled before them, a straggle of neat houses with an elongated village green splayed around a crossroads. There was no church — the Leaches must attend elsewhere, though Ashleigh didn't know where — and the former Methodist chapel just beyond the village boundary had been converted into a residential property with the blank winter windows of a holiday home. A village noticeboard stood next to a ragged play park and on the other side of the green the pub served much of the surrounding area and offered coffee and cake all day to a just-about viable trickle of walkers and cyclists. A curl of nervousness troubled her as Jude pulled up in front of the Leaches' house. Both cars were in the courtyard.

'Good that Rob's at home as well,' said Jude, though she thought she sensed a slight qualification to it. 'Maybe we can have a quiet word with him, too.'

He'd be thinking about the crime as much as the welfare of the bereaved, wondering if there was more to be gained from gauging the reactions of both Rob and Emmy separately. That wasn't how Ashleigh saw things. 'Thank goodness she'll have someone with her.'

He unclipped his seatbelt. 'I know you've got your worries about him, but I don't see any real reason for concern.'

'There's what Tino Mortimer said about him.'

'I think we've established Mortimer's hardly a disinterested observer. If you ask me, the reason he came back here at all was to do exactly what Rob Leach did to him and move in on Emmy the moment he saw a split. It hasn't happened, and I'm pretty sure it won't happen now.'

People stayed with their lovers for a long time and for a lot of reasons, and they weren't always the right ones.

Ashleigh had no doubts about Emmy's commitment to Rob and his to her, but it seemed a strange dependence, based on need not affection. A respectable marriage could be a trap and some people couldn't leave if they wanted to. 'Let's not hang around any more.'

It was Rob Leach who opened the door, his shirt sleeves rolled up and a pencil stuck behind his ear in stereotypical architect fashion. 'Sergeant O'Halloran. No disrespect but I was hoping we'd seen the last of you.' He smiled broadly, as if to make sure they knew it was a joke.

Ashleigh introduced Jude, and Rob's quizzically lifted eyebrow indicated suspicion. 'Chief Inspector, eh? Is something up?'

'We've called by with an update. Is Mrs Leach around?'

'Yes, in the kitchen. Come through. The boys in blue are here, Em!' he called ahead of them, then turned back. 'It's very thoughtful of you. Is it to tell us you've found out what happened?'

'Not exactly.' Jude nodded towards Ashleigh. He wasn't shy of taking on the difficult job of breaking bad news but they both knew she'd handle it more comfortably.

'Mrs Leach. You might want to sit down. I'm afraid we do have an update but the death is anything but solved, and I'm afraid it's rather bad news.'

Emmy had been standing at the stove poking at something delicious in a pot on top. Some kind of stew, judged Ashleigh, scenting rosemary and onion among other things. There was a dark, rich waft of red wine, too, and a half-empty bottle standing by the cooker. Emmy might not be a drinker but she clearly wasn't above putting that kind of poison in the pot.

'Well...' said Emmy, uncertainly. She looked at her husband for confirmation and, at his nod, went and sat bolt upright on one of the stools by the breakfast bar. He closed in to stand behind her, a hand resting on her shoulder. 'Go on. It can't be anything worse than the last time. Can it?' But she put a hand up to her throat and clenched her hand around the gold cross that hung around her neck.

'I'm afraid it's very bad news. I'm sorry. We've identified the body you found in the tarn.' Ashleigh paused, fractionally, and then ploughed on. Hesitation was the cruellest thing. 'I'm afraid it's Luke.'

Emmy closed her eyes for a second, then opened them again. Her face was blank. 'But that's impossible. You must be mistaken. He's dead.' She twisted round and looked up at her husband, whose expression registered the shock they'd expected. 'Isn't he?'

'Clearly not,' he said, dryly.

The colour — what was left of it — had drained away from Emmy's face. Jude stepped across to the cupboard, found a glass, filled it with water and slid it on to the breakfast bar. Still Emmy clung to her husband's finger with one hand and to the cross with the other, in silence. The clock on the wall ticked.

'There must be a mistake,' she said, after a moment. 'Mustn't there?'

'I'm afraid there's no mistake, Mrs Leach. We have DNA evidence on file from when he disappeared. There's a complete match with the body recovered from the tarn.' There had been a tiny tattoo of a snake on the man's calf as well, alongside a complicated and abstract Celtic pattern and another of a dragon chasing a demon across his shoulders. He hadn't had those when he'd last been in Blacksty.

'I won't have to identify him, will I?' Emmy wrenched her hand free from Rob's and reached for the glass. At last it dawned on her. 'Oh God. No, I'm sorry. I don't know what I'm thinking. I'd given him up for lost. I was so sure he'd gone. What was he doing there? Why didn't he come and see me? Why didn't he go and see Tino? I've always said we'd forgive him. I said it in that appeal we did for the television. I remember saying it. I said we'd forgive him anything if he did come home. He must have seen it and he didn't come. I thought he was dead.' She looked up at Rob and anger flashed up at him. 'You made me give up on him! You told me he must be dead!'

'I was sure he was dead, Em.' He dropped to his knees beside her, captured both her hands in his.

'You wished he was!'

'I never did that. We didn't get on but I never wanted him dead. How would that have helped you? But I didn't want you to go on hoping, and hoping that one day he'd appear at the door. I didn't want you wasting away with hope.'

ELEVEN

'Well, that was interesting.' Jude got back into the car and closed the door.

'Yes, wasn't it?' Ashleigh swung in beside him and slotted in her seat belt as the Mercedes crawled up past the green, past the pub towards Tino's cottage and the road back home. She felt hugely relieved that the job was over. They'd furnished Rob and Emmy with contact details for Mandy Phillips and she, for better or worse, would be the one who'd have to tread her way through the Leaches' complicated emotional issues.

Thank God Ashleigh was free of that. Emmy clung to her conscience and she was desperate to shake her off. 'So odd. Of course we don't know how she rationalised what happened to Luke. But I would have thought — surely you would have expected her to have hoped he was still alive?'

'I don't know. As you say, she has a very strong faith. I suppose it can manifest itself in two ways. It either keeps her clinging to hope in the present, or it steels her to face the worst and overcome it.'

Poor Emmy was facing the worst now. 'At least she has her husband for support.' But that nagging doubt surfaced again.

'Yes. And they'll have a body to bury. That'll help.'

Emmy had collapsed into tears shortly after they'd broken the news, so they hadn't pressed on to ask either of the Leaches if they had any idea who might have been responsible for Luke's death. Those questions had all been asked and answered fifteen years earlier. Luke had gone on to create new secrets and make new enemies and the motives for his death now surely lay in a life to which none of them had any access. Yet. 'If we ever find out who did it.' Emmy's misery had depressed Ashleigh's natural positivity. Fifteen years suddenly seemed too long to solve a cold case.

'We damned well will. Even it wasn't my first ever case I'd want it solved. It wasn't my problem back then, but I hate unfinished business.' Jude tapped his fingers on the steering wheel. 'Luke had gone to the dogs, as I think I remember hearing Rob quoted as saying at the time'.

'It looks like he was right.' And, indeed, Luke had sunk much further. There had been scars on his body, the legacy of a life saturated in drugs and violence. How would Emmy cope, knowing how he'd gone on to live without her? 'What do you think happened to him?'

'I don't think it's rocket science. Kids running away from home often fall into bad company. If I had to guess further, I might get Doddsy to reach out to his mates in the Merseyside force and see if they can make any connection between that and what was going on up at Mosedale barn on Monday night.'

'You think that's it?'

'I do. So does Faye, I think. It would explain why she's

so jumpy. She doesn't want another force muscling in on her turf.'

It made sense. Faye was defensive and territorial. 'It's just circumstantial. Because it's close to Mosedale.'

'Yes, but it's a start. He's clearly into drugs. He clearly knew something someone else thought unsustainable. That's my guess as to what was on the camera card — something that could have been used against someone. We know there was criminal activity going on in that area that night. We know we didn't catch the guys we were expecting to catch. That's the other thing. It was an operation run in a tumbledown shed up a lane in the back end of nowhere, but even after fifteen years Luke would have known the lie of the land. A bit of local knowledge is hellish useful when you're operating outside your own area. But we can talk that through later on. We've got Tino Mortimer to deal with first.'

He pulled the Mercedes up at the edge of the road, two wheels on the soft mud of the verge. By mutual consent they waited, as if to put off the evil moment. By now it was mid-afternoon, but so grey that Tino already had lights on. They could see him in what must be his study, sitting back in his office chair with his phone clamped to his ear.

'Come on then. Let's get this done.' Ashleigh got out of the car and marched up the gravelled path. In the hedge something rustled and a bird shot out with a started squeak. The temperature had dropped sharply with the first signs of the declining sun, threatening frost. It would be a treacherous drive back.

Tino took a while to come to the door. Through the glass pane in the hallway, Ashleigh saw him wandering along, still talking, but when he saw them his demeanour changed, the call ended and he wrenched the door open. 'Chief Inspector. Sorry to keep you there. I was just signing something off. Is there anything I can help you with, or is it a courtesy call?'

Some people might have made that comment sound caustic, but Tino delivered it with cheerful innocence. His smile took any sting out of it.

'Neither,' said Jude, in an appropriately sober tone. 'I'm afraid we've come to break some rather bad news to you.'

Tino stepped back to let them in. 'Oh God. It's not Emmy, is it? It can't be anything else. I don't have any close family except my parents and I was speaking to them an hour or so ago. And you wouldn't come out if it wasn't something to do with…this.'

'Mrs Leach is fine,' said Ashleigh, responding quickly to his genuine concern. 'We've just been to see her.'

Tino lifted that questioning eyebrow. 'Then…no. No, I'm not going to guess. Not at bad news. If I get it wrong it might come true later. Tell me.'

'You might like to sit down.'

He went ahead of them into the small sitting room and sat in the armchair. His eyes never left Jude's face until Ashleigh spoke. 'We have a positive ID on the body found up at Bowscale Tarn, Mr Mortimer. I'm very sorry to have to tell you that it's Luke.'

'Luke?' He sat back in open astonishment. 'Is that possible?' And then he shook his head and barked an incredulous laugh. 'No. Of course it's possible. Oh, God. I always thought he'd still be alive. I always thought he'd come back one day and all I had to do was wait. But I never thought he might—' He stopped and ran his fingers through his hair. 'I thought I'd see him again.' And something shifted beneath his natural openness and Ashleigh saw again the eyes of a liar. 'What happened to him? In the village they're saying he was murdered, but surely that can't be right. Can it?'

'He drowned.' Jude, Ashleigh could see, was watching Tino closely as she spoke. 'We don't know anything more about the circumstances yet.'

'Then it could have been an accident? But if he was up at the tarn he can only have been waiting for Emmy and me.'

Emmy had collapsed into tears and self-reproach almost instantly but Tino Mortimer, made of sterner stuff, was full of questions. If he could ask them, that surely meant he could answer them. 'Why up there rather than down in the village, do you think, Mr Mortimer?'

'I've no idea.' Tino rubbed his chin and something flickered behind his eyes again, as if he was a machine flicking from reactive to proactive mode. 'Has anyone told Chloe? And Libby?'

Libby, Ashleigh recalled, was Luke's daughter, the child who'd never known her father and now never would. She was fifteen, and the complications of Luke's reappearance and death would surely roll on into the next generation with her as collateral damage. 'Not yet. We spoke to you and Mrs Leach first.'

'Yes. And it'll be best for Chloe to break it to Libby, I suppose. Oh God. Poor kid.'

Jude appeared to have switched his attention from Tino to the garden, where a pheasant was strolling across the small patio. At this stage, he switched back again. 'Do you see your granddaughter much?'

'Occasionally. Chloe isn't that keen on us having contact. Too many harsh things were said at the time. I understand.' He shrugged. 'She won't let her see Emmy at all, and Libby doesn't seem to care. It's all a bit of a mess. Chloe places the blame for everything firmly on Emmy and Rob and the way they brought Luke up. He rebelled and Chloe only had his side of the story. I daresay she's embroidered it.'

'Does Mrs Leach know you're still seeing Libby?' asked Ashleigh.

'I've never told her. It's tricky enough keeping any line of communication with someone so hostile. I don't want to risk being accused of betraying trust in any way. Chloe is very bitter about some of the things Rob and Emmy said at the time. I don't think they were particularly kind about her.'

She'd be even more bitter when she learned that Luke had run off and left her holding the baby, that was for sure, and there would be further repercussions when she found out he was dead. Looking at Tino and his thoughtful expression, Ashleigh guessed there was more of the story to come out. 'Anything else, Mr Mortimer?'

He rubbed his chin. 'I don't know if it's relevant. And for God's sake don't mention it to Emmy. But I've had a few messages.'

'Messages?'

'Yes. On social media. I tweet a bit about work, and about places I've visited. Pictures of the countryside. Photography is a bit of a hobby of mine. Not a lot, maybe a couple of times a week. Over the past few months I've had messages from someone claiming to be my son.' He held up a hand. 'And before you ask, I've no reason to think I have another.'

Jude kept his expression fixed but Ashleigh could guess at his exasperation. Tino might only just have learned Luke was dead, but the messages should have been reported to the police straight away. 'What exactly did they say?'

Tino gave them a rueful look. 'Bugger. You're cross with me. But it was difficult.'

'Was it?' asked Jude, with a chill in his voice.

'I thought so. Because of Emmy and so on. But I can be honest with you now.' He reached for his phone and swiped the screen into life. 'Right. Okay. The first one came back in October. Here.'

He handed the phone to Jude, who scrolled through and then passed it to Ashleigh. In front of her a short thread unrolled, clumsy, badly spelt and blending innocence and threat.

Hi Dad.

A week or so later. *Dad. Can we meet?*

Hi dad. why rnt u answering?

Don't u want to c me, dad?

There were no more. Jude turned back to Tino. 'You never answered them?'

'No. I thought about it but in the end I decided against it.'

'You said you always hoped he'd come back,' said Ashleigh, more gently than Jude. whose anger was apparent. 'And yet you didn't reply.'

'I know.' Tino spread his hands in what looked like resignation. 'I always thought I'd see him again, but the messages freaked me out. You know what social media is like. My profile is public. There are some sick people out there. I think in my heart I didn't believe it was him.' He looked mournfully at the phone in Ashleigh's hand. 'I wanted to. Several times I started to reply and deleted it. It didn't feel real and it brought everything back.' He retrieved the phone from Ashleigh and laid it on the table, staring at it until the screen faded. 'I suppose I just wasn't ready, and there was nothing in the messages that convinced me it was him. They're all pretty generic, and I'm not hard to find in real life, rather than on Twitter. I wrote it off as the work of a sick prankster. And now it's something I truly regret.'

TWELVE

'I wish you'd told me.'

He was never going to let this drop. It was a constant refrain, the drip-drip of a Chinese water torture, an eternal play upon Emmy's guilt. 'I'm sorry, Rob.'

'Twenty-five years we've been married, Em. Twenty-five. I didn't think we had any secrets.'

'We don't. Not now. And I tried to be honest with you.'

'But not until you knew you were going to be found out.'

Opening the cupboard and extracting a packet of biscuits, Emmy cursed the busybody who'd seen and recognised Tino on the morning they'd discovered Luke's body. 'I've tried to explain. Here. Have a custard cream.'

'There's no need to snap at me.' He lifted an eyebrow. 'I'm not the one keeping secrets.'

Sometimes Rob's concern was suffocating. Of course Emmy loved him, but he was playing the victim with her when her heart screamed out for the kind of sympathy he couldn't, or wouldn't, give her. He'd struggled with Luke, and Luke had hated him in return. He'd done everything properly and supported her, but she'd sensed early on that he'd felt only relief after her son had gone. She'd sensed, too, that her mourning, and the inevitable guilt that accompanied it, had quickly come to irritate him; now his irritation was barely disguised and her continued association with Tino was causing that irritation to ferment into anger.

Rob was a loving man, she reminded herself, and she was in the wrong. He did everything for her. She needed to show gratitude. 'I didn't mean to.'

'I know you're grieving, Em. I am too.' She knew that was a lie. 'But let's just think about me, here. How do you think I feel, knowing you've been seeing another man?'

'That's exactly why I didn't tell you,' she said, with a sudden flash of spirit. 'Because I knew that's what you'd say and I knew that's what you'd think and it wasn't like that. It was only Tino.'

'He's not your husband. I am. If you needed help and support you should have come to me.'

But you don't understand. And it went on and on and on and round and round and would do until she'd convinced him she was suitably sorry and he had accepted her promise not to see Tino again. 'Yes. I know.' He'd made a liar of her because he couldn't accept the truth. Luke, alive or dead, would always bind her to her first love. 'I'm so sorry. I thought I was doing the right thing. I didn't want to upset you. But now I see I was wrong.'

As he looked across at her, his wounded expression softened. 'I don't mean to upset you either,' he said, extracting a custard cream, breaking it in half and dunking it in his coffee. 'I'm doing it for you. That's all. I'm only angry because I don't want you to be hurt.'

Emmy sat down opposite him. The grey streak in his

once-glossy dark hair made him look distinguished — a silver fox, as her mother (a fan) called him. He was a little older than she, nearer sixty than fifty. He'd made her happy. She should be grateful.

She reached out to touch his free hand. 'Shall we agree not to mention it again?' she asked, just as she had done the last time they'd had the discussion.

'Yes, of course,' he said, and so it was done. Until the next time, when he would turn those hurt eyes on her and say: *but how could you do it, Em? How could you deceive me after all I've done for you?*

He left his hand there for a moment, dunking the biscuit with the other, and eventually withdrew it. 'I'd better get back to work. What are your plans for the rest of the morning?'

'I might drive into town. I want to pick up some odds and ends. Do you need me to get anything?'

'I don't think so.' He considered, then gave her a sharp look. 'Just into town?'

'Yes.' She pretended not to understand what he was getting at. 'Maybe I'll drop in on Mum and Dad on the way back. Maybe not.' Her parents had moved out of Blacksty, where the steep steps of their house had been unsuitable for old age and the old building's rambling charm had grown too large for their needs and too expensive to maintain. Now they lived in a featureless modern bungalow in Penrith, from where they could walk to church and the shops. At least, she consoled herself, it couldn't have been her mother who'd spotted Tino on the road and led the police so swiftly to the right conclusion. She pushed back her chair.

'Are you sure it's just town?'

'I need to get out. That's all.' Even as she smiled at him she was plotting a small rebellion. She had vowed not to see Tino, but that was all and now it was time to pick up the offer of friendship Heather had dangled before her. 'I won't be too long.'

'Keep in touch.'

'I'll text you every half an hour.' She blew a kiss so he wouldn't take it as a challenge. When she left the room, he was laughing.

Feeling empowered, she headed for the cloakroom and unhooked her coat and scarf from the back of the door. It was raining heavily, and it was January. Heather, who was sufficiently disconnected from the rest of Emmy's life for her to say all the things she couldn't say to Rob or to her parents or even to Tino, wouldn't be working. It had taken the confirmation of her personal tragedy for Emmy to accept this, and Rob's explicit and outspoken disapproval of Heather meant acting upon it required daring. To him she was a casual employee — nothing more. When Emmy protested against this dismissiveness he doubled down; she was a chain-smoking, hard-drinking, rough woman, ex-army and tough as the boots she'd hung up almost twenty years before. She was not, he said often and loudly, the sort of woman they should be socialising with.

In her heart of hearts, Emmy thought this unreasonable, though her need for Rob's esteem was great enough that she let it dominate her and kept her plan to meet with Heather as covert as her meetings with Tino. Even under normal circumstances her gregarious nature had led her to indulge in sly chats with Heather behind the shed, over a cup of coffee she'd take out in the middle of the morning. Suitability wasn't everything, or even the biggest thing, and Emmy always tried her hardest to be open-minded. She had, after all, been attracted to Tino despite her mother's disapproval and there was a song in her soul that still sang only to him. It was his smile, or his cheerfulness, or the fact that he always remained so effortlessly happy.

Except for that time after Luke had disappeared.

Poor Tino. He'd kept his hopes up when hers had gone. Surely he wouldn't be happy now. She was tempted to call him and see how he was, but the risk was too great with Rob so concerned for her, watching every move and questioning her emotional wellbeing every fifteen minutes.

She tucked her scarf into the neck of her jacket and adjusted the zip, feeling guilty that she continued to lie to Rob despite her protestations, but she justified it. It was the whitest of white lies and she'd make time to nip into Penrith and pick up a couple of things to give it a veneer of truth. Half an hour, a quick cup of coffee and a friendly word would hurt no-one. Even if Rob found out — or if she found some way to tell him without making the mistake of a full-on confession, as she had done about her outing with Tino — it wasn't something he could hold against her for too long.

'I won't be too long. Text me if you think of anything you want.' And then she was out of the front door, breathing in the cold fresh air and feeling as if she'd escaped.

You really shouldn't feel like that about someone you loved. She walked briskly to the Renault and, safely in its shelter, called Heather. 'It's Emmy. I'm at a loose end. I don't suppose you fancy meeting for a cup of coffee or something, do you? I'm just going into town.'

'Sure. I'm at a loose end right now, too, as it happens.'

A raindrop slithered down the windscreen like the chill that ran down Emmy's spine. Heather sounded just as Rob did when Emmy had given him the answer he wanted. 'Where shall we meet?'

'Up to you.'

Emmy named a supermarket cafe, so she could be completely honest with Rob when he asked her, as he surely would, about her movements. As she turned along the road towards Penrith the thought troubled her at all sorts of levels. She shouldn't have to lie to him. He should take what she said at face value, and trust her.

When she arrived at the cafe Heather was already there, sitting at a table by the window staring down on the car park. Conscious of this visibility, Emmy found herself desperately wishing they were hidden away in a corner, but it was too late. To ask to move would seem neurotic and show Rob in a bad light; in any case, there were no spare seats in those dark back corners. Perhaps the whole of Penrith was involved in secret trysts and determined not to put their minor infidelities on show.

'Oh, Heather!' The gratitude she heard in her own voice was pathetic. 'I hope you haven't been waiting long.'

'I was in town already. No problems.'

Away from her work Heather dressed sensibly but with a feminine cast, a pale pink blouse showing at the neckline of a dove-grey cashmere jumper, a delicate silver filigree necklace with matching earrings. This vaguely surprised Emmy, too used to seeing her in jeans and wellies, and it occurred to her that she knew little about this woman who had become, by default, her friend — not even where she lived. 'Did you have to come far?'

'Not far. I live over towards Lazonby. It feels like the back end of nowhere, but I like it. I have a bit of land and I enjoy my own company.'

She must be single, then, or maybe divorced. 'Shall we order?' asked Emmy. 'I think I'd like a scone.' Not that she needed one but today was a day when she needed a treat.

'Has it been a bad week?'

Kindness surrounded Emmy like a down-filled duvet.

She blinked. She mustn't cry. 'Oh, no worse than you'd think, under the circumstances.'

'But sometimes it helps to have someone different to talk to, eh? Apart from all your other friends.'

Emmy nodded, as the waiter came to take their order. She had lots of friends, if by friends you meant the people she worked with at the food bank or socialised with at church. Most of them were friends she shared with Rob and under his eye it was impossible to talk to someone often enough, or for long enough, for them to become each other's confidante. 'I'm sure they've all heard my misery over and over,' she said, and laughed.

'I thought as much. I could see you were holding everything in. Well, I'm not going to put pressure on you to share but if you ever want to, you know I'm here.'

The waiter placed a tray on their table, and Heather took charge of unloading it, sliding plates and cups about the table. She must have been in her element in the army: competent, confident and in control. Emmy split her scone in two, spread butter and jam, and relaxed. 'I can't believe how difficult it is. It was bad enough discovering the body. When they told me it was Luke—' She stopped. 'Did you know that?'

'They said something about it in the village.' The coffee had come in a tall, clear cafetière. After a quick check of its strength, Heather pressed the plunger as if she were hitting the nuclear button. Bubbles whooshed up as the coffee grounds surged down. 'Milk? Yes. It must have been hellish for you to hear it. I'm so sorry. Sugar? Had you thought your poor lad was alive, then?'

'I knew he wasn't.' But until the DCI and his sergeant had arrived, she'd always been vulnerable to the momentary whispers of that rebel will-o'the-wisp, hope. 'Well, no. Of course I didn't know. But I was sure of it in my heart. I never thought he'd come back. I knew he wouldn't have left me for ever if he had the choice. And do you know, I don't think he did?'

'What do you mean?'

Emmy cast her mind back to that cold morning, the swell of olive-coloured nylon underneath the glassy surface of the tarn. What might have happened if Luke had lived? 'I think he came back because he wanted to see me.'

'Is that what the police think?' Heather stirred her coffee.

'What else could it have been? He wouldn't have wanted to come to the house.' Unless there had been some huge reversal to his thinking he wouldn't have wanted to come anywhere near Rob.

'They can be right bastards, the police.' Heather bit into her scone, chewed a little, and elaborated. 'Not that I've many dealings with them, but I know people who do. On at you all the time, trying to trip you up. Getting a conviction is all that matters to them, not finding out the truth. Don't let them bully you.'

'I don't suppose they can afford to be kind all the time.' The interviewing officers had been harsh with Emmy and Rob when Luke had first disappeared, less so this second time. Maybe policing had changed. Luke had been murdered, and they had to find the person who did it. She wanted them to be harsh to other possible suspects, but she, in her innocence, couldn't bear to have their searching questions roaming about in her life. 'I wonder what he wanted,' she said, and thought of him as a child, his soft cheek against her shoulder, sticky fingers on her neck.

'Maybe he just wanted to see his old mum.' Heather flashed her a sympathetic smile. 'It's a shame for you. And so near, if it was you he was trying to see. Though if it was, how did he know you were there?'

'I don't know.'

'Someone could have told him you were going up there, maybe.'

'I don't know who it could have been. Only Tino and I knew we were going.'

'You're quite sure your husband didn't?'

Emmy considered this suggestion for a moment, in a perplexed silence. Why not? For all his insistence that they had no secrets, Rob probably knew more, and did more, than he let on. She'd always thought he was honest with her, just as she'd always protested her honesty with him, but she lied, just a little, sometimes, so why shouldn't he? 'I don't know. Someone saw me with my ex-husband on Monday morning. They told the police about it. Tino and I have been up there every year for the past few years, so maybe whoever it was saw us the last time, or the time before as well.'

'And then told Rob?'

An involuntary shiver crawled up Emmy's spine. 'I don't think so. He never said anything.'

'Maybe he didn't want you to know he knew.'

'Oh but—'

'Emmy.' Heather paused in the act of lifting her scone to her mouth and her fingers tightened on it so that it crumbled. 'It's none of my business and you can tell me where to go if you want. Not that you will. You're way too nice for that.' A smile, as if to soften the blow. 'But is everything all right between you and Rob?'

'Yes. Why shouldn't it be?' Emmy could see the way Heather's mind was going. Her own was going that way too, and she didn't like it. Rob loved her to the exclusion of all else. It wasn't in his interests to have Luke back.

'He's a certain type, you know?' Heather let the crumbled scone fall to the plate and fussed about with her napkin. 'I've come across them in the army. Icily controlled all the time until they break and then it all hits the fan. I'm not saying he doesn't adore you, because it's plain he does, but love isn't always what you think it is. And it isn't always good.'

Rob was very controlled. It followed, therefore, that he was very controlling. Now here was Heather, saying exactly what Jude Satterthwaite had suggested, though much more directly. 'The detective asked me about that. But actually, you're both wrong. Rob's always been really kind to me.'

'I should bloody well hope so. You're his wife and he's supposed to love you.'

'He does love me!'

'But he shouldn't love you to the exclusion of yourself.' Heather wiped the last of the jam from her fingers. 'What else did the police say? Do they think they know who did it?'

She'd asked that before. Everyone would be asking the same thing, in the pub, in the street, in the local farm shop. They would speculate, point the finger. An enemy. A random stranger. Emmy herself. People were already looking at her in the village the way they'd done when Luke had first disappeared. 'They don't say much.'

'Did you ask?'

You didn't question the police. They questioned you. 'All I know is that it was Luke they found and they think he was murdered.'

'They don't have any idea where he's been? What he's been doing? All these years? No word of whether he's been seen around the area?'

'I suppose he must have been seen, mustn't he? Or why would someone——?' But why would someone want to kill Luke anyway? Emmy sipped her coffee and her head began to ache. She yearned to reach into her bag for paracetamol but she took too much of that these days, and it would seem an admission of weakness in front of someone as competent and effective as Heather. 'I don't know. Maybe it was an accident.'

'Could it have been?'

'I don't know. I just don't know.' Emmy dug into her pocket for a handkerchief and dabbed at her eyes. There was so much she wanted to confide to someone and Heather was ready and waiting, but her courage failed. Fear heaped itself upon her grief, a fear that the truth would kill her. 'It's been so nice to talk to you. It really has. But I need to get back. Rob will worry.'

'Text him, then. Surely he doesn't mind if you're out with your friends?'

'No, of course not. But I need to get back. We always have lunch together when he's at home.'

'One day won't hurt.'

They engaged in a battle of wills — not an antagonistic one, but a genteel tussle between Heather's persistent offer to listen and Emmy's refusal to be any more disloyal to Rob than she already was. In the end, rather to Emmy's surprise, she emerged victorious. Heather sat back and shook her head. 'If you need to go, you need to go. But why don't we do this again some time?'

'That would be lovely.'

'Soon, I mean. I'm not working much at this time of year. And I know you won't mind me speaking frankly, but you look like you need to talk to someone, even if you don't feel it's right. Just because you're married to someone it doesn't mean they have to be the be-all and the end-all of your life. You can have other friends. Otherwise it's not a healthy relationship. You know what I mean?'

For something else to do, Emmy gestured for the bill. 'Yes, but Rob and I—'

'Yeah, okay. I'm an old cynic.'

'You never married?' dared Emmy.

'No.' Heather picked at the edge of her fingernail. There was dirt still under it, ingrained from her digging and turning in other people's winter gardens. 'I never met a man who was worth my time and commitment. My money says you never did either.'

'Oh, but I did.' This time she said it with confidence, but even as she spoke she was thinking of Tino and how things might have worked out if they'd been a little more mature and not in so much of a hurry for guiltless, religiously-sanctioned sex. Now she was in her fifties she saw morality a little less strictly than she used to, but it was too late to change things, whatever her regrets. 'This was lovely, Heather. You're right. I did appreciate the chance to chat. We'll definitely do this again.'

'Let's fix a time.'

They compared diaries standing in the foyer of the cafe and fixed a date for the same time a fortnight later, and then Emmy rushed around the supermarket for a few bits and pieces to justify the exercise, before she headed back.

She drove slowly along the edge of the forest towards Blacksty, between tall stands of pine trees. What if Rob had known about her meetings with Tino? What if he'd found out and lain in wait for them? What if, somehow, he had slipped the chains of his business meeting far earlier than he claimed, and somehow come back to challenge them?

What if he'd then met Luke?

She shivered. The consequences didn't bear thinking about but Jude Satterthwaite's warning and Heather's suspicions chimed in turn with her own gut.

It wasn't a comfortable thought.

THIRTEEN

Since the discovery of Luke Mortimer's body in Bowscale Tarn, a combination of circumstances had heightened Ashleigh's anxiety. It wasn't just the long winter nights, though they played their part, but Emmy Leach's grief uncomfortably echoed and amplified Ashleigh's own mourning for the final and certain failure of her marriage. Now she was once more working closely with Jude, as if she needed a reminder that she'd ditched him for no reason other than her own folly.

The last one hurt the most, though she felt no guilt over it. Jude, who was emotionally as tough as old boots, had survived being dumped by Becca Reid and managed to deal as civilly with her as he did with Ashleigh. There was a lot Ashleigh felt she should learn from him, but though she'd rationalised her actions until she could reel off her self-justification as easily as she read a suspect their rights, she felt no better for it.

She hadn't, thank God, allowed her echoing personal failures to affect her professionalism, or she hoped not, but she dealt with human beings, too many of them suffering;

it was inevitable there would be crossover. She'd joined the force because she cared and now she thought she cared too much. On her way home she drifted down to the incident room, knowing Jude always ended his working day there to check on the progress of an investigation, certain she'd catch him.

He was standing in front of the whiteboard, staring it at it with his characteristic frown. A smile twitched at Ashleigh's lips. 'Don't you know everything on there by now? Or is there something new?'

He turned away and the frown dissipated. 'Not that I've put up on the board yet. Doddsy was telling me he's been chatting with his new best mates in Liverpool and they think they may have a lead. It's not certain, but they think there's a good shout that his face matches up to someone on their wanted list.'

There would be some grainy CCTV images, then, from some dark street, maybe years in the waiting until there was a match for a victim or a perpetrator. 'Wanted for what?'

'Supply of controlled substances.'

She perched on the edge of a desk and scanned the board again. Someone had highlighted Mosedale Barn on the OS map. It was close enough to Bowscale Tarn to invite a connection. 'Do you think it's got anything to do with the county lines inquiry?'

'It might do.' Jude allowed himself a fractious sigh, the closest he ever came to anger. 'It might be something else entirely. There are drugs everywhere, these days, and they don't just come from one gang in Liverpool. I hate those bastards. Dealing poison to kids who don't know any better. And look where we end up. Every bloody time.'

He had personal reasons for his deep dislike. Ashleigh hadn't known him when his younger brother had fallen in with the wrong crowd in exactly the way Luke Mortimer had done. Jude's partner, Becca Reid, had thought Jude's attitude high-handed and ended their relationship on the back of it; four years on, his relationship with Mikey was strained at best.

Mikey's supplier had once been Jude's closest friend. Ashleigh thought, though she didn't know, that Jude still cursed himself for not having spotted it at the time, though it was scarcely likely he could have done anything to prevent it. Now, with Adam Fleetwood out of prison and very obviously biding his time as he waited for revenge, he had a constant shadow at his back. That was why his expression darkened every time a drugs case crossed his desk.

'Yes. But we're onto them.' She gave him a sympathetic smile, one that said: *we may not be together any more but I still understand.* 'Or not us, necessarily, but someone is.'

'We knew Luke was a user,' he said, still staring at the board. 'Now it looks like he may have been a dealer as well, or at least a courier. I wonder if he did have anything to do with that gang up at Mosedale Barn. We should probably look a bit more closely.'

'Does that mean you want to bring the Merseyside force in on this?' In her turn, Ashleigh frowned at the puzzle on the board.

'Faye's reluctant to go down that route. I had a chat with her about it. We both think his presence in the dale may have something to do with the county lines operation, but she doesn't like the coincidence of where and when he was found. There's every chance his death is connected with his fake disappearance all those years ago.'

'Is that what you think, too?'

'One hundred per cent. It's good to agree with her, for once.' He grinned at her. 'The connection the Merseyside lot managed to establish is an old one. It goes back about five or six years. Realistically, all we can say is that someone who fits his description was wanted for dealing drugs in Liverpool six years ago, and that there's a Liverpool-based drugs gang operating here. That's all, really. My gut says it comes back to the parents.'

'Doesn't it always?'

'To some degree. That doesn't necessarily mean they did it.'

'It's possible someone wanted to stop him seeing them.' Ashleigh tried to imagine Luke's mindset, as he waited in the darkness or the fellside. Longing? Fear? Fury? Regret?

'I'd guess so. But that leads us to the questions of who and why, and I've no ideas on that score.' He turned away from the board and hooked his Barbour jacket off the back of a chair. 'I wish we could lay our hands on that camera card. That would shed light on it one way or another, I think. Maybe he was killed for that, rather than because he was waiting to surprise his parents.'

'Have you checked up on Rob Leach?' Ashleigh tried to sound casual. Every time she thought of Emmy she was more convinced that she was scared of her husband.

'Yes.' Jude was equally nonchalant. 'Routinely. There's nothing to make him anything more than a person of very slight interest to us. Chris tracked his movements pretty thoroughly. He definitely took the train that morning at twenty to seven and he definitely got to Manchester. Emmy says they were both at the house the previous night, but I suppose it isn't beyond the bounds of possibility he could have slipped out without her knowing.'

'It's also not beyond the bounds of possibility she knows where he was and was lying to cover it up.'

He slid his arms into the sleeves of his jacket and shrugged it up over his shoulders, then picked up his bag and turned towards the door. 'Interesting that you say that. I'd disagree with you completely if it wasn't for the fact she's already admitted lying to us. She comes across as very honest. But she isn't.'

There were good reasons for lying, as well as bad. Self-protection was one. 'I'm really worried about her.'

'We've had this conversation before. I agree her husband may be subtly coercive. I asked her about it, as sensitively as I could, and offered her support if she required it. She was adamant everything was fine. I filled in all the forms and recorded your concerns. They're my concerns, too, as it happens. It's on file, but as she's explicitly refused any help there's not much more we can do.'

'Victims of coercion often refuse help. They don't always realise they're being coerced, or they're scared.' In his statement Tino Mortimer, who perhaps had more reason than most to dislike Rob, had been adamant that Emmy's husband hadn't been violent, but he didn't have to be. Ashleigh's own ex-partner had been adept at humiliating her and subverting her, belittling her and undermining her self-esteem. It was only now she was away from him that she realised how severely it had damaged her.

'Yes.' They paced the corridor in a companionable silence, signed out of the building and went out into the car park. 'I know that. We see too much of it. But you know I've done all I can.'

'Is it enough?' The January wind hit them, the dark shadows swirled around. Ashleigh thought of Emmy, the telltale signs of her nervousness, the way Rob had been so solicitous towards her, so determined to make sure she was all right. She recalled the way he'd closed his hand on her shoulder and how she'd looked up to him. For reassurance, or to make sure she was giving the answer he wanted?

'Maybe not, but it's all we can do. I hate this scenario

as much as you do, but as it stands we don't know he's done anything wrong. He may well not have done.'

It was a trap for the police as well as the coerced. If Emmy refused help they had to wait for something to happen, and the potential consequences were unthinkable. Was Rob Leach the kind of man who might snap? 'Do we have to wait until he hurts her? I'm scared for her. Don't forget. I know all about controlling men.'

They'd reached her car by then. She reached into her bag for the key card and dropped it, sending it spinning away into the darkness at Jude's feet. He picked it up and handed it over. 'Ash. Are you okay?'

This was why he hadn't been keen for her to work with the Leaches, though she'd undoubtedly have been good at it, undoubtedly have got to the bottom of Emmy's concerns. The situation had arisen before and she'd become too engaged and involved in trying to help another woman in love with a controlling man. 'Yes. Why wouldn't I be?' And then when he didn't answer immediately, she rushed on. 'Don't you trust me to deal with Emmy?'

Another pause confirmed his view. She knew her weaknesses as well as he did. 'I haven't forgotten about last time,' she said, too quickly, 'but I've learned from it.'

'I know. It isn't that.' In the darkness she couldn't see his face. 'We haven't had a chat for a while.'

'We've seen plenty of one another this week.' Enough to remind her of how big a mistake it was, thinking someone you loved was necessarily good for you and sacrificing something wholesome on the altar of that error.

'You know that wasn't what I meant. We've talked as work colleagues, not as friends. If there's anything personal you want to talk about, I'm here.'

His forgiveness of her rejection, unspoken but obvious, was damning it its own way because it implied he didn't care. She'd seen the way he regarded Becca with narrow-lipped annoyance and registered its meaning — that he, like her, couldn't let an old love go. And how could she easily tell her ex-lover about how much she was still in love with the husband she'd been right to discard?

'I did everything right with Scott,' she said, aloud, and slopped a second, reckless quantity of wine into her glass. Some of it spilled over onto the tarot cards she'd spread out on the coffee table in front of her. A scarlet stain crept out across the Page of Cups, a card full of hope and optimism, one which reminded her of the qualities of forgiveness, yet at the same time threw up the shadow of Luke Mortimer in the cold dark waters of Bowscale Tarn. 'Everything. It hurts. It shouldn't be like this.'

The front door opened and her housemate, Lisa, clattered into the hallway. 'Ash! I hope you're feeling sinful! I brought doughnuts!'

Ashleigh swept up the deck, knocked the glass, caught it again and spilled the cards onto the floor. At least the wine was saved. 'Sinful as hell. I hope you brought a sackload. I need a treat.'

'Bad day?' Lisa arrived in the living room to the accompaniment of a swirling cloak of winter, cold and damp. There was rain on her shoulders and mud on her shoes. 'Mine was rubbish. We had a departmental IT crisis. It wasn't my fault, but I spent the day watching my screen buffering. So I thought, the only thing to cancel out frustration is doughnuts.' She cast a look at the debris, the cards on the floor, the glass in Ashleigh's hand, the puddle on the table. 'Ah, okay. It's not just me then.'

'I don't think my day was any worse than usual.'

Regaining her dignity, Ashleigh gathered up the cards that had fallen and mopped up the spillage with a tissue. The Three of Swords, the card she always associated with Scott, smiled up at her. She turned it face down, out of sorts with the cards for the first time in her life.

'No? So that's a good third of a bottle of wine you've had, by the look of it, and I don't think you're treating the cards with the usual respect.' Lisa poked fun at Ashleigh's hobby, as most people who knew about it did, but at least she had the sensitivity to understand that her friend took it seriously. 'Not that I'm judging you.'

'You're right. I shouldn't have started reading them. I'm not in the mood.'

'Is something wrong?' Lisa dropped the bag of dough-nuts on the table. 'I'll get plates. And another glass, since if you're going to be drinking on a school night because you had a bad day, you shouldn't be drinking alone.'

She disappeared to the kitchen, crashing about with the cupboards. By the time she came back with two plates and another glass, Ashleigh had calmed herself down and heaved another log on to the wood burner. 'Sorry. I'll get over it.'

'There's always something, isn't there? I couldn't do your job,' said Lisa, mournfully. She ripped open the bag of doughnuts and picked the one covered in thick pink icing and sprinkles. 'A heart attack in a paper bag, these. If I die from eating too many of them, some future me will excavate my grave and judge me for the sugary contents of my twenty-first century stomach, and I don't care. What is it today? Something nasty to do with that case up in Mungrisdale?'

Ashleigh picked a slightly more respectable doughnut, plain jam. Sugar spilled from it onto the table. It amused her how Lisa, an archaeologist, dealt so coldly with dead bodies. Hundreds or thousands of years gave some perspective, but even old bones had lived real lives, had loved and hated and feared. 'That one's fairly straight-forward.'

'What is it, then?'

She could tell Lisa anything, but today she didn't want to. There was nothing new to say, nothing that would or could change anything that had happened or the way she felt. 'It's a potential domestic violence case. I can't say any more.' The last sentence protected her from questions about the convenient untruth.

'No, of course. I won't ask.' Lisa licked her fingers and gave Ashleigh a sideways look. 'It's not because—'

'No.'

'It's just because you've been a bit on edge since Scott—'

'No.' Since she'd managed to persuade both Scott and herself that the split was final, since Lisa had managed to persuade her that it was the only thing for her. 'I'm sure we can find better things to talk about than men.'

'Oh, yeah. sure.' Still that sideways look. 'We're not talking about men, though, are we? We're talking about your general wellbeing.'

'I've already had one person today imply I can't do my job properly because I can't control my emotions. I don't need you telling me as well.' Ashleigh swigged her wine, annoyed with herself.

'I didn't say that.'

'No. Sorry.' She hadn't meant to say that, or at least not like that. And Jude hadn't said it either, or not in so many words. Fairness prompted her to add: 'You're right. I get too involved with other people's emotions. I need to step away.'

'Wine and doughnuts will do the job as well as

anything else, I suppose.' Lisa stretched her long leg out towards the fire. 'Is there a tarot card for that?'

'I wish.' Putting the glass down, Ashleigh picked up the pack and fanned it out, sorting through it until she came to the card she wanted. It was the King of Swords — stern, dominant, and controlling. She looked at it and saw Rob Leach's cool, calculating eyes and Scott's knowing smile, a dozen violent criminals now locked up, a hundred more who took their pent-out frustrations at their inadequacies out on weaker partners and walked free.

It was too much. On impulse, she tore the card in half lengthways and, under Lisa's astonished gaze, opened the wood burner and dropped it into the heart of the flames.

FOURTEEN

'I'm worried about our Ashleigh,' Doddsy said, keeping his head down over his laptop.

Jude, with whom he shared an office, looked up and swung his chair around to stare out of the window. Somewhere out there, buried in the thick blanket of cloud that obscured the distant fells, was Blencathra, with Bowscale Fell guarding its rear and sheltering the tarn. Somewhere out there was the person who'd killed Luke Mortimer.

'Is that right?' he said, trying to keep a chill in his voice.

Doddsy was his mate as well as his colleague, neither needing a warning to back off nor obliged to heed it. He couldn't be frozen out in the way someone else might be. 'You'll have noticed it, too. Seeing as you know her so much better than the rest of us.'

Despite himself, Jude grinned. 'Yes. Okay.'

'And my line of thought is that this case is upsetting her more than it usually would and that if you don't want problems further down the line, you need to take it up with her. But I think you know that.'

'I tried.' Jude swung the chair back again. The problem of Luke Mortimer was one he'd come back to in every spare moment until it was solved, but the issue of Ashleigh O'Halloran was immediate. Ashleigh was the best of the interviewers on the team, possibly the best he'd ever met. Her intuitive understanding amounted almost to mind-reading and her capacity for empathy teased information from the most reluctant witnesses and, less often, confessions from the most surprising suspects in a way none of them was able to explain. Sometimes he felt that himself. She made it easy to tell her things, and to believe she'd understand. It was one of the reasons he'd avoided her since she'd ended their relationship — because it wouldn't take ten minutes conversation on that particular subject for her to rumble how relieved he was that it had all ended. 'She wasn't very receptive.'

'I can talk to her if you like, but it'll come better from you. She doesn't need a bloke old enough to be her dad telling her she's getting too emotionally involved in a case. And if I don't do it and you don't do it, then Faye will see it and she'll do it. And we don't want that, either.'

Doddsy, who was being self-deprecating and was scarcely fifteen years Ashleigh's elder, might after all be the best one for the job. Both Jude himself and, a while before, Faye had indulged in relationships with Ashleigh. In Faye's case (according to Ashleigh's version) it had been a catastrophic error of judgement when both women were rocking at collapsing marriages and neither of them trusted a man for comfort. With him it had begun with pure lust and ended in friendship and respect. If Ashleigh didn't already know how glad he was to be free of that relationship and available for Becca if she were ever to show any interest, she'd work it out within minutes. He had his own feelings to consider; any conversation of that nature would remind him once more that Becca had turned him down again, and not gently. His pride wouldn't stand for that. 'No. That's true.' Faye and Ashleigh worked better through an intermediary.

'Then it looks like you'll have to try again.'

'What exactly do you think the problem is, then, Doddsy?' Sitting back, Jude flexed his fingers in front of him. He was pretty sure he knew, but there was never any harm in a bit of independent corroboration.

'She's got a bee in her bonnet about Emmy Leach.'

'We've spoken about that. Ashleigh thinks the Leaches' relationship is an unhealthy one, and having seen the two of them, I think she's right. I've raised it, as delicately as possible, with Emmy and been politely but firmly rebuffed. I offered her a list of contact phone numbers if she needed them and she refused to take it. I've recorded it all and placed it on the file. You can check it out.'

'I've seen it. But Ashleigh doesn't think we should leave the matter there.'

Jude sighed. The relationship was over but he still cherished what he'd learned about her character. He understood, almost certainly better than any of their colleagues, just how far the skills which made her so exceptional at one part of her job could undermine her and leave her emotionally vulnerable. 'Okay. I'll talk to her. But informally.'

'You're in the best position to do that.'

Jude drummed his fingers on the desk. 'Fair point.' Not in the mood to waste time worrying about it, he picked up his phone and called her number. 'Ash. It's a quick and unofficial call, but I wondered if you were doing anything tonight.'

Doddsy winked across the office.

'Sitting at home going through interview notes I expect,' said Ashleigh. 'Why? Is there something you need me to do?'

'I wondered if you'd help me out. Like, come and keep me company for a drink.'

'Making personal calls in office time, Chief Inspector?' she sniped back at him, but he could sense her amusement. 'That's not like you.'

'We can talk shop if you want, but I'm a bit of a Billy no-mates just now and it's my birthday. I don't fancy celebrating on my own.'

'Oh, of course. I saw the incident room was looking like a bakery. Happy birthday. Not that I ate any of the cakes you brought. Lisa bought doughnuts last night, and the sight of any baked goods will just about kill me today.'

'All the more for the rest of us, then.' Jude checked the clock quickly, looked down at his laptop to see which of the team was doing what, and when. 'Are you off out to Carlisle this afternoon? Is that right?'

'Yes. I'm going to see Chloe Ferris, Luke's ex, to see if she can add anything to what Tino Mortimer said.'

'You'd think by now she'd have told us if she'd heard anything.'

'You would, but Tino wrote the messages off as the work of a prankster, so maybe she did the same.'

They'd find out. 'Okay then. You can tell me all about it this evening. Text me when and where and I'll see you there.'

'I'm still fond of him. Of what he was, I should say.' Chloe Ferris, Luke's one-time girlfriend and the mother of his child, ran a hand through long, blue-streaked blonde hair. She'd moved on from being a wild child and a teenage mother and embraced middle-class respectability, but the blue dye indicated the free thinking of her youth persisted. These days, Ashleigh had learned, she worked part-time as office manager for a firm of accountants and was married to a PE teacher at a local secondary school. Their two children, both under school age and obviously always under her feet, were sitting in front of the television and staring intently at the bright primary colours and flashing images of an American cartoon while Ashleigh and Chloe sat at the far end of the narrow living room. 'And of course he gave me Libby. I adore Libs. She's at school right now, but she'll be back any minute.'

'Were you surprised when he disappeared?' asked Ashleigh.

'That was the thing about Luke. Nothing he did ever surprised me. It's why I liked him so much. He was a laugh, always a laugh, and he didn't give a damn about anyone. So no, I wasn't surprised. When they said he'd got lost, yeah. I rolled my eyes at that.' She shook her head. 'He wasn't the sort to get lost, unless we'd had a wee puff of the wacky baccy. He could do anything, then.' She shot a quick glance across at the two youngsters but they were still absorbed in the telly. 'I shouldn't say that, should I?'

'Nobody's going to nick you for a few rollups fifteen years ago.' Murder was different; they would bend over backwards to get someone for that, whether it was fifteen years ago or much, much longer.

But, as it had turned out, Luke hadn't been murdered fifteen years before.

'Thank God for that. We were just kids, playing about. Pushing the boundaries. It's what kids do. But some always have tougher boundaries than others and they're the ones who push hardest against them. Luke was one of those.' Chloe jumped up, plucked a tissue from a box on the mantelpiece and swooped on one of the children. The runny nose wiped, she resumed her seat.

'Who set the boundaries, then?' asked Ashleigh. 'His mother? Father? Stepfather?'

'His mam and stepdad, I think. His dad was never around to do it, and he always seemed a bit more laid back. I think Luke liked his dad, and they kept in touch, but they didn't see each other much. That's never good. His mam was a bit clingy and he found that claustrophobic. And his stepdad was always nice enough on the few times I was round there, but I always thought he was pretty cold.'

Ashleigh's impression of Chloe, now in her early thirties, was that she was the antithesis of Emmy. If her character had been set on the same lines fifteen years earlier, it was easy to see how Luke might have been attracted to such a casual, carefree approach. 'You must have missed him when he left.'

'Oh, I never thought it was for ever. I mean, of course I thought I was in love with him, because at that age you do. But I wasn't, and nor was he. When he disappeared I was gutted but it was a kind of mass hysteria, if you know what I mean. And that's another thing about his mother.'

Ashleigh waited while Chloe ran a judgemental eye over her two younger offspring, decided no action was required, and settled back into her chair. 'Go on.'

'I always know where Libby is. I always sense when this pair aren't well, even if they're with someone else. I'm their mam. I think I'd know...' Her voice had dropped to a whisper, in case the children overheard her. '...if something terrible happened to them. Even if I didn't know for sure, if I hadn't seen it for myself I'd never, ever stop believing they'd come back.'

'But Luke's mother—?'

'She's different. Maybe it's her faith. Maybe she just thinks what will be will be. I don't know. But I thought she gave up on him very easily.'

Emmy, Ashleigh recalled, had so obviously been convinced of her son's death. 'What about his stepfather?'

'I remember going over all this in my head at the time, when I was sitting up in the wee small hours with Libby. Over and over. God, Luke hated that man. I never understood at the time, but later on I saw a couple of documentaries on psychology. It was the two of them competing for his mam's attention, I bet, and her sitting in the middle like the ice queen, letting them fight over her.' Chloe shook her head.

It was a depressingly familiar scenario. 'Do you keep in touch with them?'

'We did, for a while. I was never that fond of any of them, God knows, but we owed it to Libs to keep up contact with her dad's family. Emmy came to visit sometimes, and her man with her, sitting watching over her like some kind of jailer, but they soon stopped coming. She wasn't good with kids, I don't think. She never understood them, never relaxed with them. And she didn't approve of the way I was bringing Libs up. With her it was all good behaviour and church on Sundays and always doing things for other people.' She turned an adoring smile on her children. 'Whereas I always think, when you're a kid you need a bit of fun. Oh, you've to teach them good manners and to be polite to other people and not do them any harm, sure, but that doesn't mean they can't enjoy themselves. I cut Libs a bit of slack, and she turned out all right.' She beamed. 'If I say it myself. But she's got a good stepdad. That makes all the difference.'

'So you stopped seeing Luke's parents completely…when?'

'It was a few years ago. They didn't come much when Libby was little and it was down to Christmas and birthdays pretty soon. When she was about ten she decided she didn't want to see them any more. I stopped inviting them round and they never asked to come. It all kind of fell away. I haven't seen either of them for years.'

'And his father?'

'Tino? He's a different kettle of fish altogether, him.' Chloe laughed. 'He has that knack some people have. He knows when to come and when to leave. He understands there's a distance to keep. Luke got on okay with him, and I see why. He'd be much easier to be friends with and he never interfered. As Libs got older, I left it up to her to decide how often she sees him, just as I did with Emmy. They meet up every now and then. He always takes her out for a slap-up tea on her birthday. I daresay they're in touch all the rest of the time as well. But that's how it should be. There's no obligation and no interference. If Libby wants to talk to me about him, she knows she can.'

The cartoon came to a raucous end. Chloe glanced quickly at the clock as the credits rolled. 'Is there anything else?'

'No. Thanks for your time.' Ashleigh had never thought the interview would yield much. 'By the way, did Emmy and Rob get on?'

'God, it 's such a funny set up with that pair. You never know. Luke said they didn't but he wasn't exactly a detached observer. He hated his stepdad so much he was bound to think he made his mam miserable, even if he didn't. I know myself it's possible to argue with the person you love and still love them. That's what kids do to you. They stretch you thin.' She laughed. 'Maybe he was right. I never saw it myself, but I hardly knew them before Libby was born. I wasn't the right sort of person. My dad's always been a bit of a drinker and a swearer, though that doesn't make him bad.' That laugh again. 'It's always difficult to tell when folk are happy, though, isn't it? We have such different ideas of happiness.'

She guided Ashleigh towards the door. 'You'll laugh, but for a while I wondered if his stepdad might have had something to do with him disappearing. Time proved me wrong on that one, though. Poor Luke. I suppose I'll see his parents at the funeral, whenever that is. That'll be weird. I wonder where he was all that time? And never in touch.'

'Not at all?'

Chloe looked wistful. 'No. I used to think I saw him sometimes, but it always turned out to be someone else.' She blinked away a tear. 'Funny how the mind plays tricks.'

'There weren't any messages?'

'No,' said Chloe definitely. 'And now there never will be. You make damn sure you catch the beggar that did for him.' She opened the door and Ashleigh was barely out of it before Chloe closed it on her, firmly, just in time to stop one of the toddlers darting out.

Ashleigh had parked about fifty yards along from the neat modern semi where Chloe and her family lived. A knot of teenagers in school uniform lounged against the wall at the end of the street, laughing, some of them smoking, and she paused to give them half a look. These kids were pushing boundaries just as Luke had done. Most would settle down pretty quickly but some of them, maybe, would progress from nicotine to other narcotics and cross her path in less innocent circumstances, years down the line.

She hadn't told Chloe that Luke, an occasional drug user in his teens, had moved on to harder things. She turned her back on the teenagers and headed for the car, but by the time she got there she saw in the wing mirror that someone was behind her. One of the group, a slender girl with her school skirt rolled over at the waist to bring it as high above her knees as she dared, and with two buttons of her school shirt undone and obvious inside the open front of her blazer, had detached herself from her peers and was heading towards her.

It was a fair bet who this was. The girl had Chloe Ferris's wide brown eyes, and the narrow lips were evident in the pictures of Luke, alive and dead, on the whiteboard in the incident room.

'Are you the police?' the girl asked.

'Yes. And are you Libby?'

Such simple deduction had an immediate effect. Libby Ferris looked mightily impressed. 'You've been to see my mam, haven't you? About my dad.'

'That's right.' Ashleigh looked her up and down. Libby had gone pink in the face and the group she'd left were all watching them with interest, as if they'd dared her to go up and speak and now, having completed the dare, she wanted to cut and run. 'I know you never met him, but your dad's always your dad. You must have been upset to hear about it. I'm so sorry.'

'Yeah. That's it.' Libby picked at the fraying sleeve of her blazer. 'I never talked to Mam about him, because I thought she'd be upset, but I always hoped he'd come back one day. Maybe when I saw Granddad on my birthday he might just turn up to surprise me. But he never did and now he never will.' The faintest tear sparkled in her eye. Her mascara was already smudged. This wasn't the first time that day that Libby Ferris had been crying.

'I know it doesn't make it any easier,' said Ashleigh, even more gently than she'd been with Chloe, 'but we will find out who did it.' It was a high-risk promise, but she was sure they'd make it good.

'Yeah. But you know.' Libby looked down at her feet and her black ankle boots scuffed the pavement. 'There's something else. Something I didn't tell anyone. I think he might have been trying to get in touch with me.'

'Recently?' Chloe had claimed to have received no messages, and Ashleigh was sure she hadn't been lying. That meant she was out of the loop, whomever that loop involved. Tino, Libby...and Luke?

'Yeah. In the last couple of weeks. I didn't answer it. It was just some random bloke, I thought. You get these sickos on social media.' As if Ashleigh was unaware of it. 'I get a lot of weirdos sending PMs and dick pics on Insta and the rest of it. We all do. But these came on Messenger.'

She got out her phone and showed it to Ashleigh. 'Here. I don't want to give it to you, obvs. But this is what it said.'

FIFTEEN

When Jude arrived at the wine bar Ashleigh was already at the counter, chatting to the manager. He took off his coat and dropped it at the table in the window where she'd left her jacket and bag, and sat down as she came back. Doing so spared him the difficult decision of how to greet her — with an air kiss, a peck on the cheek or nothing at all — and so define the current state of their relationship. 'Sorry I'm late. Things came up. You know how it is.'

'I got you a red wine,' she said, 'though it's cheeky of me to order for you and if you'd rather have something else I can go back and stop them pouring it. But they have a really meaty Rioja and the barman talked me into getting you to try it.'

'That sounds perfect.' She'd read his mind again. Sometimes he liked a Guinness or a pint of Loweswater Gold, but a cold winter night called for a strong red wine. 'Sorry, again. I was in with Faye. She likes to keep me late. I think she does it deliberately.'

'There was me thinking you were held up by the weight of birthday greetings wedging your front door shut.'

'Ha.' Jude allowed himself the wryest of smiles and could tell by the look on Ashleigh's face that she'd seen it. He didn't know why he was surprised. She always did. 'If only.'

The barman came over with the drinks and nibbles and set them down on the table. 'And?' persisted Ashleigh. 'What's the story? Did everyone but me forget your birthday?'

'I was being self-indulgent. My greatest fan sends me a present every year. Thirty pieces of silver. Chocolate. Left over from Christmas.'

'A cheapskate, then.'

'As well as everything else.' He stopped for a moment to think of what else Adam Fleetwood was — a former friend, an ex-convict, a one-time drug dealer and a continuing bad influence on Mikey.

'So small-minded,' said Ashleigh, sympathetically.

'I'm used to it by now. I expect he'll drift past here, any moment. He lives at the bottom of my street and keeps track of my movements.' Adam had dated Becca, briefly, in a move surely calculated to provoke. 'On the bright side, the chocolate keeps the mousetraps baited for a few weeks.' He lifted his glass. 'Cheers.'

'Happy birthday.'

They clinked glasses. He noticed Ashleigh closing in on her drink as if she were desperate, her fingers gripping the stem of the glass. 'Thank you. And before we talk about anything else can I be boring and ask you how you got on with Chloe Ferris this afternoon?'

'You won't have had a chance to see my briefing note if you've been in with Faye all afternoon.'

He raised an eyebrow. 'I saw you'd circulated something.'

'What, and you managed to resist the temptation to read it? You're losing your cutting edge.'

He'd already been running late when he'd seen it. 'There was no point, when I knew I can get it straight from the horse's mouth.'

'Thanks for the compliment.' She put down her glass, picked it up again, swirled the gin round in it and set it down once more. 'It was interesting. I don't mean the interview with Chloe herself. She'd nothing to add except a few regrets and a fair amount of disrespect for Emmy Leach. But when I was leaving, her daughter — Luke's daughter — stopped me.'

'Libby?'

'Yes. I thought she seemed pretty cut up about everything, which is to be expected.' She helped herself to a couple of peanuts from the portion which had arrived with the drinks.

'I get that. He was her dad, and that matters. You don't have to know someone to have a relationship with them, in your head at least.' Even when you chose to end a relationship, it still existed. Mikey hadn't spoken to their father for ten years and yet the chasm between father and son grew darker, deeper and more bitter with every failure of communication. 'She might have idolised him.'

'Not idolised, perhaps, but she probably focussed on his virtues rather than his faults. And it looks as if she might have come closer to a relationship with him than she thought. She's been getting messages from someone claiming to be her dad.'

Jude sat up at that. 'Is that right? Just like Tino. What did she say? Did she ever meet him? Agree to?'

'No. Like Tino, she thought it was probably an internet

troll. And the contact didn't amount to much, just a couple of messages and no background information. She was reluctant to give me the phone. Which is fair enough. Kids these days.'

Jude smothered a grin. He could imagine. All sorts of things went on on teenagers' phones, most of it harmless but embarrassing, though some of it was undoubtedly dangerous and he'd seen enough transcripts to have sour thoughts along with the amusement. 'I bet. Fifteen, is she? Jeez. I'm sure she doesn't want any adult to look too closely. I don't think I'd want to. Though obviously we can go back to her if we have to, but if there's no reason to suppose she's hiding anything I don't think there's any benefit in being heavy-handed.'

'Indeed. I hope we don't have to do that, because I think it took her a lot of courage to speak to me. Anyway, she agreed to let me have some screenshots, and I got her to agree to take the phone in to the police station in Carlisle and they'll download the relevant data so they can follow it up. There was no profile picture for the sender, though of course we have the number. He told her his name was Luke but he was going about under the alias of Colin Caton.'

'Did you get a chance to follow that up?'

'Only very quickly. Chris is going to look tomorrow and see what he comes up with. He's also going to see if he can find anything else — a phone registered to that name, for example, or an email address.'

'If it was Luke, and if he was up to anything criminal, he'd have used a burner phone.'

'Yes, but he may have used his own phone for his own business. I've passed the details on to Doddsy and he's sent them off to his friends in Liverpool, but it looks to me as if we may have found Luke's alias, and that gives us a lead on to where he's been and what he's been up to for the last few years.'

There was every chance Luke's past would shine a light onto a web of dodgy dealings. Jude lifted his glass and immediately, looking out into the dark, regretted having sat at the table Ashleigh had chosen. As he'd expected, the figure of Adam Fleetwood ghosted past, lifted a hand in recognition, smiled and drifted on. He turned his back. 'Sorry. What?'

'You weren't kidding about Adam, were you?' Ashleigh had seen him, too. Her expression was sympathetic.

Adam was a thorn in his flesh, the source of a series of trivial and easily-discounted complaints drip-fed to the Professional Standards department at regular but not-too-frequent intervals. They were carefully timed so Jude's superiors were beginning to tire of the waste of time and resources required to investigate them, even though they knew he'd be guiltless. Adam was like that: clever, and patient. He clung to friendships with both Becca and Mikey, surely for the dual purpose of irritating his former friend and ensuring their paths crossed regularly, a reminder that he hadn't forgotten his grievance.

To hell with it. Jude considered himself at least as clever and twice as patient. Eventually Adam would tire of the game and give up, or overstep the mark and find himself on the wrong side of the law. 'No. But I'm used to him by now. He doesn't bother me.'

'Is that right?'

'He irritates me, like a gnat. That's all.' Adam would have seen him with Ashleigh and a false whisper would get back to Becca that their relationship was on again, quelling any faint hope he'd ever had of reigniting their romance. 'Enough about me.' He kept his back resolutely turned, though still caring enough to watch in the reflection in the window to be sure Adam had gone. 'How about you? I'm sensing you're a little on edge these days, and I don't think I'm the only one. I wanted to make sure everything was okay. But not as—'

'— my boss. As a friend. You said.' She picked the glass up and sipped. He judged she was deciding whether to confide, and in the end the gin, and the fact that they still liked each other and didn't have to deal with the fallout if either of them had ever deluded themselves they were in love, seemed to do the trick. 'I never did like January. It's a vile, dead month and there's nothing in it to look forward to. And yes, I know you'll ask what I mean. I suppose I'm just having a bit of a wobble about Scott.'

It had been obvious. Ashleigh was a fidget at the best of times, but the constant byplay with the gin glass had betrayed just how unsettled she was. 'I thought it was all over.'

'It is. It literally is. I gave him one last chance and of course he blew it. There was one last mistake with one last pretty girl, and one last plea for forgiveness. And that was it. For my own health, he had to go. But I did love him. I knew it would be hard.'

Jude thought of Emmy and Tino, Chloe and Libby, all wondering where Luke had gone, all clinging to a last hope that they might one day see him again. Sometimes when people did come back and relationships were rekindled, the dream wasn't the same as the past had been. If Luke had come home he would have brought his problems, whatever they might be, with him. 'But not this hard, eh?'

Ashleigh must have been thinking along the same lines. 'You know how it is. I've been speaking to all these people who knew Luke. If he'd come back I don't think it would have gone well, do you? From what we know of him already he'd fallen into bad company. My money says he wasn't just here for fun, either, even if he did take the chance to look up old friends and relatives while he was here. It all ended horribly. And of course there was Emmy.'

Jude had got to the bottom of his glass sooner than he'd expected. At Ashleigh's nod in return to his questioning look he got up, crossed to the bar and ordered more drinks. 'Yes,' he said, resuming his seat. 'Poor Emmy.'

'There. You see it too.'

'Was Scott ever violent?' he asked her, something he'd often wondered about but never felt able to express. Now there was enough distance between them for it not to sound in any way jealous or possessive.

'No.' She shifted in her seat. He judged it wasn't quite a lie, but nor was it the whole truth. 'Not physically. But there are all sorts of ways of harming people. You know that. I don't think he even realised he was doing it. It's just some people have such a strange idea of love. It's all-consuming, and that's the way they think it ought to be. Maybe I'm as much to blame. He always used to accuse me of being possessive, because I wasn't prepared to put up with the other women.'

Scott, Jude knew, had worked for a sailing firm in the Mediterranean and had seemed to regard the long line of bikini-clad beauties who crossed the decks as both a perk of the job and a way to fill the time he was apart from his wife. Some long-distance marriages worked but Ashleigh's, where one partner strayed and expected the other to remain faithful, had never had a chance. 'You were quite right.'

'I know. But that's the thing about people like Scott. Not just men. I've seen it in women as well. They make people doubt themselves. That's what he did to me. Until that happened I never did doubt myself, and most of the time I still don't.' She drank again. 'Let's not pretend. I know the real reason you asked me out.'

'I asked you out because it's my birthday and I thought you might want to have a drink with me to celebrate.'

She giggled. 'You said that with a straight face. I wasn't born yesterday. You want to give me a ticking off about Emmy.'

'No, not that.' He studied her face and she looked back at him, with nothing to hide. It was all there in her eyes. 'I wanted to make sure you were all right and I wanted to reassure you — again — that as far as Emmy is concerned, we've done everything possible to help.'

'She absolutely triggered me,' Ashleigh confessed. 'That's what it was. When I said Scott hadn't been violent that was true, but only up to a point. He was never violent with me. If he had been I'd have gone like a shot and never looked back. But he could be violent with others.'

'I see.'

'It isn't even recent. It was before we married and I didn't find out about it until later. When he was drunk he got into some brawl or other in a taverna somewhere in Rhodes and there was a court appearance and a hefty fine. But he was much younger, then, and I thought he'd reformed.'

'And had he?'

'In that sense, yes. I think so. It hasn't happened again. But later, when he became more confrontational and when he'd had a drink I always thought of that. I always knew he was capable of hurting me.' She stared down into her glass again, unable to meet Jude's eye. 'That's what it was about Emmy Leach that troubles me so much. I think she feels exactly the same about her husband, and that's why I think she's afraid of him. It's not because of anything he's done, but what she thinks he might do if she gives him what he thinks is reason. I bet he stopped her from seeing Libby. But before you ask I've no evidence for it and that's why I never said.'

Jude rubbed his chin. A few months earlier he'd have taken her hand for consolation, but these days they inhabited a different world. It didn't mean her expression pained him any less, but only that there was little he could do about it without overstepping boundaries. 'Okay. I understand now why you got stressed out. And I think it was right not to allocate you as Emmy's FLO.' Faye couldn't have known the background to Ashleigh's marriage, or if she did she hadn't realised its significance. Or, knowing Faye, she knew and was trying to make a point about public service, without stopping to think about her duty of care.

'You're probably right. At the time I was keen to do it but I thought it needed someone who understood. I thought I might be able to help her. She might talk to me.'

'I told you. I raised the matter with her and she turned down my offers of help outright. She wouldn't even take a contact number.'

'Yes, because he might find it and then he'd know.'

'Nevertheless.' Jude thought again of Emmy, cool, steadfast and suppressing apparent outrage at the idea she might need help. 'I'll warn Mandy, and tell her what I've said and that you formed the same impression. She can take it on. And I promise you that if anyone else needs to go and see Emmy — or Rob, come to that — outside of the routine FLO visits, I'll do it myself.'

She seemed mollified. 'You've way more important things to do than that, surely.'

'Yes, but I can make an exception in this case.'

'Okay then. Though I suppose you're right and if she won't play ball there's nothing more we can do.'

Jude turned back to his drink. Neither of them said it but he was sure she was thinking the same as he was — that if she was right there was one very obvious thing that might trigger Rob Leach's anger, and that was the meetings with Tino that Emmy had kept secret for so long.

SIXTEEN

'**D**o you have any plans for the afternoon?'

Emmy picked up the soup plates and carried them over to the dishwasher, glad of the chance to turn her back on her husband. These days his constant watchfulness made her both nervous and guilty. 'Not what you'd call plans. Is there something you want me to do?'

'No, not especially. I'm just worried about you.'

She closed the dishwasher and made herself face him. 'About me?'

'You seem a bit on edge.' He gave her his best reassuring smile, but still she sensed his disapproval. 'That's all.'

Since the possibility of Rob having killed Luke had come into her head, Emmy hadn't been able to settle. It was a ludicrous idea. She knew that. She'd dropped him off at the station and gone straight to her assignation with Tino. It surely wasn't possible that he'd got there before her, but she couldn't swear to his movements every second of the preceding night. Rob liked to be in charge in his own home and had hated the challenges Luke had constantly thrown at him. They would have increased tenfold if her boy had come home a man.

'Would you like something sweet to follow up?' she asked, to distract him. 'There's some of that lemon cake I made yesterday.' Like a 1950s housewife, because she knew he liked her to look after his every possible desire. 'Or there's fruit.'

'No thanks. I'd better get back to work. I promised to get some drawings across to a client by close of play today and they're not coming together. I need to get my head down.' He looked across at her. 'Why don't you go down to the studio? You haven't been there for a bit.'

He probably thought she could do no harm in the studio, alone with her thoughts. 'I could do.' It was cold down there in the winter and these days her creativity had become limited. After Luke's disappearance Rob had encouraged her to harness her enthusiasm for pottery and indulged her with a fully-equipped studio where, she now saw, she could be under his eye. She enjoyed throwing pots and lamps that raised a little bit of money when she sold them in the craft shops in Keswick and Caldbeck — enough to justify the exercise, if not to make a living. Her career was a game but it suited both of them for her to pretend she had some kind of autonomy. *My wife is a potter*, Rob would explain to people who he felt were judging them for exercising their choice to have a breadwinner and a homemaker.

It might have been a little less old-fashioned if they'd had children of their own, but she hadn't been ready for another child for a while after their marriage and then they'd been so consumed by Luke's hostility that neither of them could face the thought of the chaos a competing sibling might bring. After Luke's disappearance she couldn't handle Rob's tentative suggestion they should start a family. That would imply a replacement for Luke; and Luke, for all his faults, was irreplaceable.

'It'll be a distraction for you.' He got up. 'I like those pale blue dishes you did the last time for the craft fair. The ones my mum likes so much.'

Blue was a summer colour, or so Emmy thought. Winter was a time to hide herself in greys and browns and whites — hard, unforgiving shades. 'Yes, why not? I'll go down and have a go.'

'What time's tea?'

'It's vegetable bake. I'll have it ready by six.'

She unhooked her jacket from the back of the door in the utility room, and thrust her hands into her gloves. There was an electric heater and the studio would take a while to warm up, but she could spend the time making plans, tidying and thinking about what she'd do. It was futile, because she'd almost certainly do nothing, but it was better than dwelling on what Rob might have done, in the cold and dark above the tarn.

And yet, inevitably, as she passed along the gravel path down the side of the garden, that was exactly what she was thinking about. The grey blades of crocuses were reaching tentatively upwards at the edge of the path and she stopped to appreciate their dogged elegance, their muted colours blending into the yellow of the moss that riddled the grass and the golden brown of the last of the beech leaves, stuck to the path. More early daffodils were easing through to replace those she'd sacrificed, that day up at the tarn.

What would have happened to her if Luke had come back? She'd have wanted him to stay with them, at least in the short term, and Rob surely wouldn't have coped, like an ageing stag facing up to the challenge of the young buck. Had he known? Had he seen — or feared — how things would pan out and taken drastic action?

Impossible. Just impossible.

The detective had left his number in case either she or Rob thought of anything else that might be interesting to him and she hadn't refused that one the way she'd turned down the insult of a helpline for domestic abuse. She could call him. But what would she say? He'd been nice enough but his rank was intimidating. It might be easier to speak to Ashleigh O'Halloran, who'd had a comforting and unshakeable confidence about her, as if there was no situation that would or could faze her, and who'd managed to seem so understanding when Emmy had shed a tear for Luke.

If she called, what would she say? She had nothing to share but a suspicion and an old secret she didn't dare reveal. If she called them they'd come back and ask Rob about his movements and, when he'd been able to prove he was on his way to Manchester on the Monday morning, he'd think it through and realise she was the only person who could have betrayed him.

Unthinkable. *Oh God, but Luke. If he killed Luke what else could he do? What will he do to me?*

Ruling out the police left Heather, who would understand and had spotted Rob's ruthless streak even though she'd misinterpreted it, but Heather would advise her to go to the police, as her own conscience was doing. Every avenue brought her back to her central fear: Rob's knowledge, and Rob's response.

She reached the studio and stood in front of it for a moment, squaring her shoulders. She needed to regain control of her common sense. There was no point in talking to anybody about it; Rob hadn't done it. He might have wanted to, and he might be capable of it, but wishing someone's death was a sin not a crime and as for being able to do it… well. Everybody was capable of murder but very few committed the crime.

On another day she'd call Tino for reassurance but today, with Rob's attention closely on her, she didn't dare. She stood for a moment and looked at the water dripping down from the guttering. Soon there would be birds nesting in it, and spring would come. She smiled, turned the key and slipped into the studio.

She knew at once that someone else had been there. It was her space and no-one else ever came there, but she hadn't been there for some time except that brief moment on the day after Luke's death. Today there was a freshness about the place, as if a breeze had recently blown through it and cleared away weeks' worth of clay dust. There were dry leaves on the floor, too, as though they'd swirled in on a breeze in a moment when someone had opened the door. She was sure they hadn't been there before.

Stepping inside, she closed the door and stood with her back against it, scanning the space. The kiln seemed undisturbed. The rack of pots she'd been working on still stood by the window. The blocks of clay, sealed in plastic, sat under the table on which she kept her tubes of paint, in rainbow order. There was a package on the workbench next to her wheel.

Her heart rate increased and, once more, she fought her fears and wrestled her irrational mind into submission. Perhaps someone had come to ask about buying her work? But what prospective customer would creep into her studio without asking? There was no sign of forced entry so they must have had the key, but as there were two keys and she kept both, someone must have been in the house.

Someone hates me, said Emmy's rational self, in her head, *but that doesn't mean they want to hurt me.* She took a cautious step forward. The package wasn't as bulky as she'd first thought, just a brown A4 envelope but (she approached it circumspectly) one that looked as if it might have a sheaf of papers in it, and something else, just big enough to lift the overall shape from flat. There was no name and no address written on it.

Curious, and yet filled with dread, she moved forward. Could it be from Tino? He knew the studio was her space and hers alone, but surely he'd have found some other way to get in touch. She lifted the packet and slid out the contents. A USB stick dropped to the floor. A sheaf of photographs fanned out onto the table and followed it to the ground.

She felt sick. Even before she'd seen them she knew what they were, and though the idea revolted her, she couldn't help but look at them. The top one was a close up of herself, head and bare shoulders, head thrown back, laughing. Its clarity revealed the ecstasy of the moment, her joy in the act of physical love etched in every line of her face. As for the others — a cursory scan was enough. Image after image of herself and Tino, making love, deep in the woods of the estate in a pool of summer sun.

She panicked, backed out of the studio and locked the door. Then she almost ran up the path. She couldn't tell Rob. She had to think. Gathering her thoughts, she crept along to the door of his study. Good: he was on the phone. She pushed open the door.

'Changed my mind,' she mouthed to him. 'Going for a walk.' And in reply to his slightly puzzled nod and thumbs up, she closed the door again and almost ran to the car.

She needed breathing space. She needed fresh air and a moment to think. Who had done it? Who had known, all this time? And what would happen now?

There was only one place where she felt she could snatch a breathing space, and that was where she headed — back up to Mungrisdale and Bowscale Tarn. The path was an easy one, well-marked and not too steep, and she walked it often. On that cold January afternoon she met no-one. There had been a few cars parked at the end of the path, but if any of those belonged to walkers they were dispersed into the landscape, and the only sign she saw of them was a couple of red dots moving down along the path to the abandoned mines beyond Roundhouse. It wasn't until she reached the tarn and was secure in her isolation that she dared get out her phone and call Tino.

'You have to help me,' she said, her bottom lip quivering. 'Something terrible has happened.'

'Yeah. I know. I wanted to phone you but I didn't dare. I didn't know who'd overhear. And I wasn't sure if you'd got a package too, but you must have done.'

'Yes,' whispered Emmy, bitter with regret at his love and her folly

'Was it the same as I got? Photographs?'

She ran her tongue over her lips. It was the cold wind that made her eyes stream; her soul was still and resolute and she wouldn't cry. Her sins had found her out, that was all. It was inevitable. 'Yes. From last summer.'

'From that day in the woods?'

She nodded, as if he could see her. There had been several days in the woods, most of them innocent, some spilling over into passion. There had been other days, too, when Rob had been out of the house and the temptation to be with Tino, just for an hour or so, had been irresistible.

Someone had known. Who, and for how long? 'And a flash drive.'

'I got one too. Haven't dared look at it.' His voice was dark. 'Not until I've made sure it doesn't have a program that's going to hack into my laptop, anyway.'

Vaguely, Emmy wondered what a hacker might find to incriminate them. Their messages would be enough. She sat down on the rock and looked at the shoreline of the tarn. The jam jar was still there but the wind and the cold had taken their toll on the daffodils; their still-yellow petals were ragged and the stems snapped, so they drooped over the edge of the jar. 'I should have brought more flowers.'

'What?'

'More daffodils. I'm up at the tarn. I had to get away where no-one would find me.' She'd have to explain that to Rob later, but she hadn't thought about anything except getting away, hadn't even stopped to check the package closely. 'Was there a note?'

'No.'

'It'll be blackmail. It has to be.' Someone must have heard that she and Tino had been seen together and was taking the chance to pounce. 'Who was it? Do you think it was the person who reported you to the police?'

'I doubt it. This person has had that evidence for months. They'll have been waiting their moment and thought this was their last chance to say something before it came out any other way. They probably think they can bounce us into whatever they want.'

'It'll be money, surely.'

'Probably. I'm not made of the stuff, but I've got something put aside.'

'Tino. We shouldn't pay.' Maybe the threat was on the flash drive. She pictured a shady, hooded figure, voice disguised by some kind of electronic software, reading out a list of terms and conditions. 'You don't pay blackmailers.' She loved him, beyond words, but sometimes his lack of courage infuriated her.

'I wouldn't pay,' he said with certainty, 'if it was just me. But it isn't just me, is it? It's you.'

Her reputation. Her marriage. 'Rob will be furious.' Oh, he would be. He would go white with silent anger and he'd reproach her, and her own conscience would be her punishment. Or maybe today would be the day he snapped and raised a hand to her and maybe, in his anger, he would kill her. 'I can't tell him.' It had been hard enough to confess that she and Tino had gone to the tarn together.

'No. You mustn't. Don't tell anyone. We'll think of something.'

'Yes, but what?'

'I'll come and get you.'

'But the scandal—'

'Emmy. For the love of God. I love you. That's what matters. Do you think I care about the scandal?'

He didn't. She did. She couldn't face a congregation who knew what she'd done and would damn her with their silent judgement. She was liked and respected locally and it mattered to her. 'But the people at church—'

'Don't give me that. They can keep their false outrage. If we did anything wrong it was breaking the vows we made the first time round. We made our mistake but in the eyes of God, you're still my wife.'

She wrapped her jacket around her. A fell runner slithered down the path at the edge of the crags but he paid her no attention, too busy scrambling down the scree and down towards the soft, flat bog of the dale. 'Maybe.' That was how she justified it to herself. She wasn't such a fool as to think he was as devout as she, and she thought he didn't need that justification.

'Shall I come up and get you?' he repeated. 'It doesn't matter what people think. If Rob wants to come and challenge me over it he can try. I'm a match for him. I can look after you. We can be together, the way we should have been all along, if it hadn't been for your mother.'

'Oh, Tino.' she shook her head, affectionately. She could quite see why he riled her mother so much. 'Don't be an idiot.'

'Why is it idiotic to want the two of us to be together? We love one another. Don't we?'

She thought back to those summer days in the woods, when they'd thought it was secret. Dappled sunshine delicious on her skin, the consuming touch of his hand and his lips, the coming-together of their bodies. She thought about it often, always with pleasure, but now the memory was tainted. Someone had been watching them, maybe more than once. 'We do.' But love was never easy. 'Let me think about it.'

'Any time you need me, you can give me a call. Whatever I'm doing, I'll come at once.'

'Goodbye, my darling.'

She cut the call off, the matter unresolved. *Not yet*, she should have said. The longer she lived with Rob the more she knew she wanted to be with Tino, but it was never easy to shake yourself free. Through the years of her second marriage she'd never realised how the bonds were tightening around her mind and her heart until she didn't know how to slip free of them.

Now there was something else to worry about. Only one thing was certain. She would never go back into her studio, now it was imprinted with the memory of a sinister and ill-willed stranger.

She had both keys to the studio in her pocket, on a key ring Rob had bought her in Paris, on their honeymoon. A raised image of the Eiffel Tower gleamed on a heavy metal tag. She flung it, as far as she could, and had turned her back on it long before it fell to the water with a satisfying splash.

SEVENTEEN

'I don't know how many times I've been over this.' Jude was at the table in the incident room, with Doddsy, Ashleigh and Chris. He frowned. 'The answer's in here somewhere but I can't see it. Nothing.' Every word of a once-cold case, revisited late into the night — every witness statement, lacking in any information; every interview; every aspect of Luke's character; every step Jude himself had taken in that bare fellside fifteen years before.

'Let's try it once more.' Doddsy rubbed his chin, thoughtfully. It was obvious the echo of an old case troubled him as much as it did Jude. 'Luke was off the rails, probably driven off them by an overly strict upbringing but that's neither here nor there.' He was a churchgoer himself. He would know many people as devout and uptight as the Leaches, Jude thought, and yet it always struck him that his friend was remarkably tolerant of others. 'He made life hell for his mother and his stepfather. He was aggressive and abusive. He'd disappear from home for days at a time and come back drunk. He stole from his family. He did drugs. He ran with a very dodgy crowd.'

'The parents were considered as potential suspects, obviously,' said Chris, thinking aloud. 'Equally obviously they were cleared. Rightly so, as they didn't do it, or at least not at the time. But if their kid was such a nightmare, who's to say they wanted him back?'

When Luke hadn't been found within a few days the number of officers on the ground had rapidly reduced and most, including Jude, had returned to other duties. It had become common currency locally that he'd got lost and come to harm. Unofficially, the police had concluded he'd run away and now that looked to be the case. Jude sighed. There was a pattern. Luke had left home before and for all his bumptiousness he'd never stayed away more than a couple of nights and always came home when he needed a meal. The thing that had attracted official attention to that final disappearance was the abandonment of his bicycle, of all his possessions and the lack of any subsequent trace of him.

'I remember Groves — he was the senior investigating officer — saying he'd turn up, years down the line.' Jude nodded. He'd never got on with Groves, but the man had been right in this instance. 'He never specified whether he thought he'd be alive or not, I grant you. But he was right. So why?' He shifted his chair closer to the table, remembering Faye and her warning about him and Doddsy fighting old battles. It was new information that counted. 'Chris. I know you've been liaising with the folks down in Liverpool. Do they have anything that can help us fill in the gaps?'

'Not a fifteen year gap.' Chris flicked his iPad open with a broad grin. He was never happier than when he had information to dispense and a story to tell. 'He — or someone claiming to be him — was in contact with his father and with Libby using the name Colin Caton, and we've managed to find that account. It looks like a fairly recent alias, set up on social media about two years ago with an email account used only for that purpose. The Merseyside force have managed to link that back to another account in the name Joe Pardoe. The two were set up on the same computer, about five years apart. So if Colin is Luke, he's probably also Joe.'

'Those two aliases take us back seven years. So for the eight years after he left, are you saying we don't know who he was or where he was?' asked Ashleigh.

'I'm saying we don't know yet. The tech lads in Liverpool are still trying to unpick all this, but they're drawing a blank so far.'

'Are we certain these two are him?' asked Jude. 'He might have been lying low and just kept off social media. He might have been on there under other identities we just haven't yet found.'

'Yeah, that's a problem. The messages to Tino and Libby came from that account, but he was careful never to use a photograph of himself, and neither of them engaged with him. He never offered any proof of his identity. It's possible the account wasn't his but a malicious prankster.'

'God knows why.' Doddsy's face showed the contempt they all felt for the anonymous internet troll. 'Unless it was a criminal double-bluffing.'

'Waiting two years after setting up the account? That would take a lot of thought.' Chris lifted an eyebrow.

'I've known criminals take longer,' said Doddsy, with a sigh. 'I can't think of a reason why, though. If it wasn't Luke, who stood to gain from it? Is there anything else?'

'Oh yes. I don't need to tell you people leave clues all over social media, even if they don't intend to. Quite how much we can learn from it is another matter entirely.'

Jude stifled a smile. Chris had a tendency to patronise

his older colleagues. Jude had only just turned thirty-seven but sometimes it felt as if there was a generation between them. 'Who were his friends and followers?'

'They're still tracing back through them. One or two distinctly shady characters with records for aggravated burglary and the like. A couple have done time. No big-time criminals, no-one we'd have heard of.'

No serious criminal would be so stupid as to leave clues in plain sight. They would have their own online aliases, or other people to deal with these things for them, or they would avoid the elephant traps of the internet altogether. Unpicking this network of friends and contacts, and the next layer back, and the next layer, would be a painstaking and time-consuming task and one that required specialist digital forensic skills that went beyond even Chris's talents when it came to the web.

'Go on,' Jude said, leaving that for the experts to worry about. 'I can tell you've got something you think might be of interest. What kind of content was he putting up?'

'The posts he left are all pretty innocent, or seem so. If he was using social media to communicate with users or dealers, he probably wouldn't even do it by private message. We haven't been able to trace any contacts on his phone, but as you've pointed out, there's every chance he's got more than one and he'd be careful what he put on it.'

'And how.' If Luke had used WhatsApp, his messages would be encrypted and inaccessible. 'So what have you got?'

Chris loved a bit of theatre. He laid the iPad on the table and then sat back while Ashleigh, Doddsy and Chris leaned in. 'He posted some things on multiple channels — Facebook, Twitter and Instagram. I made a slide show of his images, in date order. Flick through and see what you think. Remember, we started two years back. The first image is from two Christmases ago.'

There were photos of Christmas trees. A few, blurred, from a train window, of Preston Station in the rain, almost as if the author had been testing — or trying to muddy — the water. Then the first surprise.

'Wait,' said Jude, homing on the screen and using two fingers to zoom in. 'Well, well. That's Bowscale Tarn.'

'Interesting, isn't it?' Chris was enjoying himself. 'Look at the next one.'

Jude flipped on. There was a photograph of a bunch of daffodils — shop-bought, this time, so it must have been too early for Emmy to pick them from the garden — lying at the base of the rock. The next image was a close up of the message, the same as before. *To darling Luke, with all our love.* 'This was two years ago?'

'Yes.'

'That's answered one question, then,' said Ashleigh, 'or I think it has. If he was up there, for whatever reason, just after the anniversary of his disappearance then he'll know they came up there. Maybe he'll have guessed they came every year. Maybe he missed them last year, and that's why he camped out.'

Jude was aware of tension in her voice. She'd be thinking of Luke, trying to decide whether or not to confront his parents, or of Emmy who might soon learn how close she'd been to seeing him and confronting the reality that he'd decided, in the end, not to contact her. He looked across at her, thankful the other two were still concentrating on the screen, with what he hoped was a warning glance.

She raised a slight hand in acknowledgement, gave him a rueful smile that said *I know, I know.*

'I'm intrigued to see where this leads us,' he said, turning his attention back to the photographs.

'You will be. But if you can draw any conclusions from it, I'd love to hear them.'

He flipped on. The next was a more general view, of the route down to Mosedale from the tarn. A snap of a bicycle, propped against a crumbling but unidentifiable stone wall. A series of shots along the fellside route that Jude had driven on the way back from his overnight reconnaissance on the morning Luke's body had been found. Then a few scenic shots of the village of Caldbeck.

Jude sat back. 'He's too smart to post any pictures of Mosedale Barn, of course, but you can see it lurking there in the background. I wonder. This seems to be as good a way of sharing the lie of the land as any other. His profile is public, so anyone can see them.'

'There are captions,' said Chris, 'though they don't show on this slideshow. They're mostly pretty generic. *Landscape with cows* and so on. That one says *valley with barn*.'

'This is clever. If anyone needs to know where the barn is, that's all they need to do. Check in here, flick through the images and there it is. You can see everything you need to see and no-one needs to know you've looked.'

'We reckon the operation had been running up at the barn for a couple of years,' said Doddsy, 'so again, that fits. He'd have a new, clean identity for a new operation. Anyone can see the account and you don't have to compromise your own identity by letting them into your group chats.'

A lot of the pictures were good, some almost professional in composition and exposure. 'Is there much interaction on them?' asked Jude.

'Several likes and retweets.'

With a little more analysis they'd probably be able to

see more. There might be clues about how someone might approach the barn, or pick up points for drugs, or hiding places in case of pursuit, but it would be time-consuming and almost impossible to separate likes and retweets into interested parties or casual scrollers, and anyone with criminal intent would be wise not to interact at all. 'I'm going to assume there are lots more of these.'

'You'd be right. I think a lot of them will be completely irrelevant — just a load of landscape shots and so on, to create a bit of white noise. You'd need to know what's significant and what isn't. If someone has a spare day or so and a huge amount of patience, they might be able to use them to put together a trail of where he's been.'

Jude flicked through a few more. Wisely, Luke had always chosen landscapes, never people. There were some arty shots of trees, images of crocuses coming up in a lush green lawn behind a vegetable patch. He looked twice, but it wasn't the Leaches'. And then, a few pictures on, he paused. 'This looks vaguely familiar to me,'

'Right.' Doddsy was also looking keenly at it.

'That's the Pennines.' It was a stunning photograph, a long line of sunlit hills riding above shaded layers of fog. 'That's the sun on Cross Fell, and Dufton Pike below it. I'm not sure exactly where it was taken but it wouldn't take long to find out. Certainly somewhere in the Eden Valley, judging by the scale. Doddsy, is this your neck of the woods?'

Doddsy inspected the picture. 'It's somewhere a bit further down the river from where I am.'

'Have we got a map? Let's have a look.'

The map on the board, with Bowscale Tarn marked, extended as far as the River Eden in the east. Getting up, Jude scanned it. His finger hovered over it, north of Doddsy's home village of Temple Sowerby. 'Somewhere up here, maybe. Beacon Hill, perhaps? Langwathby? It's certainly along that way.'

'There are a few the same as this,' Chris said. 'It's the ones of Mungrisdale and the barn that get a few more likes. The more generic ones get the odd admiring comment, but that's all.'

'Surely the tech people can find out who's liked what pictures?' asked Ashleigh.

'Yeah, but that'll take a hell of a long time, and even then you can bet the house that most of them will be ordinary punters who just like the pics. They're good. And the rest will be fake profiles.'

'There'll be one who slips up, though,' said Doddsy. 'There always is.'

'I'll be interested to know who they are.' Ashleigh again. 'Because don't forget. There are a couple of likely lads already charged in connection with the Mosedale Barn operation. It'll be interesting to see if they've thrown a sneaky little like Luke's way.'

'Good shout.' Jude sat back and pushed the iPad away. 'Doddsy, you might want to raise that with your Scouse mates. In the meantime, Chris, would you mind sending these pictures on to me? I'll have a look through them when I've got a bit of time.' Later that evening, probably, when everything more pressing was done. 'If nothing else, I think this might give us some idea of where Luke has been hanging out in the time he's been missing.'

'Certainly for the past couple of years,' Doddsy agreed.

Jude closed the file and laid it on the desk. As the team drifted off to their respective desks and offices, he put in a quick call to Faye with an update, then headed back to his own office via the coffee machine.

Doddsy was sitting back in his chair, hands behind his

head and a cheerful expression on his face. 'I wondered where you'd got to.'

'Fetching you a coffee.' Jude set one cardboard cup of coffee on Doddsy's desk and sipped from the other, taking a moment to stand and look out towards the Eden Valley. You couldn't see the Pennines from their window — couldn't see much, indeed, beyond a gleam of green between buildings.

'Ta.' Doddsy inspected the contents of the cup, with a little less than enthusiasm. 'I called down to the Merseyside lads as you suggested, to check in. They've been running a few things for us, too.'

'And?'

'They've got CCTV footage from Lime Street Station. Luke, or it looks like him, getting on a train bound for Preston. A couple of weeks ago. With a rucksack.'

From Preston, it was little more than an hour to Penrith and only another fifteen minutes to Carlisle. 'And is there any chance of CCTV—?'

'I've requested a look at anything they have at Preston, to see if we can catch him changing trains, or at Penrith. The latter's more likely, I think, or certainly we're more likely to get it reasonably soon. If that's where he was going, and if he did go via Preston, there won't be too many trains he could have got or places he could have got off.'

'With a rucksack, you say.' Luke hadn't been sleeping rough for long, certainly not for a week. 'I suppose he could have been sleeping up at the barn and just happened not to be there the night we raided it.' Maybe he should have been. Instead he'd been lying dead beneath the surface of Bowscale Tarn, his appointment missed.

'Or his paymasters could have done away with him because he wanted out. And he was on the run from them and went to Bowscale because he knew he'd find his parents there and could ask them for help. I'm thinking aloud, here, you understand.'

'Apart from the sleeping bag, he had no kit. He had virtually nothing in the way of food. A couple of bottles of water. No spare clothing, no cooking equipment.' The rucksack that had been retrieved from the sodden wreckage of Luke's tent had been all but empty. 'That was an overnight bivvy if ever I saw one. No more.' And certainly not the set-up of someone on the run.

'Don't forget the camera,' Doddsy reminded him.

'Yeah. Clearly whoever he was working for knew he was taking photographs if they were going up on Face-book, but maybe they thought he was taking photos of something else. Or maybe someone else.'

'A rival gang might have done the job.'

'It doesn't feel right, though, does it?' Jude shook his head. 'I wonder how he got there? If he was nipping about between the Eden Valley and Mungrisdale he must have had some form of transport. There are no buses up there at this time of year. He'd hardly take a rucksack on a bike, though most of the pictures might have been taken on a cycle ride, I suppose. I think there's a bike in the back-ground of one of them.'

'A car, then.' Doddsy scratched his thinning grey hair. 'There aren't any abandoned vehicles in that area. I checked, though he could have walked a fair distance if he'd wanted to. He was young enough, and reasonably fit, for all the drug use. According to the PM, anyway.'

Jude cast his mind back to the early stage of the investi-gation. They'd checked for abandoned vehicles in all the possible areas where Luke might have started his walk, not just the obvious place at Mosedale but further afield, at Bassenthwaite, Threlkeld and Caldbeck. Nothing had come to light and no-one had seen him. 'Right. But the other thing we have to consider is that he had an accomplice who was giving him a lift and possibly someone he was staying with. That person must know he was there and maybe they knew why.'

'Aye,' said Doddsy, with a deep sigh, 'and maybe, for whatever reason, they killed him.'

EIGHTEEN

L ater that afternoon, Jude sent Ashleigh down to Blacksty to see if there was anything more to be gleaned from the village.

'It's not exactly on a whim,' he'd said to her, 'but you'll be good at it. You've got an honest face and people talk to you. Go and sit in the pub for a couple of hours. Put your coffee on expenses. Folk are nosy and they'll come to see what's going on. I just have a feeling there's something we need to know and someone is bound to tell us what it is.'

It made sense. Based on the evidence of the photographs they could be reasonably sure Luke had been around Blacksty, off and on, for a couple of years. As she sat in the bar with her cold coffee Ashleigh thought back to the images of him, his dead face bloated and waxen from hours in the water, and compared it with the grainy images from the CCTV that had tracked his journey at Liverpool, Preston and Penrith stations. It was unlikely anyone in Blacksty would connect the recent, near-skinhead Luke and his drug-addict boniness with the floppy-haired, well-fed youth who'd left fifteen years earlier. If he'd spoken, or asked the wrong sort of questions, they might have put two and two together, but there was every chance Luke had learned all the tricks in the book about avoiding detection. When he'd passed through Blacksty, as one image he'd uploaded to Facebook indicated he had done, he must have done so fleetingly and with care. A cyclist swathed in Lycra, perhaps, helmeted and goggled, slowing down for pedestrians and horse riders as he cruised through the village; or a walker in sunglasses, with a bandana pulled up to conceal his face as he sauntered past his former home.

But no-one, it appeared, had seen him. The landlord, delighted at the prospect of an increase in custom on a winter Thursday, had happily made a table available for her in the bar for the afternoon and supplied her with coffee. Probably because of her presence, the place was busy with men in overalls and wellies, and a couple of clusters of women pretending they came down every Thursday afternoon for a cup of tea and a chat. The news that the detective sergeant was there asking questions about Luke had spread through the scattering of houses and it seemed everyone wanted to come and play their part in the mystery. Everyone, of course, except Tino and Rob and Emmy.

'His dad would know if he'd been here,' the umpteenth villager said after giving another account in which Luke made no appearance, answering the same series of questions with the same obvious and futile answers as everyone else. 'Tino Mortimer, I mean, not Rob. You'd need to ask. He might be in. He sometimes comes by at lunchtime for a sandwich and a bit of company. But not Luke's mam and stepdad. They're not the type to come in to the pub.'

'It's odd to think,' said a woman, striding through the bar to the table and latching on to the conversation, 'that the lad might have been right through the village. You'd think someone would have recognised him, wouldn't you? I'm not a villager myself and I never met the poor kid. But yes, I think if I was around and I saw someone who looked like him I might have looked twice. Knowing the story.'

Ashleigh took a moment to size up this newcomer, who was tall, sturdy and dressed in mud-spattered overalls. She hadn't been greeted by the throng at the bar and hadn't paused to nod to them in acknowledgement. She must, therefore, be there because she had information. 'You must have been in the area a long time,' she said, inviting confidence. She gave the man a half-look and he, having said his piece, lost interest and slid back to the comfort of the bar.

The woman smiled. 'Yes, all right. I sound a bit of a know-all. I don't live here, but I work here. I didn't know him, but I know what he looked like, and yes.' She lowered her voice. 'I think I've seen him.'

'Is that right?'

'I bet everyone says the same. It makes them seem interesting.' She jerked her head at the group behind her. 'But I might. I work for his mam.'

'Is that right?' Ashleigh cast her mind back to the kitchen and hallways, all she'd seen of Blacksty Farmhouse. There had been, she recalled, no pictures of Luke. 'Have a seat. Tell me about it.'

'Poor Emmy was cut up when he was lost, so she tells me, and I can tell that's true by the way it nearly broke her when he was found. She showed me pictures of him last time I was here. He was a difficult lad, but he had such an expressive face.' She pulled up a chair. 'My name's Heather Short.'

Ashleigh had brought photographs of Luke, as a lost teenager and as an adult and placed them on the table.

The photographs of his body were too gruesome for public consumption. 'These are Luke. Does that help?'

Heather put the photos side by side, then switched them around. 'This is one of the photos she showed me. I help Rob and Emmy keep tabs on that jungle of a garden they have. I was about to call in on her and make sure she's okay but they said in the shop you were asking more questions. So I came here instead.'

'It's routine.' Ashleigh thought, very briefly, of Emmy and her misery, and what she must be going through if she knew the police were still asking and guessed what they might be saying. She pulled herself up. Faye had appointed Mandy Phillips to probe more closely into Emmy and Rob's grief, but Mandy was rushed off her feet and had only managed a half-hour visit. 'We have some reason to believe Luke may have intended to come back to Blacksty and it's possible he did so before he died. We want to establish if that happened.'

Heather Short regarded her keenly, the kind of look that Ashleigh herself turned on people when she wanted to appear steely, and which Jude employed to indicate scepticism. Heather looked the no-nonsense type, with dirt under her fingernails and mud on her boots. She had on denim overalls and her greying hair was cut to a short bob. Ashleigh judged her to be somewhere in her early fifties. 'I doubt I can help much. What happened to the poor lad?'

'I can't tell you. The details have still to be signed off.'

'That's what Emmy said. She hates all this police-speak. I know she'd rest a bit easier if she knew the truth.'

They all would. Ashleigh turned on her bright dealing-with-the-public smile. 'Thankfully she has a family liaison officer to offer her support. She and Luke's father will be told everything we know as soon as we're able to tell them.'

If Emmy wanted to satisfy her gardener's evident curiosity after that, it was up to her.

'When will the rest of us know?'

'When the case comes to court, I would imagine. There's a process for these things.'

'Sorry.' Heather sat back. 'I probably sounded a bit aggressive there. I'm ex-army. They teach you to be assertive.'

Assertive was one word for it. Ashleigh moved on, though she filed that detail away to pass back up to Jude in her report on the day's interviews. 'So you think you might have seen Luke?'

'We should be less worried about the lad than about who killed him, shouldn't we?' Heather tapped a finger on the table. 'I don't know for certain if I've seen him at all. But I did see someone, and it might be him or it might have been someone else.'

'Go on.'

'As I said. I'm Emmy's gardener.' *Emmy's*, noted Ashleigh, immediately detecting an animosity to Rob. 'I do a day a week for her over the summer, a day a month in the winter. It was back in the autumn. I had my leaf blower and I was clearing up the leaves in that bit of ground they've got at the bottom. Emmy calls it the orchard and I think it was once, but it's just a few scraggy apple trees now. Have you been out into the garden?'

'I haven't, no.'

'The police were all over it when he disappeared, Emmy said. Looking for him, in case they'd done away with him and buried him there. Right. So you have the garden.' She withdrew a pen from her pocket and reached for the sheet of paper that Ashleigh passed to her, and then she began to sketch. Under her fingers the Leaches' property spun into life, even her casual sketch revealing scale and location. 'Here's the house. The lawn. The vegetable garden. Then we're into the orchard. That backs onto the fields on this side.' A few curls of the pen produced an animated and slightly surprised-looking sheep. 'Then there's a hedge — an old one, a bit broken down. Rob had a fence put in to back it up, and there's a row of barbed wire on it on the far side.'

'He thought they needed barbed wire?'

'I wouldn't have thought so myself, but he's an odd one, is Rob.' As she looked up, Ashleigh recognised malice. There was no love lost, then, between Rob Leach and the woman who had befriended his wife. 'I bet he's got a few secrets. They're well off. They've some nice stuff. I think she has some of Rob's grandmother's jewellery, and there are some nice pictures in there. Original art, Emmy says, though I'm no judge of that kind of thing. Now. On this side there's a boundary to the woods.' A few trees and a squirrel eating a nut ornamented the map. 'And it was in the woods I saw someone.'

'In the autumn? Can you be any more precise?'

'It would have been October. I usually do them on the second Monday of the month so it would have been the 12th, maybe. I was clearing the leaves when I realised there was someone standing in the trees, watching the house.'

'What was this person like?'

'I didn't like to look too closely, so I carried on with what I was doing and tried to sneak a peek, but they ducked into the trees before I could get a good look. I'd say a man, but I could be wrong about that. Khaki trousers. Green top. Black woolly hat. It was a chilly day, as I remember. He was standing, watching. I went to put a load of leaves in the compost and when I came back he'd gone. I didn't see where.'

She sat back and pushed the paper over to Ashleigh.

'You can hold on to that if it's any use. Do you think that could have been Luke?'

'It's impossible to say for certain.' Ashleigh looked at the paper, trying to reconcile the plan with the fleeting glimpse of the garden she'd had from the Leaches' kitchen. 'Is it fairly easy to get into that bit of the woods?'

'Not easy. I'd say, but people do go there. There's a footpath but it's not a public right of way and it's always closed during shooting season, so he shouldn't have been there.'

'Did you mention it to Mr or Mrs Leach?'

Heather didn't meet her gaze. 'I decided not to, in the end. The poor woman has enough to trouble her. And I might have been mistaken.' She picked up the two photos and considered them again. 'I can't say I'd recognise him even I'd had a better look at the time. But he's the right height and the right build. And the hat is the same.'

There might have been thousands of people mooching around the Lakes on a cold autumn day in a mass-produced black hat, but it was something, no matter how tenuous the link. 'That's a start.'

'It'll be no help to you, but there's no way I'd say for certain it wasn't him.' Heather put the photos down, picked up the one of young Luke again.

Over her career in the force, Ashleigh had seen a hundred or more witnesses with information to give and not feeling able to give it, either through fear or because they thought what they knew was so trivial as to be useless. She took a quick look towards the door. There was no-one obviously waiting to see her and no-one within earshot. Even the barman, busy wiping down the polished wooded bar, was at the far end of the long room. 'Is there something else, Ms Short?'

'I doubt it's relevant. But I've often wondered since I

saw the lad. About whether he wasn't so much casing the joint as checking out Rob Leach.'

It was an extraordinary leap of the imagination. 'What makes you say that?'

Heather gave a sidelong look at the barman. 'As I say, I'm not local to here.'

'Where do you stay?'

'I have a smallholding just outside Lazonby. When I left the army twenty years ago I set up my own little gardening and landscaping business and it's been doing fine. When Emmy's gardener retired they were looking for someone else and it was through another of my customers that I came here. He knows Rob from somewhere. Work, I would imagine.' She fidgeted. 'He did warn me Rob isn't quite the nice cuddly character he tries to pretend he is, but I can handle his type. Not that there's anything wrong with him, and most of the time he keeps the facade going, but there's a temper under that calm exterior. You can see it.'

Yet more evidence of Emmy's vulnerability. Ashleigh made a mental note to alert Mandy to it. 'What sort of things set him off?'

'Nothing I do, for sure. I talk to Emmy rather than him where I can, though I daresay he has the last word over everything that goes on. But I remember once he came out to the garden, looking for her. She'd gone into Penrith, I think, and not told him because he was on the phone and she didn't want to disturb him. And oh, he was mad. Icily polite to me. He wouldn't have dared not be.' She squared her shoulders at the memory. 'There was a vein pulsing in his temple, like it always says in the books, you know? About half an hour later she came back and he was shouting at her in the house so I headed up to see if she was okay. But by the time I got there everything was fine and she was acting as if there was nothing wrong.'

'You never mentioned it to her?'

'Oh, sure.' Heather gave her a sidelong look, as if affronted by the suggestion she wouldn't intervene. 'I've tried to sound her out a couple of times to see if she's all right. But it only came to me recently, after they found Luke. It's the way she keeps looking at him. She's afraid.'

Ashleigh had seen it. She remembered the fearful look Emmy had given Rob when they heard Luke's body had been identified. It chimed too closely with her own experience. 'Why, exactly, do you think she's so scared?'

'I'm not sure I'd take it seriously if someone suggested it. But the more I think about it, the more convinced I am that she thinks he did it.'

'You mean, killed Luke?'

'Yes. Like I said, I didn't know the Leaches back then, but it makes sense. By all accounts they didn't get on and Luke was a difficult little bugger. Rob hates a challenge but he'll never refuse one. And before you say the obvious, yeah. I know. Obviously he didn't kill Luke back then, but he might have wanted to, or Luke might have thought he wanted to, and that's why he left. And if Emmy guessed that, what was she to think, except that Rob might have done it? Who would she tell?'

Ashleigh's mind was working overtime. If it was true, there was every chance Emmy would have confided in Tino, but how would he have reacted to the suggestion that the man who supplanted him in Emmy's affections might have wanted to kill his son? Surely there would have been more from him than silence. But her job was not to think but to listen, so she kept her expression neutral and her thoughts to herself. 'Did she ever say anything to you about her suspicions?'

'No, though I had coffee with her the other day and I think she nearly did. I know it's not evidence. I know I can't prove anything. But I think she thinks if he didn't get him that time, he got him when he came back. He might have seen him lurking about the place and arranged to meet him. Lured him up to the tarn and then did for him.' She looked at Ashleigh, expectantly. 'That's all I've got for you.'

'Was Mr Leach there the day you saw the figure in the woods?'

'No, but just because I only saw the lad once doesn't mean he was only there once. You should know that.'

Ashleigh did know it, and was used to being patronised by members of the public who played too much Cluedo or read too many whodunnits. 'That's very interesting. Thank you, Ms Short.'

'I just want to be damn sure nothing happens to Emmy. That's all I care about.' Heather pushed back her chair and stood up. 'Contact me any time. Here's my number.' She wrote it on the map she'd sketched and headed away.

When she'd gone, Ashleigh hung on for another ten minutes, but it became clear that anyone who had anything to say to her had already done so. She gathered up all her bits and pieces and took them to the car, but before she headed back in to the office she took a stroll along to the end of the village and called Jude.

'Productive?' he asked. He was in the incident room, she judged, by the sounds in the background. Someone seemed to have found something to laugh about.

'I don't know. I've got one possible sighting of Luke in the village.' She filled him in on Heather's input. 'I know I've not to get too involved and there's Mandy, and I know you said you'd deal with Emmy directly, but that reinforces what I thought about Emmy and Rob, doesn't it?' And her fears.

'Up to a point. It's possible she's afraid of him because

she thought he'd killed Luke but he obviously didn't, so that fear would be misplaced. And, as you've previously pointed out, once she believed he was capable of violence she'd find it very easy to convince herself he did in fact have a second go, and was successful. Whereas in fact we know he didn't, because he wasn't anywhere near. He was on a train to Manchester and we have CCTV to prove it.'

Unless, of course, he'd done it the night before. Jude would know that, too, and if he hadn't mentioned it, it was to calm her anxiety. She was annoyed with herself for having shown him her weakness that night in the wine bar, and with him for responding to it. She didn't need protection. 'He could have hired some else to do it.'

'He could. Either way, it doesn't mean he's any danger to Emmy just because she thinks he is.'

'Or that he isn't.' Now at the edge of the village, she turned and walked back. There were no lights on in Tino's cottage and the driveway was empty. 'What about the man she saw in the woods?'

'That could have been anyone. Blacksty Farmhouse definitely counts as property porn, even if you aren't casing the joint. If I remember correctly there's a footpath that goes through the woods and round the back of it. So maybe the person she saw was just taking an amble up through the woods to get a look at the autumn colour.'

'I'm just at the start of the path now. I can't see where it goes from here. It looks as if it turns away into the woods.'

'Let me check the map,' he said, and there was a moment's silence, broken by the clack-clack-clack of a pheasant in the woods. 'Yes, it does, but then it cuts back. It doesn't go close to the Leaches' property, but probably close enough. Anyone who wanted a good look could wander off the path.'

'Shall I go and have a look?'

'I might do it myself, next time I have a free half day. It must be starting to get dark up there and it's probably not smart to go lurking in the shadows in pheasant shooting season. I wouldn't want you to end up as an accident statistic.'

'Right. I'll get back in to the office. Will you be around?'

'No. I've got a meeting. But we can catch up later. In the meantime I'll get Chris to have a dig into Heather's background, when he has a minute. What did you make of her?'

'Shifty,' Ashleigh said after a moment, lowering her voice as she strolled past Blacksty Farmhouse. 'But I wondered if that's because she wasn't quite comfortable ratting on Rob. I couldn't make my mind up whether she genuinely thinks he's guilty of anything or whether she just dislikes him so much she's determined to believe it. It could be either.'

'It could indeed,' agreed Jude, and ended the call.

NINETEEN

As Tino had driven home from work in the dark he'd passed Rob's Audi, parked in the lay-by on the edge of the village, just fifty yards from his home. When he pulled up outside his house he turned back along the road instead of going in. He was normally a calm man, and generally a happy one, but the package of photographs that had come through his door had put the fear of God into him, and the fact that Emmy had had the same had led him close to panic.

There was an obvious candidate for putting them there, and that was Rob, but something didn't make sense. Tino himself wasn't a devious person and he couldn't get into Rob's head. In his place he'd have confronted Emmy and then stormed down to swing a few punches at Tino himself, and that would have been it, but Rob was cold, calculating and controlled. If he knew, he'd known for a long time and now he was choosing to let them know he knew. Why?

One thing was for certain: it was piling misery on Emmy. It didn't seem to have occurred to her that her husband might be responsible and Tino was in no hurry to enlighten her, but they had to be very careful indeed. Quite what Rob's end game was, he had no idea. It might be the satisfaction of surprising the two of them when they met to talk about it, or just the pure pleasure of watching Emmy grow increasingly stressed while he continued to offer her support and, eventually turned on her.

If Rob knew, there was nothing they could do about it, but if his plan was to put his wife — and Tino himself — under psychological pressure, there must be some way they could stop him. For all his much-vaunted Christian virtues and extensive good works, Rob Leach was a twisted bastard with the sick mind of a sociopath.

Tino approached the Audi with extreme care and no plan. Rob was taking a call and in the light from the phone Tino saw him running his hands through his hair in distraction, as if the conversation was both important and concerning. Serve him right. With luck, some huge flaw in an architectural plan would have knock-on costs his professional indemnity insurance wouldn't cover and his business would go under, taking his career and reputation with it. Tino slowed, his breath crystallising in a ghostly cloud. Frost gathered in the air and caught at his lungs as he walked. He hovered at the end of the lay-by, still in the shadows but where Rob would surely see him when he looked up.

He did. Their eyes met and Rob's startled expression narrowed into one of cold anger. He ended the call and tossed the phone down on the passenger seat. Then he opened the car and got out. 'What do you want?'

Too late, Tino realised that his conviction that Rob was behind the packages wasn't a certainty. If it wasn't him, he didn't dare give him cause for suspicion. 'Out for a walk,' he said, scratching about for a more subtle way to challenge his successor in Emmy's bed. 'There's no law against it.'

'Right. You think I didn't see you drive past a few minutes ago? Why come back up here? Because if you think you can frighten me, Mortimer, you're wrong.' He laid a hand on the back of the car door, as if he was using it as a shield and pulled himself to his full height.

He was a tall man. Disadvantaged by three or four inches, Tino nevertheless curled his fingers into fists and told himself he wasn't scared. He didn't know what he could say to give Rob Leach something to go away and think about and, hopefully, steer him away from any violence towards his wife; he no longer knew who to trust, who was too interested in his activities, who was a voyeur. He didn't know what Rob knew or planned or, worse, what he was capable of. 'I'm here to say something I should have said years ago. If you have anything to do with what happened to my lad, you'll pay for it.'

'Your lad? The boy you left for a mother barely out of her teens to look after on her own? That's a good line, Tino, but no-one will buy it. Emmy knows the truth of it, and so do I.'

In the darkness Rob seemed a dominant figure, a madman. Tino's courage began to seep away. 'You listen to me,' he said, his breath catching in his chest.

'No. You can listen. It's bad enough you seducing her into going up to the tarn with you when she should have been going with me—'

'Luke was my son!'

'I brought him up. I gave him everything he could want, including discipline, though he didn't thank me for it. I was endlessly patient with him, for his mother's sake. Don't you ever accuse me of failing that young man!'

But he had failed him. They all had, and Tino was by

no means least among them. 'I'm not accusing you of failing him. I'm accusing you of killing him.'

He thought Rob froze, as if he'd somehow hit home. 'I'm done with this conversation. You can think yourself lucky I'm a good Christian man, or I wouldn't answer for what happens to you. Don't think I don't know where your interest lies. You keep away from my wife, okay? Or you'll be sorry.'

He slid back into the car and closed the door in a swift, fluid movement, and then everything happened very fast. The engine leapt into life and the powerful Audi surged forward.

Tino jumped for his life. The wing mirror caught his elbow and tipped him off his feet and he fell, towards the verge rather than the road. He rolled over just as Rob manoeuvred the car, stumbling to his feet, slipping again and rolling to the ground at the mercy of Rob's fury and the mean black weapon he drove. And then, thank God, more car headlights came along the long road through the woods and Rob stopped, and headed the car out of the lay-by and back into the village.

Tino sat while the second car went past, entertaining half a thought of flagging it down and alerting a witness to the crime, but the possibilities that raised were too complicated and Emmy would surely suffer for them. He sat for a while, assessing the damage. With luck the swelling pain in his elbow would turn out to be a bruise not a break, and the mud into which he'd slithered so inelegantly would wash off his clothes. After a moment he scrambled gingerly to his feet and picked a careful way home along the muddy verge.

TWENTY

Thank God, Jude thought as he parked the car, they'd struggled through to Saturday without further incident, and there had been nothing to detain him in the office on a scheduled rest day. The Luke Mortimer case was slow-moving and it had fallen to Doddsy to nurse it over the weekend, so that Jude had a chance to switch off and reset.

Not that he ever really switched off. He was still churning the case over in his head as he walked up towards Brunton Park to meet up with his father. In theory they met there fortnightly, spent a casual couple of hours watching the football and then went and discussed it for an hour or so afterwards in the pub. In reality, the arrangement too often fell victim to Jude's workload and he barely got the money's worth from his season ticket. Today the stars aligned: not only did Jude manage to reach the stadium, but did so in time to be part of a packed crowd to see a Premier League side stutter against Carlisle United in the FA Cup fourth round.

'We did ourselves proud, holding them for so long,'

David Satterthwaite was saying, as they left the ground. 'It's a shame they took us out at the end but there's no way we can compete with resources like that. Superior fitness always tells.'

'Accidents do happen,' Jude agreed, half his mind elsewhere. He twisted around, trying not to attract his father's attention. He was right. Out of the corner of his eye he'd spotted his brother. Mikey had a season ticket, too, though he made sure he was seated in a different part of the ground from his father and brother, so it was hardly a surprise to see him. Now, forewarned, Jude would be able to steer them away from him. He got on well enough with Mikey, but that was more than could be said for his father. David's injured innocence when he periodically extended an olive branch to his antagonistic younger son was inevitably met with recriminations and the same accusations, repeated again and again, about his failings as a father.

On another day Jude might have taken his chance, but Mikey was with Adam Fleetwood, so avoiding him became paramount. Adam was a man as capable of provoking someone else to cause trouble for his own amusement as he was of causing it for himself. It was better, therefore, to make sure they didn't meet.

'Dad,' said Jude, cutting across his father's analysis of all the what-ifs that came with a striker missing an open goal. 'Let's get a drink.' He dodged sideways towards the nearest pub. Normally they found somewhere closer to the city centre but Mikey and Adam had slowed down and if they pressed on they'd catch up with them.

'We can go somewhere a bit further—'

'I'm parked just along here. This is handy.' Jude surged into the pub and headed straight to the bar. He'd commandeered a table and ordered a pint for his father and a tall

Diet Coke for himself before David had a chance to argue. 'It can get busy further on.'

He settled with his back to the wall — a copper's habit that allowed him to watch the room — and was rewarded by the sight of Adam, pushing his way in with Mikey in his shadow.

'You should come on the train next time,' said David, mercifully oblivious. 'Then you can have a drink.'

'You know I prefer to drive.' Hoist by his own petard, Jude cursed. Adam and Mikey had joined the crowd at the bar, now, and seemed to have found some acquaintances.

'Busy with the Luke Mortimer case, were you?' asked David, lifting his pint. 'I'm surprised you didn't ask me about it. I had your colleagues all over it at the time he disappeared. I'm sure they thought I was a suspect.' He was notoriously over-dramatic, and it was perfectly possible that he'd believed that, for a while. Everyone did, even the innocent. In reality David's name had cropped up in the files as no more than a footnote, a teacher who'd taught Luke a few terms' worth of history. No more.

'I did want to chat about him, as it happens. Just to freshen my memory.'

'For God's sake, lad. Your memory will be a bit better than mine on that.'

'I never met him, though.'

'I only taught him a year and a half and he was bunking off for the last term.'

'Did you ever come across the parents?'

'I see so many parents it's hard to match them up with the kids, sometimes. But Luke disappearing fixed them in my head if you know what I mean. So yes, I did.'

'Caring parents?' asked Jude, still keeping an eye on Mikey.

'I'd say so. I know Luke didn't see his dad that much.

He was living away by then, but he made an effort to come up at least once a year to a parents' evening. The stepfather was charm itself. Luke did a bit of drama for the first couple of years, so our paths crossed then. After that he got into bad company. You know the rest.'

Jude had read the file on Luke's disappearance at least three times since his body had been found, and nothing had offered him any help. 'Were you surprised about what happened?'

David considered. 'Only up to a point. He was getting wilder and wilder. I mean, he was a nice enough kid, as I say, but by the time he got to sixteen it was all about challenging authority. You couldn't say anything to him. I never thought he'd sit his exams — if he hadn't walked out of the place he'd have been thrown out. But yeah, when he disappeared I don't know I was that surprised. The only thing I wondered about is that he never came back.' He drank and flicked his gaze around the bar. Mercifully, Adam was chatting to a mate and Mikey was looking down at his phone.

'Would it surprise you if I said there's every chance he did come back?'

'Not at all. When?'

'There's some evidence he may have been knocking around the area off and on for the last couple of years. Maybe even longer.' Jude clinked the ice in his glass. Thank God David and Mikey hadn't spotted one another.

'Not earlier? There was always a bit of chat about it. A couple of years after he went someone turned up at a classmate's eighteenth birthday party pretending to be him, or so I heard — really cleverly made up, and everybody freaked out. And people spread stories. Even before we all became quite as obsessed with social media as we are these days, there was stuff. Someone thought it would be a laugh to make a Facebook page in his name and there was trouble about that. So although he was gone it never really felt like it. He became a bit of a local legend.' David drew a forefinger across his top lip. 'And it's interesting you say that, because a couple of years ago I thought I saw him.'

David had as sharp powers of both observation and recall as did Jude himself. 'Where was that?'

'I was driving the back road between Plumpton and Lazonby, giving some of the guys from the amateur dramatic society a lift. One of them was a colleague of mine, and knew him better than I did. He pointed the lad out.'

Jude visualised the road in question. Sometimes he ran along it. He hadn't had time to try and pick out the locations from which the photos on Facebook had been taken but it was the right area. 'Interesting stuff. No-one thought to mention it to the police?'

'We never thought. People assumed he was dead by then. You should ask Becca about it. I think Tino Mortimer used to play football with her dad.'

'I might do that.' He wouldn't make a point of it, but Becca was bound to cross his path at some point, like an unlucky black cat. She always did; or maybe that was because he never attempted to avoid her.

'Tino Mortimer always struck me as a decent sort,' went on David. 'I think he'd have handled matters better than the stepdad did. There's a bit more spark about him. According to my colleagues he always seemed to know when to fight his battles and when to let someone else win. I don't think the mum and stepdad were bad parents. Just not the right ones for Luke.'

Jude had been keeping a constant eye on the packed bar and now trouble was brewing. Mikey was shouldering his way through the crowd with a pint in his hand and

Adam, always an *agent provocateur*, was nudging him over in their direction. David was still oblivious, but there seemed no escape.

'Dad,' said Jude, picking and choosing his challenges just as Tino did. 'Maybe drink up and we could try another pub.'

'Why? You were the one who was so keen to come to this one.'

'It's getting busy. We could stop somewhere on the way home and get a bar meal or something.'

'We've got a seat. And I was telling you about Luke. It's difficult enough for kids when their parents split up. You know that.' He managed a shrug, but it was one that sloughed off any responsibility for the emotional carnage that had followed his own failed marriage. 'These things happen. It's bad news when kids end up as collateral damage, but it happens all the time and most of them survive. It doesn't seem to have done you any harm.'

'Collateral damage?' Mikey had been close enough to hear. He lunged forward and slammed his drink down on their table. Jude flung out a hand to stop the glass as it skidded across the surface and missed. The table rocked, the pint spilled itself into his lap and the glass smashed on the floor.

In an instant Jude was on his feet, dripping beer, and flung out an arm in case Mikey followed up with a punch. David, astonished, remained seated.

'Right.' In the silence and the circle of interested faces that Mikey had created, Jude acted. 'That's enough, Mikey. Outside.'

'You've no right to tell me what to do!'

Jude lowered his voice. 'I'm not having you done for assault. Now get outside. I'm taking you back home before you can cause any trouble.'

Mikey tried to shove past him. Still David sat, gaping. Had the man not even enough sense to get out of the way? 'Sitting there going on about parents. Good parents, bad parents, the wrong parents. Collateral damage? Are you for real?'

He surged forward again. There was alcohol on his breath and Jude guessed the story. There would have been a few pints before the game, a rising tide of excitement during it, and the needling presence of Adam Fleetwood, like a devil in his ear. 'Mikey. Enough!'

'Who do you think you are?' someone said in the background, and Adam's voice, satisfied and amused, said: 'Batman, I think. Or some such. Some kind of superhero, anyway.'

Jude manoeuvred Mikey back out of their father's reach and placed himself firmly between them. 'Don't start thinking I can't get you out of here by force if I have to. You know I can.'

However much alcohol Mikey had shipped before the match, it had been long enough ago for the edge of his aggression to be blunted. He shuffled back. 'I want to talk to him.'

'Aye, I bet you do.' Jude couldn't keep the sarcasm out of his tone. In the years since their parents' divorce Mikey had steadfastly rejected every approach David had made, snuffing out Jude's regular attempts to broker some sort of rapprochement. 'This isn't the time and it isn't the place. If you're serious about it, arrange something for some other time, when there's no drink. I'll come along and keep the peace. But not here and not now.'

He grabbed Mikey's arm and led him out of the bar. David, he could see, had finally realised the best place to be was somewhere else and had disappeared from the bar. Out in the street he caught a glimpse of him, walking briskly along towards the city centre where, no doubt, he would find less antagonistic company in another pub and then get the train home.

In the meantime, there was Mikey. He'd seen David disappearing, too, and pulled a little in that direction like a half-trained dog tugging at a lead. Wise to the tricks, and aware of what might be going through Mikey's head, Jude kept a tight hold until the was sure David was too far away to be caught even if they could find him, and that Mikey had given up any idea of pursuit.

'Right, our kid,' he said with a sigh. 'Let's take you home.'

TWENTY-ONE

'I can't do it!' read Linda Satterthwaite, from the script in front of her. 'How can I kill such a sweet thing as you? No matter what the Queen wants me to do, I won't do the wrong thing!'

'But what shall I do?' Becca Reid, who was supposed to know the words, snatched a quick look at her script to check the next line.

'You must run into the woods. I'll tell the Queen I've killed a deer and take her its heart.' Linda laid down the script as the front door opened. 'Mikey, is that you?' Turning to Becca she gave a tiny shrug. Their peaceful evening of script-reading was over. 'Sorry. That's an end to it. I wasn't expecting him back so soon. Someone must have given him a lift. At least it saves me the trip to the station to fetch him.'

Mikey wasn't alone. Becca's heart quickened as she recognised a second voice in the hallway. Jude. Damn. She should have guessed. 'Never mind. We can always try again some other time. It'll give me a chance to learn my lines a bit better.' Next time they were going over the script she'd see if Linda wanted to come over to her place. If, by some unfortunate turn of events, Jude turned up, at least she'd be on her own territory.

The living room door burst open and Mikey bounced through it, red in the face and fizzing with anger. 'Jude's brought me home to be grounded,' he said, coming to a halt in the middle of the room and addressing himself to his mother, arms folded, 'for being drunk and disorderly in a public place or whatever he calls it. And keeping bad company. And trying to knock Dad's block off.'

'Oh dear.' Linda, who had been the injured party in the divorce, was always sympathetic to Mikey when it came to his father. 'I take it the afternoon didn't go quite as well as expected?'

'Dad and I bumped into Mikey in the Crown,' said Jude, appearing in the doorway and seeming, or so Becca thought, a little amused. He gave her a slight nod and she returned it and then looked away, picking up her script again and slipping it into the polypocket in which she'd brought it. 'But it's okay. Disaster was averted.'

'There wouldn't have been a disaster. I just wanted to talk to him.'

'I'm sure. We all know how that would have ended.'

'You didn't have to drag me out of there like a kid misbehaving in the park. You humiliated me in public. Who do you think you are?'

Becca stood up. 'I'll head home.' Mikey's anger was obvious and she had no wish to get caught up in a family row.

'There's no need.' Linda's voice was rich with irritation, though Becca thought it was more to do with her ex-husband than either of her sons. 'I'm sure Jude and Mikey—'

'If he stays I'm heading back out!'

'On that note,' said Jude, 'I'll leave you to explain what happened, or not, as you see fit. I'm off home to salvage the rest of my evening. As far as I'm concerned, that's it. It never happened.'

'Why don't you pop round tomorrow afternoon?' asked Linda, frowning at Mikey, now. 'Didn't you say you were off all weekend?'

'I was, but I changed shifts. I'm off on Wednesday. I'll pop in for a cuppa then.'

He hovered in the hall while Becca scooped her coat off the newel post where she'd deposited it, and shrugged it over her shoulders. She only lived over the road but the evening was cold and there had been a touch of sleet about when she'd arrived. 'Did the football go okay?'

'Oh, we lost of course.' He laughed. 'As Dad kept saying, we were one good shot away from a giant killing, but I can't be doing with all this *what-if* nonsense. So what if we'd equalised? We'd still have lost.'

'That's a shame.'

'Not at all. I was enjoying it. Up to a point.' He opened the front door for her.

'What happened?' Becca asked, lowering her voice although she was sure they couldn't be heard from indoors, 'with Mikey?'

'It was fairly straightforward.' He followed her down the path into the darkness. 'As I said. Dad and I went for a drink after the game and we bumped into him. That's all.'

A sly, grey shape detached itself from the shadows and trotted in Becca's footsteps. Her cat, Holmes. She clicked her fingers at him, fruitlessly. You couldn't chain Holmes's free spirit. 'Did he really hit your dad?'

'No. But he tried, and he would have done, if I hadn't stopped him.'

Jude was a decent man. Becca knew that, from the time

when she'd been in love with him. The problem was that his decency was strait-laced and unforgiving and he'd probably taken a harder line with Mikey than their father would have done, but today she still sensed that degree of tolerance and amusement she'd felt in the house. Mikey appreciated Jude's attentions, probably more than either of them thought he did. He'd get over it. 'What did your dad do?'

'The sensible thing. Cleared off. Eventually.'

Still they lingered, and Holmes sat on the path and regarded them with interest. 'It's a shame it spoiled your evening out.'

'And your evening in. I'm sorry we interrupted. I didn't know Mum had a visitor, or I'd have driven Mikey around for an hour to give him a bit more time to cool off.'

'It wasn't really a social occasion. Linda was just helping me read through my script for the panto.'

'The panto? In January? Or are you starting early for next Christmas?'

She and Jude had always teased one another, even after their relationship ended, but these days he poked fun at her very gently. She hid her smile. 'You know I do the Brownies in the village. They wanted to do a panto but there was too much going on before Christmas — school nativity plays and parties and so on. So we're doing it for Easter instead.'

'Sounds fun.'

'It is. They've put together a script — with help, of course — and we're doing Snow White and the Seven Dwarves.'

'Which one of them gets to be Snow White?'

She giggled. 'Me. That was their idea, too. But they're doing all the rest of the roles themselves, except the wicked queen. None of them wanted that part, so Jess gets that.

She's Tawny Owl.' But he'd know that. He made a point of knowing everything and everyone.

'I'll put it in my diary.'

'Let's hope you don't have to cancel,' said Becca, and regretted it immediately. She often sounded waspish when she spoke to Jude, even though she never meant to. It was just that the words always seemed to come out wrong, as if her own better judgement was trying to keep him at bay.

She was fond of him, that was the thing. They'd been together a long time and there was a part of her that would dearly like to be with him again, but that was the problem. She couldn't handle his single-minded devotion to the job and she didn't trust him to put her first whenever she might need him; no-one with any self-respect would want to be judged as harshly for their shortcomings as he might judge her, or come second to the needs of strangers.

'Let's hope I don't,' he said, as if he hadn't picked up on her sharpness. 'I'll do my best, though. I wouldn't miss it for the world.'

'You must be busy just now,' said Becca, trying to erase her harshness with kindness and interest. 'With the Luke Mortimer thing, I suppose?'

'No busier than usual. But yes, that's the thing on my mind the most at the moment.'

Becca understood why. So often the stories you read on the news gave off uncomfortable echoes in your own home life. She remembered Luke, at a distance, because his disappearance had been a big story, a gap in the heart of the community. 'Did you know I was at school at the same time as him?'

'I didn't think of that. But of course. You would have been.'

'Only just. He would have been a few years below me and I didn't know him. I'd left the school by the time he disappeared.' In a small and close community like theirs, in the narrow strip of Cumbria between the Pennines and the Lakes, a large area nurtured a relatively small number of people. The loss of one echoed in the lives of everyone, and everyone knew the family, or knew someone who did. 'I met Emmy Leach, once, you know.'

'I didn't know that.' That caught his interest. That might have been why she said it, although anything she thought she could contribute would be trivial, utterly irrelevant to the case.

'She came to talk to the WI last spring about the work she does with the food bank. I was talking to her afterwards. I really liked her and she seemed a genuinely lovely woman.'

'That's good to know,' he said, his usual bland response to a comment that wasn't of interest.

She sensed he was wound up, for all the blandness and the false amusement. 'Is everything all right?'

'Of course.'

If anything was wrong it was probably her. She knew he still cared, and part of her thought it was kinder just to cut him off, but there was another thought, too, the one which said it had been right between them once and maybe it could be again. Just not yet. 'Are you worried about Mikey?'

'Up to a point. He nearly made a complete idiot of himself and if I hadn't been there he could have got himself into trouble. But all's well that ends well. He's mad with me now but when he calms down he'll realise I had no choice.'

'He said you brought him home for keeping bad company,' she said, and waited for his dismissive laugh.

It didn't come. 'I never said anything along those lines. He was with Adam, as it happens, and I'm pretty sure he'll have been poking and prodding away behind the scenes, trying to make trouble. That was the reason I was so high-handed with Mikey. Probably too much so, but the alternative was walking away and leaving him and Dad to fight it out. As Mikey keeps telling me, I'm his brother not his dad.'

They stood for a moment on the pavement in the darkness. A mist was rising from the River Lowther half a mile away beyond the road, and the half moon shimmered in the clouds. It was a landscape wrapped in ghosts. 'Yes.'

'Dad's bloody clueless about Mikey. He doesn't understand. Someone had to try and there was no-one but me.'

Becca thought of the *what-if*. *What if we'd equalised*, Jude had asked, rhetorically, about the football. Life was riddled with much more complicated counterfactuals. What if she'd been more patient with him? What if she'd been honest? What if she hadn't left him?

For a few months, she'd dated Adam Fleetwood. It had been long enough to see beneath the charm and the professed good intentions to the rock-hard determination and desire for revenge that lurked beneath. 'Do you know, Jude, I think I owe you an apology.'

'Oh?'

'About Adam. I was wrong about him. I don't think he was that hard done by after all.'

'He was never hard done by.' Even in the darkness Jude chose not to face her, and turned sideways so all she could see was his profile, fine-drawn against the the thin moonlight. 'I'm sorry. If you deal drugs, you deserve to go to prison.'

Her soul quivered a little. 'Yes. And thinking about it, maybe Mikey deserved a firm hand.' That was where thinking about Luke had brought her — to consideration of everything that had happened, and how in the end

Mikey had enough respect for his brother to survive his hard line. Everyone reacted differently to events and at the moment Mikey had needed discipline there had been no-one to offer it but Jude.

'That's big of you,' he said, and though the words were prim, she thought she sensed that old amusement under them.

'Come in and have a coffee,' she said, after a moment. 'Or even a bite to eat.'

'I won't, if you don't mind. Mikey spilled his drink over me so I'll need to get home and get changed. And I'd probably better get out of the village before he comes after me. It isn't big enough for both of us when he's in that kind of temper. But I'll see you around.'

'Goodbye then.'

'Goodbye.' And he strode off towards his Mercedes, got in and the car roared away. Only when he was out of the village and the lights had turned back towards Penrith did Becca head up the path toward the house with Holmes at her heels.

What if...? Jude had asked, and answered his own question. *We'd still have lost.*

TWENTY-TWO

Emmy waited until the Monday morning before she cracked — five days in which everything she said to Rob had to be carefully thought out, phrased and rephrased to keep him sweet, until she sensed him eyeing her with suspicion. Church on Sunday had been impossible. That was what broke her resolve — a visiting preacher who chose to deliver an hour-long sermon on the certainty that her sins would find her out.

Everyone else's sins will be found out, too, Emmy reminded herself over coffee on the Monday morning, going back over the sermon and trying in vain to allow her rational mind to pick up and repair the threads left by her distress. That would include Rob's sins, whatever they might be, and those of the vicar, who had looked on solemnly and nodded throughout the sermon, and the mother of three in the back pew who looked far too exhausted to have any sins to answer for. None of those people faced the threat that hung over her and over Tino — that someone knew of their infidelity and, for whatever reason, was biding their time until…when?

Rob was out and even though she knew there was no chance of him creeping back she didn't dare call Tino, as she so desperately wished to do. If she called, she might weaken, give in and ask him to take her away. In the short term there would be scandal and then there would be relief and happiness, but once the dust had settled, they would confront the long shadow of Rob's fury.

She picked away at her previously immaculate finger-nails and looked out at the garden. They still didn't know what this potential blackmailer wanted. Now she regretted having thrown the keys to the studio away without looking to see if there was something to be done, a message or instructions that would give them a way out of the situation. Perhaps Tino had found one, but was as fearful of contacting her as she was of contacting him. Perhaps even now he was negotiating with whoever it was, and would find a way round it.

Deep down she knew Tino was no superhero. She shook her head over her cup of coffee, remembering how he'd left her to deal with the recovery of the body. Whatever his claims about acting in her interests rather than his own, when it came to it he'd been the one to run away from the potential scandal. There was every chance he wouldn't be taking the initiative but was lying low and hoping it would all go away so that, months down the line, they could pick up where they'd left off.

It was just as it had been up at Bowscale Tarn. If there was something to be done, she would have to do it.

A pale sun was shimmering through the mist, a promise of a brighter afternoon, and the early frost had decayed to a shining carpet of dew. Emmy let herself out of the back door and took a childish pleasure in walking across the grass, leaving a trail of dark green footsteps behind her. The studio was locked and she regretted throwing away the key, so she must look elsewhere for help. She peered in at the window and could just about see that the pictures were spread out on the table but, thank God, she'd tossed the brown envelope on top of them and they were on the far side of the studio, so there was no way anyone could see them without going inside.

With chilled fingers, she removed Jude Satterthwaite's card from her phone case. She walked down to the orchard where the frail phone signal was at its strongest and stood among the thrusting green spikes of the daffodils, feeling the sun on her face. It was the last day of the pheasant shooting season and someone was making the most of it, the pop of a gun in the distance indicating that there would be game in somebody's pot, some evening soon. 'Is that Chief Inspector Satterthwaite?'

'Speaking!' he said, cheerfully.

When she'd outlined what had happened, he was brisk and sharp. 'I'll get down as soon as I can, Mrs Leach. It sounds as if we'll have to force entry to the studio, but you were right to call me.' There was a fractional hesitation. 'Is your husband there?'

'No.' Emmy drew a long, even breath. 'Rob is out today and won't be back until later.'

'Does he know what you've found?'

She licked her lips. 'No. Though of course he'll have to.'

'Not necessarily. We'll be as discreet as we can.'

'I mean, I'll have to tell him. Because he's my husband and because he's going to find out one way or another.'

There was a long pause, as if he was thinking of how to answer. 'I'll be with you in twenty minutes,' he said eventually, a response that was somehow both optimistic and disappointing.

Emmy lingered in the orchard for a while. If you

walked up to the top of the hill you could see the sprawl of Penrith on the slopes of Beacon Hill away to the east. It wasn't so far, but she was hardly an emergency and they wouldn't put the blue lights on for her, even if he hadn't promised discretion. Nevertheless, she counted the minutes until they arrived.

It took twenty-three minutes before Jude Satterthwaite's Mercedes drew up in the courtyard at the side of the house. He'd brought a younger man with him, blond and seemingly trying not to be too enthusiastic, whom he introduced as Detective Sergeant Chris Marshall.

'Chris has some dark talents,' he said, as Emmy led the two of them to the studio, 'and one of them is breaking and entering as quickly and unobtrusively as possible. Normally I'd call a locksmith but I'm guessing you don't want us hanging around so this way, with luck, we can be in and out of here pretty quickly.' A pause. 'When do you expect your husband back?'

'Not for a couple of hours.' Emmy wasn't quite sure why she was afraid of Rob, and she knew it was wrong to be so, but somehow she was more afraid of him than she was of the scandal or her own conscience. She was sure the chief inspector understood that, and while they watched Chris Marshall examining the lock, poking at it for a few moments and then, like a magician, turning the handle and opening the door, she almost told him, but she didn't. It would solve the problem in the present but amplify it further down the line.

Jude Satterthwaite was watching her with an unashamed question in his eyes, but when Chris Marshall opened the door he moved swiftly inside the studio. Without touching the pictures, he scanned them carefully, lifted his eyebrows very slightly in a way she thought he didn't intend her to see, then produced an evidence bag and a pair of disposable gloves and swept the photos and the USB stick into the bag. 'Do you know when these were taken, Mrs Leach?'

That reproached her, as if he assumed there had been many occasions such as that when there had only been a few. 'In the summer. At the beginning of July.'

'Was your husband away at the time?'

It was an obvious question, and of course he must considered that Rob was the photographer, but it couldn't have been him. She'd have known. She nodded.

'And where were they taken?'

'In the woods, less than a mile from here. There's a path at the end of the village, into the woods. There are rhododendrons and so on. It's well-concealed.' Though not well enough. 'I used to meet my ex-husband at the stile by the path and we'd walk up to the woods together.' And then slip through the bushes and disappear, as if into another world.

'Often?'

'Two or three times, maybe. Sometimes we went else-where. But we didn't always… you know. Mostly it was just to walk and talk.' And kiss. They had always shared a kiss, as they had done up at Bowscale Tarn while their son's body floated yards away from them, like a dormant curse.

'I'd normally get someone to do a sweep for finger-prints,' he said, 'but—'

'No. Please. There's no need for any fuss.'

'I doubt there would be much to find,' he said, acqui-escing, 'and if there is I expect it'll be in here.' He tapped the evidence bag, then peeled off the gloves and pocketed them, firing off a few more questions as he did so. Had she looked through all the pictures? Had she handled the enve-lope much? Had she viewed the contents the flash drive? She shook her head at them all.

His parting shot was one she'd been expecting, and he saved it for when they were on their way back to the car. 'You say Mr Mortimer received something similar?'

'I believe so. But we didn't speak much about it, and I haven't seen or spoken to him since that call. That was Wednesday.'

'Okay, Mrs Leach. Thank you. We'll call in on him now, then, if he's there. And by the way.'

It was coming. She nodded.

'I'd like to repeat what I said to you last time. If you've any concerns at all about your safety you can call 999 and we'll get someone out to you. I promise you we'll take it seriously.'

'Thank you,' she said, perfectly composed, 'but I have no concerns. My husband is a good Christian man.'

'Is there any other sort?' He smiled at her, as if something about that amused him. 'Do remember, though. Any time. You can call for help in an emergency and if you need to chat you have Constable Phillips's number. And of course, you can always call me.'

He got into the passenger seat clutching the evidence bag, and the sergeant drove off, spinning the wheels of the Mercedes so that a loose piece of gravel spat across the sandstone slabs of the yard. She watched them go with regret. It would have been the time to talk to them, to mention that she was afraid, that Rob had never been violent but things might change now someone knew she was an adulteress.

Calling the liaison officer was out of the question, because Emmy hadn't taken to the woman at all. If the blonde sergeant, Ashleigh O'Halloran, had been there she might have succumbed because Sergeant O'Halloran had given off the sort of vibes that begged her to confide, and the two men had been more forbidding and impossible to confide in. It was as well because a confession would have led to all sorts of complications. Whatever came her way she deserved it, because she was either married twice in the eyes of God or else she'd broken her vows to her second husband. *I'm a sinner whatever way*, Emmy told herself, but as she turned back into the house she was relieved and apprehensive in equal measure.

TWENTY-THREE

'I've had a look at the video,' Jude said, to the usual group of Doddsy, Ashleigh and Chris. 'It wasn't an easy watch. Whether it's got anything to do with Luke's death I can't say. It may just be a nasty piece of voyeurism.'

'Was it...' Ashleigh, who hadn't seen the video, made a face, '...worse than you might expect?'

'Whatever that means. I've seen much worse,' said Doddsy, with a sigh. 'The photos aren't that bad, and I'm not saying there was anything particularly hardcore in the video itself. But I don't get my kicks out of watching a couple having — let's face it — perfectly normal sex.'

Jude nodded. 'I thought the same.' There was something distasteful about the idea that someone had been filming Emmy and Tino without their knowledge, and Emmy's mortification had been painful to watch. Maybe he was just getting over-fastidious in his old age. 'I got the sense someone had been waiting for them. You could see the camera was in position before they arrived.'

'It wasn't a camera trap was it? One of those auto-mated things they use for wildlife?' Chris leaned forward.

'No.' The photos had covered the entire period from Emmy and Tino arriving, hand in hand like the teenage sweethearts they'd once been, until their departure the better part of an hour later. 'There was a bit of shifting of focus and some of the shots zoomed in. The time stamp on the images shows they were taken on July 8th of last year, between one and two o'clock. It wasn't a video camera, so the video quality isn't that great. But it's good enough.'

'And whoever took the pictures waited six months before doing anything about it.' Ashleigh was frowning.

'I'd very much like to know where Rob Leach was at that time,' said Doddsy, pre-empting Jude's own thought.

'I'm on to that.' Chris wrote it down. 'Do we know anything more about the photos and the video, Doddsy? On the technical side, I mean.'

'Yes. The photos were taken on a Canon 1100.'

'There are thousands of those bloody things around,' Chris said, somewhat mutinously. 'We can't go around the whole of Cumbria looking for one with those images on.'

The camera in question was a popular model but Chris had missed the point entirely. So had Ashleigh, who was already scribbling on her pad: *RL camera make?* Doddsy's expression was neutral. Jude was surprised at them. It was the first thing he'd thought of when he'd checked his emails that morning. 'We don't need to. You're right, Chris. They're ten a penny. But we already have a camera that fits that spec. It's the one we retrieved from Bowscale Tarn. What we don't have is the card that went with it.'

Doddsy laid his pen down. 'Well,' was all he said.

'I'll follow up with the manufacturer,' said Chris, always busy and adding another thing to his list, 'and see if it's been registered with them for a warranty and email updates and so forth. That'll tell us who it belongs to and, if it's Luke, where he lived and maybe some more. If it isn't his, it may give us a contact for him, and that's of interest in itself.'

'And the missing card?' said Ashleigh. The photos of Emmy and Tino were in the brown envelope on the table and she tapped her finger on it. 'I think we know what's on it, don't we? These photos.'

'Maybe,' said Jude. 'There could have been more. Remember Heather Short said she'd seen someone she thought might have been Luke hanging around in those woods in the autumn. If he was the one who did the filming, the question we have to ask ourselves is why, and how they got from Luke's camera to his parents nearly two weeks after his death.'

'Can we be sure they weren't there before?' asked Chris. 'It looked to me as if that studio hadn't been touched in a long time.'

Jude jotted that down. 'I'll ask Mandy to raise it with Emmy, next time she's down there.' Though that wouldn't be until later on in the week. Mandy Phillips's time was fully accounted for, as was that of every other FLO in the department. He wasn't sure they'd get much feedback from the visit anyway; Mandy had indicated that Rob had not only been present throughout every second of her first visit but had also insisted on cancelling a meeting so he could be present at the next. It was another warning, but one to be considered on a different occasion. Jude returned to the point of fact. 'If she hadn't been in there since Luke's death, it's possible he left it there. In that case it might be that she knew about it and did nothing.'

'Why do that, though, if she was scared?'

'We don't know she was. Remember, she claimed to have waited five days before she called us.'

'His dad, though.' Chris was still frowning, probably at himself for having missed the obvious. 'Tino Mortimer, I mean. He said he found the photos and USB stick in among some papers on his desk but he thought he might have picked them up with the post and brought them in to the office. But they might have been put there before.'

'It's possible.' Tino had been a furtive interviewee, showing signs of embarrassment rather than shame and full of claims that he'd been about to call the police but that Emmy had beaten him to it. 'I suspect a rather more simple explanation. Someone knew what Luke had on the memory card and they killed him for it, but he used the camera a lot. It seems to have been one of the tools of his trade. What we see here isn't necessarily what they were after.'

'Ah, of course.' Ashleigh's expression cleared. 'Someone got the card, maybe found what they were looking for, maybe not. Either way, they stumbled on the pictures of Emmy and Tino, and saw a way of making a fast buck. Is that it?'

He nodded his head towards her. 'Exactly. And there's one other thing to go with it. I doubt if Emmy noticed it, so we'll have to get Mandy to ask her. On the back of one of the pictures someone had written *keep quiet*. Very faint, in pencil. But it was there.'

'Wait.' Doddsy sighed. 'Maybe it wasn't money after all. Why the hell are people so complicated?'

'Maybe it wasn't. Or maybe Emmy was meant to keep quiet about the photos. The pictures sent to Tino Mortimer were identical and one of those had the same message on the back.' Jude pushed his chair back. 'There's plenty for all of us to do. I'd like a little more information on Heather Short and her background, Chris, if you can. She's the only person who claims to have seen Luke, or someone who might have been him, and she seems to have an insight into what's going on in the Leaches' marriage. Whether or not she does is immaterial, but I'm interested that she thinks she does.'

The meeting broke up and Ashleigh, on the pretext (or so Jude thought) of heading to the coffee machine for a cup of coffee, followed him to the door. 'You saw Emmy, didn't you? And have you caught up with Mandy since she went down to see them? What did she say?'

'I can't read people as well as you do. When Chris and I saw Emmy yesterday she seemed pretty stoical about the whole thing. Mandy reckoned the same. She finds Emmy calm and polite but she doesn't confide.'

'I suppose it's that faith she has. My gran was the same. Brought up in the church, lived through the War, sat back and let whatever came at her, come at her. She lost friends and family in the blitz and in the fighting but hey. At the end of it, Gran was still there.' She frowned. 'I bet Rob hates having an FLO around.'

'I'm sure he does. Hence he was so keen to make sure he was there.' Tino, Mandy had reported, had been gloriously casual. *Pop in any time you like*, he'd said. *Any of you. Kettle's always on.*

Ashleigh lingered. He knew what she was thinking, understood her concerns. He understood, too, that she couldn't say them aloud. She thought, as he did, that she'd have done a far better job of putting Emmy at her ease.

'When Chris and I were at Blacksty yesterday I offered Emmy another chance to talk,' he said, to ease her concerns, 'and I told her again that if she has any worries about her safety she should call immediately. You're right, as it happens. I think there are red flags all over that relationship. But it's not for us to force her to report her husband for coercion, or to try and get her away from him.'

'I do know that. But I was lying awake last night worrying about her.'

He wouldn't go so far as to say Emmy's situation worried him quite that much but it had been on his mind, too. He was able to keep a more sensible perspective on these things than Ashleigh. 'You should have called me.'

'Maybe I will, next time.' She moved to the machine and slid a couple of coins into the slot and he headed back to the office, musing on the pieces of the jigsaw that would lead them, eventually, to Luke Mortimer's killer.

TWENTY-FOUR

Heather was loading her tools into the van as the cold dawn broke over the rim of the Pennines. It was just before dawn and she stood and watched for a while as the winter sun raised its head above the ridge, flashed a broad spill of rays down the slopes and into the valley, and then disappeared almost immediately into the low cloud. After the brief brightening, the sky darkened again.

The courtyard was eerily quiet, as the birds which had woken with the light seemed to settle back again in confusion. She turned to see headlights on the curving track that led to the converted farm buildings where she lived. That would be Richard, the young Polish man who brought his mop, bucket, and the endless supply of smiles which adequately compensated for his limited English, whenever Heather felt the need to give the place a going-over. Richard was always on time and that suited Heather, who was an early bird herself. With the van loaded, she stood and watched the headlights strobing through the decaying hedge as the car made its way up the uneven track.

Either Richard had a new car, or it wasn't him. She cocked her head to one side and listened. Very few people came up to the smallholding. That was how she liked it; it was easy to go into the village and be matey and chatty with the locals without giving away too much. The postman delivered to a box fixed to the post at the end of the lane, and she picked up her parcels from the delivery office in Penrith. Even Emmy didn't know her address.

The sun made another determined attempt on the darkness as the car purred to the end of the lane. This wasn't the rust bucket of a Vauxhall Corsa Richard had nursed all the way from some one-horse town outside Gniezno, in search of opportunity a few years before. She was pretty certain he hadn't done well enough for himself to acquire a new Audi in the few weeks since she'd last seen him.

A new black Audi. Rob Leach, then. She was only surprised it had taken him this long. With an ear out for Richard's approach behind him, Heather prepared herself, waiting until he'd stopped the car and got out, then striding across the courtyard towards him. 'Good morning, Rob. I'd offer you a coffee, but as you can see, I'm on my way out.'

'I wouldn't mind a coffee,' he said, so for a moment she thought he'd misheard her, then realised he was looking for trouble. 'I'm sure you'll spare me some time to talk. I have quite a lot to say and there's even more for you to say to me.'

'I don't think so.' She flicked the rear door of the van shut. 'If you don't mind, I'll be off. Daylight's short at this time of year. I'd have left before, but I'm waiting for someone.'

'Oh, is that right?' He didn't believe her, and it was only by chance it was true, but he cast a nervous glance back along the road just in case. And there, thank God, came the second set of lights, the ones that ensured Rob would soon be on his way because he wouldn't know Richard's English was poor and he wouldn't dare say what he had to say in front of anyone who might repeat it. 'Ah, damn.'

'No need for blasphemy,' she mocked him. People like Rob stuck in her craw. Emmy was all right, a genuine Christian racked with unnecessary guilt, but Rob was the worst sort, wearing his religion as a cloak of public respectability and never acting on it. He was a very unpleasant person indeed, and she was the only one who knew just how evil he was.

It wasn't a comforting thought, in that crisp near-darkness. 'Here's Richard now. It's a shame you don't have time to chat.'

He got back into the car. 'You can make yourself available. I've got things to say to you.'

Not on your life, thought Heather, but when she looked at him again she saw in his eyes exactly what Emmy had feared. Rob could carry a grudge for decades and never forgave those who offended him. She wasn't prepared to give him the satisfaction of thinking he had her on the run. 'It's to rain tomorrow. I'm not working then. We can meet in town.'

'We'll meet this afternoon. You can come to the house. Pretend you want to talk about what plants to put in the border or something.'

'What will Emmy say?'

'Emmy won't care. She's going to pieces. She didn't get up this morning. We'll have a chance to speak in private.'

Reviewing the suggestion as the Corsa came closer, Heather decided it was as well to go along with him. A matter of a few hours didn't give her much time to sort out alternative options, but if he was foolish enough to meet her in the relatively public surroundings of Blacksty, where help was only a nosy neighbour away, she wasn't going to come to any harm. Discretion, in this case, was the better part of valour. 'Okay.'

'Good morning, Meesis Short,' sang Richard in his cheeriest voice, as he jumped out of the car. He beamed at Rob. 'Your friend?'

'No,' Heather said, as Rob got into the Audi and reversed in a series of short sharp manoeuvres, a multi-point turn that sprayed up mud as he headed for home. 'Anything but.'

'Not friend who stay? Friend is gone?'

'Yes, he's gone.' She opened the front door for him. 'I'll make you a coffee and you can get started. I won't be back until later. Just pop the keys through the door when you're done.'

Rob Leach was clever and he had the mean mind of a psychopath, but he was mistaken if he thought he could get the better of her.

'I don't know what you're doing here,' said Doddsy, with a faint trace of irritation. 'I have you down in the book as on a day off.'

'I am. But I needed to come in and sign something off with Faye, so I thought I'd drop by.' It wasn't unusual for Jude to be in the office on his days off. Becca had hated that and it was a habit he knew he should break. 'What's the problem? Are you planning a coup?'

Doddsy laughed. His method of working closely followed Jude's own, and when Jude had appeared in the incident room he'd been holding a brainstorming session with Chris and Mandy Phillips, the FLO. 'I don't need your job as well as my own. I'd leave, if I were you, before I find you something to do.'

'You know me. I can't pass a meeting without wanting to know what's going on. You carry on. I'll listen and then I'll go.'

'I'm starting to feel things coming together.' Doddsy looked down at his notes. 'Chris. I know you've put a lot of time into this.' It was obvious from the sergeant's smug expression that the effort had been well rewarded. 'What have you got?'

'As usual, Ash's instincts were correct. I've been drilling away and Ms Heather Short is a most interesting character.'

Jude looked around the room. He'd forgotten that Ashleigh was on a rest day, too. When they were together their free time had rarely coincided and these days he had no idea when she was scheduled to be off or what her plans were. Her place at the table had been taken by Mandy Phillips, who looked as if she'd unloaded her opinions already and was bored with the procedural stuff — and he had some sympathy with that.

'Is Heather Short her real name?' asked Jude. 'From what Ashleigh said she was keen to talk about her recent past and very vague about where she was before.'

'No, you're right. It's an alias. Do you want to put any more guesses on the table about her?'

Jude waved a hand in the general direction of the whiteboard. A sample of the images from Luke's Facebook page had been printed off and added to the clutter that made up the puzzle. 'Yes, why not? I think I'm going to guess she lives somewhere in the area those photos were taken from.'

'That's not a guess, though.' Doddsy shook his head at

him as if he were cheating in a parlour game. 'We know she lives in that area. She told us she had a patch of land over at Lazonby, didn't she, and I know you've nothing better to do in the evenings than sit down with an OS map and Google Earth and those photos and try and work out where it is.'

'Guilty as charged. That's exactly what I did.' It had taken his mind off the recurring nightmare that was Mikey and David and their eternal, father-son feud. The scene after the football echoed too closely with what had gone on between Luke and Rob, this vicious hatred of the one for the other. 'And I have an answer.' He pulled over the map he'd been working on the previous evening and unfolded it. He'd marked it with lines of sight and they converged, or nearly so, on a rough area a couple of miles from Lazonby on the Plumpton road. 'Here. Do I win the prize?'

'Bloody hell,' said Chris, impressed. 'Never mind wasting your time on management. I could use you on the desk work. You might make a difference.'

'I had a clue. My dad saw someone matching Luke's description wandering up that way, years ago.' His brow creased once more in annoyance at Mikey's interruption. David could ramble on for hours but he had the gift of noticing things and accruing knowledge from others. Most of it was valueless but there might have been some other detail to emerge if Jude had had the chance to talk him through it.

'Is the boss right, then?' asked Doddsy of Chris, and laughed. 'There's always a first time.'

'Yes, spot on. That's a place called Wildrigg Farm. The farmhouse is long gone and most of the land was swallowed up by one of the neighbouring operations years back. There's the main barn, which has been converted into a residential property, and the outbuildings are still there. There's about an acre of land. That's where the woman we know as Heather Short lives.'

'Who is she really?' asked Jude.

'She changed her name from Marian Tate when she left the army twenty years ago. Though when I say *left* I should say *dishonourably discharged*. There were allegations of bullying and some suggestion of theft and also of blackmail and extortion, though no charges were brought.'

'I see where this is going. Is there any drugs connection?'

'One of possession with intent to supply, but that was immediately after she left the army. She was given a suspended sentence and it lapsed long ago.'

'Interesting. And then?'

'Everything went quiet for a bit, but she set up a security business and moved to Liverpool, where she seems to have made connections with some of the lads who are now suspected of running the county lines operations. By connections, I don't mean she did anything illegal. She supplied the security for some warehouses that were later busted and found to be used to store drugs and, in one of the cases, as a cannabis farm. Her involvement was very much at arms' length but they knew her and she knew them.'

'Did I hear somewhere that she was a connection of Rob Leach's?' asked Doddsy.

'Yes. Heather mentioned it to Ashleigh. She said they came across one another way back, but they didn't get on.'

Chris tapped the table with his pen, as if to bring them back to attention. He loved the drama of a briefing meeting far more than the excitement of a chase on the street. 'She worked as part of the security team on a development project in Liverpool Docklands, and that project involved the firm Leach was working with at the time.

There's no suggestion of anything illicit. She did a lot of work with squeaky clean organisations as well as the occasional dodgy one. But there's every chance that's where they originally met.'

'When was that?'

Chris turned a bland expression on them. 'About six months before Luke vanished. About a year after that she was earning enough money from somewhere to buy a significant and expensive property in Liverpool, which she still owns. When I say significant she paid about a quarter of a million for it. The previous year she'd invested in the run-down remnants of Wildrigg Farm, which she proceeded to do up over the years. And, by the way, just before Luke vanished, Rob Leach came into a large inheritance from his father.'

Jude picked up a pen and began doodling, furiously. 'Okay. Let's think this through. Connection with Liverpool drug dealers? Makes sense. Connection with Rob Leach? Coincidental. Contact with Rob Leach just when things were getting a bit hot on the drugs front? I think we might call that initiative on her part, especially if they had a local connection. She might have had a recce up here and spotted the potential. Then…what? Are we really suggesting Rob Leach paid her to kill his stepson, just because they both had an influx of cash about that time?' He looked around the table and judged that was exactly what they all thought. 'Let's have a look at why we think that. And then look at why she didn't do it.' Because she hadn't. Luke had lived.

'As I see it,' Doddsy said, 'there's no need for a drugs connection for that contract to be taken out. All that's required is that the two of them met and spoke. I'd like to know the source of the money for her new property. I'd like to look at Leach's financial situation following the inheritance. But she certainly came into a large amount of unexpected income at the same time as Luke disappeared.'

'We're already following up the finances,' said Chris, 'but that might take a while. I had to get Faye to lean on the banks. They don't like letting us have that sort of stuff.'

That might pay dividends. If Rob had, indeed, taken out a contract on his son it was unlikely he had the skills to weave the transaction into a web of others. 'Fine. That's a good start. But she didn't do it.'

'I wonder why not? wondered Doddsy, aloud. 'She's ex-army. She did a couple of tours of duty in Iraq. She'd hardly be squeamish about killing a young kid, or you'd think not.'

A memory formed in Jude's mind, of arriving in his mother's house on Saturday evening and hearing Becca declaiming from the panto script. Becca, whose heart was as soft as butter, could never have killed anyone but Heather wouldn't have spared Luke for any reason other than cold-hearted self-interest. 'I reckon he was more use to her alive than dead. That's where opportunity comes in.' He twirled his pen between his fingers.

'Probably.' Chris looked down at his notes with a lurking smile. That meant there was more to come. 'She seems to have been a smart operator. Her army record isn't bad, if you take out the disciplinary issues. She was NCO material, by the sound of it.'

'So here's Luke,' persisted Doddsy. 'He's on the wild side. He smokes a bit of this and sells a bit of that and possibly injects a bit of the other. He's unhappy at home, pushing the boundaries and desperate to show himself up as a man rather than a boy, and put one over on his stepfather on the way. Short approaches him and offers him a chance to get away. She doesn't mention any kind of contract with his stepfather. She just says she can help him disappear. He can come and stay with her for a bit, maybe help her do up this place up at Lazonby.'

'A bit close to home, don't you think?' asked Chris.

'Maybe. Maybe he came later, or not at all. But I think we can be pretty certain she subsequently offered him the chance to make a bit of money by running drugs for her, with a bit of cash or maybe payment in kind.'

It was what Jude had feared for Mikey. Thank God that had never happened, that Adam Fleetwood had gone to prison before he could be too closely tied into it and had had the good fortune, or so it appeared, to come out rehabilitated. He could see how Heather, whose youth bore evidence of a wild streak Luke would surely have recognised, might inspire trust in a troubled teenager. 'There's no evidence she was staying with him all the time, is there?'

'No. For a lot of the time he was in some doss house in Toxteth with a lot of other no-hopers. The bosses must have decided to expand their operations and they'd need someone on the ground. And there's Heather, who they know and has local connections — and they can do business with. She knows the area and she has Luke to do the running around. And so… bingo.'

'Rob believed he was dead, though.' Jude narrowed his eyes, trying to recreate a moment in the past. 'I saw the look on his face when we broke the news to Emmy. He tried to pretend it was all about her, but he was absolutely gobsmacked, though he recovered pretty quickly. Mandy. What do you reckon?'

She shifted in her seat, defensively, he thought. 'By the time I got to see him he'd had plenty of time to think about what not to say.'

'What about Emmy?' Jude persisted. 'If she suspects he killed Luke, that would explain why she's so scared of him.'

'I didn't see anything except some kind of god-awful superiority. Cold as ice, the pair of them.'

Jude looked at his watch. It was late morning. 'Someone needs to talk to Heather.' He'd speak to Faye. There was a clear case for a search warrant, to see if there was any evidence that Luke had stayed there. 'Doddsy, what do you think of Mosedale Barn? Do we have any update?'

'As far as I know that's gone quiet. The two lads you took in that night haven't had anything to say and it seems they genuinely know nothing. That makes sense. You'd keep them in the dark. I'll go back to the guys and see if they can ask them directly if they've ever come across Luke or Heather Short. We know Luke had at least two aliases. But it certainly seems plausible there may be a connection.'

Jude had come across Heather's type before, the facilitators who kept themselves out of the worst of the trouble and paid others to do their dirty work. 'Am I right in thinking you were expecting more people to turn up at Mosedale Barn that night?'

'We didn't know,' Doddsy said, 'but the boys you helped pick up seemed to be hanging around waiting for whoever it was.'

'Right. And maybe the person they were waiting for was up at Bowscale Tarn that night.'

'Luke's hardly a kingpin, though,' objected Chris. 'He was a user and an addict. If he was supposed to be there it would have been to pick the stuff up and get it out on the streets, I'd have thought.'

'I didn't mean him. I meant Heather.' Jude doodled further. 'But I struggle to see why she'd kill him then, when she didn't before.'

'Perhaps she wanted the camera card and he wouldn't give it to her.'

Jude was still shaking his head. It made sense, but only to a certain point. Beyond that, there was confusion. 'It's worth a look, certainly.'

'Do you want me to go down to Lazonby and see if she's there?' asked Doddsy.

'Yes. I'll get a warrant drawn up and you can see if there's anything of interest there. I imagine she'll be too smart to keep drugs on the premises but if we can I'd like a look at her laptop, if nothing else. And I think maybe I'll go down to Blacksty and have a chat with Rob Leach.'

Jude was almost at his car before he decided on the issue that had been niggling at him ever since he'd realised Ashleigh wasn't there. He'd missed her insight. Mandy was, no doubt, highly competent at her job but she couldn't produce the input to the team meeting that they were used to and it was clear she'd taken a dislike to both the Leaches. He got out his phone and dialled Ashleigh's number. 'Morning.'

'Is something wrong?' she asked.

He reached the Mercedes and leaned against the side of it. 'That's a fine way to talk to me. No, nothing more than usual. I just popped by the office and now I'm on my way for a walk. Any plans for your day off?'

He pictured her, thinking it through with a slight frown on her face. 'None. It's a fairly grim kind of day, isn't it? I was going to sit here and think about life, the universe and who killed Luke Mortimer.'

'I thought you might. I was planning to head up to Blacksty for a walk. Fancy coming along? We can have lunch afterwards.'

'Hmm.' Another pause, another moment for him to try

and work out what she was thinking. 'Is there good walking up there? Or do you just want to check out the lie of the land?'

'Got it in one,' he said, and laughed. There was no longer any romance but he valued her friendship and enjoyed her company. 'The walking's pretty dull, unless you like wet woodlands. But I quite fancy having a look around under no time pressure. That was all.'

'It sounds very sensible to me. Shall I meet you there?'

'I'll pick you up,' he said, and rang off.

TWENTY-FIVE

Doddsy took Chris and a couple of uniformed constables with him down to Wildrigg Farm, more in hope than in the expectation of catching Heather Short at home. Though it was January, the weather was dry and there was every chance she'd be out at work.

'That's another thing,' he said to Chris as they turned off the road from Penrith and drove up the rutted lane ahead of the marked patrol car. 'You don't earn a lot from gardening in the winter. I couldn't find any suggestion she's got a second job.'

'It'll be good to get a look at her bank statements, if we can.' Chris's enthusiasm, as always, bubbled up. 'Though you never know. A lottery win, maybe. Or an inheritance. But if it's all above board she'll be able to prove it and if she doesn't want to help us by answering that kind of question she's probably got something to hide.'

'Maybe.' On the whole Doddsy took a more relaxed view of people's natural reluctance to share their private affairs with the police. He'd been in the force a long time

228

and had known a couple of bent coppers who didn't always use the information the way they should. 'I don't think we have enough evidence to go after her bank accounts just yet.' That might come.

'Either way, this is a nice pad.' Chris brought the car to a halt in the courtyard and looked around at the barn. 'Look at it. Lovely piece of work.'

Doddsy took a look. You could see where the new building had been grafted on to the old, where the rough stone of the original barn gave way to local sandstone that looked to be of the same age but clearly more finely built. The stones were better dressed and, he judged, came from the original, long-gone farmhouse. The outbuildings were neat and heavily padlocked.

'It looks like someone's home.' Chris got out of the car and looked at the battered white Vauxhall Corsa parked in front of the house. The two constables got out behind then and stared around. 'This doesn't fit with the moneyed image, though.'

'Maybe it's not her.' There was a light on in the house, even though it was late morning, but the building faced north and the weather was grey. 'We'll find out.'

He headed up the path and rang the bell. It echoed in the depths of the building and a moment later the door opened and a young man stood in the doorway.

'We're looking for Heather Short.' Doddsy flashed his warrant card. 'DI Dodd and DS Marshall. Cumbria Police.' He fingered the document in his pocket. 'We have a warrant here to search this property. May we come in?'

The man gaped at them and, behind them, at the marked police car. 'Meesis Short not here.' He waved a gesture in the vague direction of the hills.

'Your name?' asked Doddsy, as he stepped across the threshold.

'Richard,' said the young man, now even more confused. 'I clean house. She pay.' He rubbed his fingers together to indicate cash. 'Legal.'

'Where do you live, Richard?'

'Penrith. I clean…a month. A week. Four hours.' He stuck up four fingers for verification. Learned phrases, all he needed to get by. 'Fair pay.'

'Okay. Thank you, Richard. And Ms Short lives here by herself, is that right?' Doddsy took out the warrant and showed it to the cleaner, for all the difference it made, and then he and Chris stepped over the bucket that stood in the slate-floored hall and into the kitchen.

'A man,' said Richard, articulating carefully, as if he were struggling to remember the words and knew the importance of getting it right. 'When I come. And other time.'

'When did you last come to clean here?'

'Three weeks,' said the man, triumphantly.

'And this other man? He was there then?'

Chris was reaching for his iPad as he spoke, bringing up a picture of Luke Mortimer. He said nothing, only showed it to Richard. They watched as a frown spread over his face, followed by a nod of recognition.

'Yes,' he said. 'This man.'

'Look,' said Ashleigh. Anxiety gripped her as Jude pulled the Mercedes up at the side of the road. In the distance Tino and Emmy were having a painful and obvious public conversation from opposite sides of Blacksty's main street.

'I see them.' Jude put his hand on her arm, as if he thought she was going to intervene. If she'd thought it necessary she wouldn't have hesitated, but she was more precipitate than he. Thank God she trusted his good sense. He moved the conversation on. 'I thought we could take that path up through the woods. Then maybe we can get some lunch.'

'What if we bump into someone?' Ashleigh got out of the car and looked along the long village street. It was a dank, grey morning and the wet leaves were black and slippery underfoot. She sniffed the air. She could have been lounging at home with a coffee and a book, but she hadn't been able to resist the urge to come out and pursue the case. On that basis alone, she and Jude were a perfect match. It was a pity relationships didn't thrive on trust and friendship alone. It was a pity they needed that unidentifiable, uncontrollable wild card called love.

'We're birdwatchers,' he said, and dug into his pocket for a pair of mini binoculars.

'You think of everything. But I wondered. If we just went down… Emmy might be a bit more relaxed if we're off duty.' Or not. Emmy had looked drawn even before they'd identified Luke's body.

Jude looked, swiftly, down the road. Emmy had turned her back on them now, and on Tino. 'I doubt she'll be keen to chat, even if Rob's not there.'

'I can't stop thinking about her.'

Jude stepped towards the footpath. He'd parked the Mercedes at the edge of the village. Someone would see it, eventually, and put two and two together, but by this time they should be used to seeing the police around the village, even if they were so obviously off duty. 'I'd like to see if someone would be able to see the house from where Heather says she saw this man.'

Ashleigh considered Heather, robust and determined. 'Do you think she was lying?'

'I don't know. Possibly. Possibly not. But do you know what?'

'What?'

'If it's all falling out as we think — if Heather managed to get hold of Luke as a drug runner — it was very much in her interests he didn't get back in touch with his parents. If she did see him, maybe she wasn't meant to. She might not have told him she worked for them.'

Control of information was important. If Luke had been an addict, Heather would have been foolish to trust him with anything that might bring him any cash. 'She might have. We know he or someone claiming to be him has been in touch with both Tino and Chloe. It's such a pity they didn't take it seriously.'

'I don't think we can blame them.' They'd reached the stile by then, and he clambered over it and held out a hand to help Ashleigh down. She took it, though she didn't need it, and a connection she'd thought was lost was instantly re-established. 'The path goes round in a loop. Let's follow it. It brings us back along the edge of the woods and that's where Heather says she saw him.'

The path was faint, thick with tough grass and a layer of leaves and pine needles. They walked in a companionable silence for the first few hundred yards, then rounded the shoulder of the hill and emerged from the woods. Blacksty lay just below them, crouched low and sprawling along the road, and a few miles to the west Mungrisdale glowered through a thick mist that clamped down on the upper slopes of the fells.

'Bowscale is over there,' said Jude, 'though of course we can't see it. It's easy to see how people believed Luke might have got lost up there. You don't need much mist to lose sight of where you're going and once you're off the track it's all too easy to lose your bearings.'

'Look.' Ashleigh stopped and the woods to their right gave way. 'There's Blacksty Farmhouse.'

The Leaches' home was about a hundred yards away, visible as the path emerged from the trees then cut immediately back into the woods.

'There could have been someone,' said Jude, looking at it, 'but yes. If it was Luke, he'd have had to make a determined effort to get to where Heather said he was. Look at that undergrowth. And it was wet all autumn, so it would have been hellish muddy. But it could definitely be done.'

'I bet these woods have seen a thing or two,' said Ashleigh as they approached the thick pine woods at the centre of the plantation. 'Not just Emmy and Tino getting up to a bit of how's-your-father, either.'

'When we searched the woods after Luke disappeared, we uncovered a lot of cans, fag ends, the like. Kids always find somewhere to hang out, and this is perfect for them. If anyone came along they didn't want to see, they could all disappear within seconds.'

'Do you think Luke really did want to come back?' Ashleigh asked. The path had narrowed by then and she'd moved ahead, but she stopped for a second to look back.

'Possibly.'

'Well. I wonder. Perhaps Rob saw him.'

'There's no evidence Luke tried to contact Emmy, though, is there? Which is odd, because she's his mother and she so obviously loved him. You'd think he'd have cared.'

'He tried to get in touch with both Tino and Chloe via social media. Emmy isn't on any social media at all. I don't imagine she's kept the same phone number for fifteen years, and she may have changed her email address. That might explain why he didn't.'

'Or he may have tried and she didn't tell us.' Jude

caught her up where the path broadened. He was always more cynical about things than she.

'Unlikely, I'd have thought. And that's the other thing I was wondering about. Maybe Rob did know he was back. He could have seen him but if, for example, Luke had written to his mother, who's to say Rob didn't intercept it?'

'It's a thought.'

They walked on in silence. The path was short and circular and it wasn't long before they were back on the road into the village. The street was empty. Emmy and Tino's awkwardly public conversation had ended and there was no sign of either of them.

'Let's go and get some lunch,' said Jude. 'It's years since I've eaten here, but I remember they do good fish and chips.'

'Good shout.' And Ashleigh began to make her way down along the street that led past Blacksty Farmhouse and towards the pub.

TWENTY-SIX

When Emmy got into the house, she caught a glimpse of her face in the mirror in the hallway. She was as white as a sheet. In public Tino was brave enough, quite happy to be seen talking to her across the street and content for anybody to overhear the platitudes he had for her about the weather. When matters came to the crunch, his courage let him down. In the trivialities of their conversation (the logging lorry had caught fire up at the common the previous day; someone had said they'd seen grey squirrels in the plantation, which meant the nature warden would be out in the woods with his gun) she could sense, beneath his usual sunny disposition, a degree of irritation that she'd told the police what they'd been sent.

Someone had to, she defended herself, or it would been hanging over them and driven them both to distraction. While there were many things in her fears and her conscience that kept her awake, the photographs weren't one of them. They were the police's problem and she trusted them.

Her other problems wouldn't go away. She stared at herself in the mirror. She'd always liked to think of herself as well-preserved, but now the renewal of her grief had tipped her over the edge and she was faint and fading, thin around the face and with a shaded expression of discontent, so she looked like her mother. She made a face at herself, like a child, just so she could look like someone else. Her mother was loving and well-intentioned, but if only she hadn't taken against Tino all those years before, would the marriage have survived? Could the two of them have kept Luke on the rails and would he, as a result, still be alive and the three of them happy? They would have embraced Chloe and little Libby, welcomed them into the family, and who knew? Maybe there would have been more babies and the house would have overflowed with love and laughter, rather than Rob's chilling disapproval and reproach.

Libby had been a sweet child and, Tino said, had grown into a bright girl, on track to be a promising young woman. Emmy wished she'd had the courage to get in touch, but that would have been a transgression too far. Rob thought it was better to cut off all contact and she couldn't afford to keep any more secrets from him. To keep the peace she'd had to let Libby, the last living reminder of Luke, slip away.

For what? Rob might already know her biggest secret. It was a matter of time, of how he reacted and how he would make her pay, of whether she had the courage to call for help before she got hurt. She rearranged her hair in the mirror and waited for him to call out to her from the office, but there was silence. With a sudden rush of anxiety her face fell back into the foreshadowing of her mother's. She sighed, took her coat to the cloakroom and headed for the kitchen.

Out in the courtyard, Rob was getting into the Audi. He lifted a hand in a cheery wave and a smile accompanied it. Despite the warmth from the underfloor heating, Emmy shivered as he drove away. For something to do, she made herself a mug of coffee she didn't want and switched on the radio. Classic FM swarmed into the room, a Tchaikovsky serenade that wrapped her in a soft, sweet cocoon of strings.

Rob hadn't been out of the courtyard for five minutes when another vehicle appeared. This time it was Heather's van. She pulled up, got out, looked around her as if to see who was in, and then strode to the front door.

Coffee in hand, Emmy rushed to welcome a friendly soul. 'Come on in. You timed it perfectly. I've just made coffee. I wasn't expecting you today.'

'No. I was in the area and I thought I'd pop by. Rob asked me to drop in. But I can't see his car.'

'No, he's just gone out. He didn't say where. He never mentioned he'd asked you to come.' That was unlike him. 'He must have forgotten. Did he say what it was about?'

Heather turned away from her and looked out of the window towards the end of the garden. 'No.'

'He keeps talking about redoing that big border down the side, the one with those things that keep growing and whose name I can't remember.' Conscious that she was rambling, Emmy made coffee. As she did so it dawned on her that Heather was equally distracted. She placed the second mug on the breakfast bar.

'Rogersia.' The ping from Heather's pocket warned of a notification, and she took out her phone and glanced down at a text. A frown followed, and she stared at the screen for a while longer, as if in thought. 'That's what it's called.'

'Oh, yes. I remember.'

There was a short silence. 'I don't imagine he'll be long,' said Emmy, to break it. 'Maybe he went down to the farm to get some milk.'

'Look, Emmy.' Heather placed her phone on the table, face down. 'I need to talk to you.'

'Yes, of course.'

'I'm going to need your help.'

Heather had offered friendship, so the least Emmy could do was reciprocate, even if it wasn't her Christian and civic duty. 'Of course. Just let me know what I can do.'

'That was Rob. He asked me to come along here for a chat, but he's changed his plan. Now he wants me to meet him up at Bowscale Tarn.'

'The tarn? But—'

'Yes. It seems weird to me.'

'Of course, you won't go.' Emmy's stomach turned, a weird, sinking sense that everything had finally spun out of control, just as she'd feared for so long. 'That's so strange. Why would he do that?'

Heather's gaze was steady. 'He's hinted a couple of times that he thinks I had something to do with Luke disappearing. Or reappearing. Which is nonsense.'

'He thinks you killed Luke?' This was ridiculous. For years Rob's behaviour had made Emmy fearful for her sanity. For the first time she saw a different perspective. Perhaps it wasn't she who was the problem.

'I don't know what he thinks. But I don't want to meet him on my own. He's less likely to… make unfounded accusations… if there's someone else there.'

Unfounded accusations? Emmy thought of the photos. Was Rob really that unhinged? 'I don't think you should go. You should call the police. You've told me what you think he's like. I'm sure they'd take it seriously. I'll call them for you.'

'You wouldn't want me to go to the police.' Heather fidgeted with the phone and her frown told tale of a decision in the making. 'Rob might get into serious trouble. Do you want that?'

To her shock, Emmy found herself thinking that if Rob were to get into trouble with the law it might turn out to her advantage. Tino, who was more relaxed and more fun, had always behaved impeccably except in the little matter of their adulterous affair, and even that could be morally justified if she turned her mind to it. Rob in trouble with the police, especially with that underlying hint of aggression, was a different matter, and then she might have what she needed: the germ of a reason to leave him.

She stifled a smile. If she so much as mentioned that to Tino he'd immediately construct an argument sound enough to persuade her, but that was all speculation and right now she was dealing with Heather and quite a different problem. 'I don't know. If you have any concerns, you really shouldn't go at all. I think that's what I would do.'

'I need to show him he can't mess me around. And that I'm not afraid of him.'

Afraid of him? The conversation was taking a strange turn. It was Emmy who was afraid of Rob not strong, competent Heather. 'Then definitely don't go. Didn't he say he'd be here? You turned up and he wasn't. Pretend you didn't get his message.'

Heather turned her phone upwards. 'I've already replied. I've told him I'll be there as soon as possible. The question is, whether or not you come with me.'

Emmy put her coffee mug down. Heather had always been good to her, always offered her a friendly ear, even when all Emmy needed to do was talk to someone without an agenda, but this was all wrong. 'No. Really, I don't want to. I'm afraid Rob's been a little unreliable lately, and I don't know that I want to—'

'Emmy.' Heather's voice had hardened, just a little. 'I need you to come with me.'

This must have been what Heather was like in the army, Emmy realised with a shock. She always found it too easy to respond when someone was ordering her about but this time all the alarm bells were ringing. She might be too scared to challenge her husband, but Heather was different. 'I'm sorry. I hate to let you down.'

'No, Emmy. You don't understand. You're coming with me, whether you like it or not. If you don't I'll be giving Rob a piece of information you really don't want him to hear. If you come with me as my insurance policy, so to speak, then I'll keep quiet and you can carry on playing away with Tino Mortimer for as long as you like, as far as I'm concerned.'

Realisation hit Emmy like a cold wave. Behind the shock came an overwhelming sense of betrayal at how Heather had offered her friendship, and how cynically she had played Emmy's timid acceptance of it. Now she knew the action she'd taken — that Tino had been too timid to take — had just spared her from a difficult decision, she discovered a new resolve. She still had to deal with the fallout of the affair, to decide whether to stay or whether to go, and she still had to deal with Rob's reaction to the inevitable discovery, but it would be a mess of her own making, not one into which she'd been teased and trapped by a pretence at friendship. 'That was you? The photos?'

She had her phone in her pocket. Half-turning, she managed to flick open the WhatsApp chat she'd made for Tino and herself, and hit the call button, taking the precaution of flicking it onto mute. Tino was always a great help, at a distance. He always knew what to do for the best, even if he let other people do it, but most importantly he was the only person she could trust.

'Who else did you think it was?'

'I didn't know.' The phone buzzed in her pocket. Tino would be shouting into the phone, thinking it was a pocket call. She prayed he'd stop and listen. 'I couldn't think who might have done it.' Now it was obvious. Heather could have sneaked in there and left it the last time she was there or, more likely, filched the key over coffee in the kitchen and made an impression of it. Or perhaps in the army she'd learned unlikely tricks, and could pick a lock as easily as the young detective had done. It didn't matter: it was done. Emmy's mind whirled. What should she say? Should she meet Heather's dishonesty with lies of her own? But she was a poor liar and so, as she always did in the end, she opted for the truth. 'I've turned the photos over to the police.'

'What?'

'Yes. Because I didn't know who put them there. I thought someone would come after me for money and I don't have any.'

Heather swept an appraising glance around the kitchen with its slate floor and gleaming appliances, at the garden. 'Aye, right.'

'The money's Rob's, not mine. I can't give you anything without him knowing. I knew he'd find out eventually so I thought it was better to do the right thing.' It always was, no matter how painful. 'If you've got any sense you'll tell the police about it yourself. Because they'll find you. And you've admitted it.' Both Jude Satterthwaite and his sympathetic sergeant would take her seriously. She thought she'd seen them in the village when she'd been talking to Tino, but she hadn't been sure. If she was right they were off duty, because they were in casual clothes, but he'd said she could call him any time and she'd believed him. *Crime, violence and abuse don't only happen nine to five* he'd said.

'I think you'd better go.' Now she understood what Heather was capable of, a second doubt crept into her mind. Maybe Rob was right and Heather was in some way culpable for Luke's death. She pulled her phone out of her pocket, wishing she'd programmed Jude Satterthwaite's number into her contacts. 'Heather. I want you to leave. Now. If you don't I'm going to call the police.'

Heather's hand shot out and the iron grip twisted the phone away. 'You're coming with me. Your man says Bowscale Tarn and it's Bowscale Tarn we're going to. I told you. You're my insurance policy.'

'Take your hands off me!' But Emmy was slight and Heather strong and wiry, at a huge advantage even without a knowledge of combat training. All she could do was shout and hope Tino heard and, for once in his life, acted. 'I'm not going with you!'

It was no surprise, as the elements of Heather's criminality fell into place and showed the true scale of her badness, that the hand that went to the pocket of her overalls emerged with a gun. Emmy had never seen a hand gun before, still less one as mean-looking as that, but her nerve held. 'I'm not going.'

'Yes, Emmy. You are.' Keeping hold of her wrist, Heather raised the gun. 'Your man won't hurt me if you're there. Maybe I won't have to hurt him. But if you don't… you don't know it, Emmy, but I've killed before.'

Holding her breath, Emmy stared down the barrel into the void and saw her punishment, a battle of wills only the gun could win. Trusting her life to Tino and to the good Lord, she let out a long sigh of defeat and preceded Heather from the house.

TWENTY-SEVEN

'Fish and chips for lunch is a good shout.' Ashleigh brushed a hand through her damp hair. The weather was closing in and the mist, which had been clamped down on the Skiddaw massif all day, had rapidly expanded to full-blown fog. From the middle of Blacksty, where the view normally opened up the whole of Mungrisdale, you could now see nothing beyond the last of the houses, and the trees were dripping with latent damp. 'I know it wasn't much of a walk but I managed to work up a hunger.'

She paused at the side of the road. Twenty yards behind, Jude had stopped and was fiddling with his phone. 'What are you doing?'

'Trying to get a signal. Give me a minute. I think I've got one.'

'Is it important?'

'I don't know. It's a message from Doddsy.' He was clamping his phone to his ear as he spoke.

Doddsy, who was a better guardian of Jude's wellbeing than he was himself, wouldn't have called on a rest day if it

243

wasn't important. 'My hunger will have to wait, then. But for heaven's sake hurry up, or I'll be catching a squirrel and eating that.'

'A pheasant would be easier to catch.' He grinned at her, took a few steps this way and a few more that. 'It's just as well I'm out with you, not Becca. She'd be rolling her eyes at me by now for taking a phone call on my day off, never mind having gone into work first thing.'

It had been Jude's idea to spend a day off trudging round in the wet woods on the trail of the phantom that might have been Luke Mortimer or might have been a chimera, a figment of Heather's imagination, but Ashleigh had entertained a passing thought of doing the same, so she could hardly complain. She drifted a few yards in the direction of the village centre and took a peek into the courtyard at Rob and Emmy's house. Neither the Audi nor the Renault was in there but there was a white van parked where they normally stood.

Interesting. There was no sign of any tradesmen working outside and no lights on inside. Emmy had certainly been around when they set off for their short circular walk, in that painfully obvious encounter with Tino. She must have headed out immediately afterwards. Nevertheless Ashleigh made herself visible, on the off chance that Emmy hadn't gone far, would drive past on her way home and be tempted to stop.

It was as well Jude was busy on the phone or he'd guess what she was thinking. Maybe he already had. She could predict his reaction; he'd hustle her into the pub as soon as he was off the phone and follow up with a gentle reminder that she mustn't get too emotionally involved.

She smiled. These days she was more optimistic about life in general. Jude was right. There was nothing they could do unless Emmy asked them to intervene and even then she would go directly to Mandy Phillips rather than to Ashleigh herself. Reviewing her relationship with Scott with as much coolness as she could manage, Ashleigh understood why Emmy stayed with her husband but also why, when the time was right, she might choose to leave. Emmy Leach was a woman who did what she believed was the right thing, at the right time.

The trouble was, one person's right thing was another's utter folly. Still she watched the house, as if the stones could tell her something of what went on inside.

'That was interesting.' Jude had finished the call, pocketed the phone and was striding towards her.

'Did they find Heather?'

'No. She wasn't there. There was some young Polish lad in doing her cleaning and he didn't know where she was and barely spoke any English, though he did know enough for them to be able to execute the search warrant and have a look around. They found her laptop, and that'll be interesting.'

'I bet they find those pictures on them.'

'I bet they do, though that won't tell us whether it was she or Luke who took them. The really interesting thing — or rather, one of two really interesting things — is that the cleaner was able to tell them Heather had had a visitor with her recently. A young man who'd been sleeping in the guest annexe and generally keeping out of sight. He only saw him a couple of times and Heather had told him he was a nephew, helping out around the place.'

'His English can't have been that bad,' said Ashleigh, 'unless Doddsy speaks better Polish than I gave him credit for.'

'His English is terrible, apparently, but Chris used his head and got to work with Google translate so they managed to work something out, though I daresay it was a bit contorted. They'll get a translator up there to take a statement from him, but he was able to identify the visitor from some of the photos they showed him. And yes, it was Luke.'

That was no surprise. 'I wonder how often he stayed there?' Out of the corner of her eye Ashleigh saw Tino jogging down the street towards them. 'It'll be fascinating to cross-refer that with the pattern of activity at Mosedale Barn.'

'It will. And here's something even more fascinating. Doddsy also managed to get through to the camera manufacturers and yes, the purchaser of the camera did register it for a warranty.'

'And was it Luke?'

'It wasn't. It was our friend Ms Short. It looks like you were right and she was behind the photographs and the attempted blackmail, if that's what it was. The story about having seen Luke may just have been to try and shift suspicion away from her and onto him, The dead can't deny anything. But we have the camera and the search turned up a zoom lens that's compatible with it. With the registration document and the cleaner's testimony we're starting to build up a tight case against her. But I'm not sure what for.'

'God, yes. Of course. Only for knowing Luke and an attempt at extortion. Though looking at the way things are unfolding, I bet she's got a hell of a lot of other things to answer for.'

'Me too. We just need to find out what they are. And prove it.' Jude had turned at the sound of running feet as Tino got closer. 'Ey up, as Doddsy would say. What's this?'

They stood and watched as Tino, focussed only on Blacksty Farm, turned off the road and into the courtyard. He raced up to the front door and hammered on it with his fist, his free hand crashing on the bell. 'Emmy! Emmy, where are you?'

Without thought, both Jude and Ashleigh broke into a run. She, being slightly nearer, got there first. 'Mr Mortimer. Is everything okay?'

He spun round, looked them up and down, and seemed to take a moment to recognise them. 'Ah, thank God! You must be on to them. We need to move fast—'

'We're not here on business, just for a walk and some lunch,' said Jude. There was a sharp edge to his voice. 'Is there something we can help you with?'

'I just had the craziest call from Emmy. I was speaking to her earlier and she seemed fine, but after that I was up on the hill at the back of the house, just getting a breath of fresh air. I thought it was a pocket call, and it kept breaking up, but there was something really weird going on. Someone talking, like a radio play, but not the radio. It was on in the background.' He paused to gather his breath. 'That's Emmy's gardener's van. Shit. That means it's true.'

'What's true?' Jude's voice rang with concern. 'Is Mrs Leach in any danger?'

'I don't know. As I said, it kept breaking up, I thought I heard Heather — that's the gardener woman — talking about meeting someone at Bowscale Tarn but I didn't hear who. And then I thought I heard Emmy say she wasn't going and Heather say she'd have to. Then they vanished but the line stayed on and all I could hear was the music.' He flourished the phone. 'That's all I can hear now.'

Ashleigh crossed to the kitchen window. Inside, the breakfast bar displayed signs of chaos — a spilled cup of coffee, Emmy's handbag knocked to the floor, her phone lying on the table. The strains of Classic FM streamed out from Tino's phone.

'Did you dial 999?' asked Jude, already fingering his phone.

'No. I wasn't sure what was going on. And I didn't want to risk cutting Emmy off if there was something wrong.'

'I'll call.' Ashleigh was already dialling. 'We'll need to get up to the tarn, I think.'

'Let's move,' Jude said.

'We'll take my car,' said Tino, 'if it's quicker. I can—'

'I'm just along here.' Jude broke into a jog, Ashleigh alongside him. Tino ran with them. 'Mr Mortimer, I think you should stay here.'

'They'll have gone the tourist route but we can get there ahead of them. Don't think I'm letting you go up there without me if there's a risk to Emmy.'

'I think we know what we're doing,' said Jude, with an edge to his voice that showed he was struggling to balance a need to reassure with a degree of irritation.

'Yes. And I'm coming with you.'

Jude, Ashleigh thought as she reported the incident to the control room, had probably given up the argument on the basis of ease. It might be easier to order Tino away or give him something else to do when they got there, rather than waste valuable time arguing; it was unlikely a patrol car would get there before them. Besides, the journey would give them the chance to find out what else Tino Mortimer might know. 'That's the blue lights on the way.' She signed off the call as they reached Jude's Mercedes, and got into the back. Tino, uninvited, slid into the passenger seat.

'Brilliant,' said Jude, started the engine and launched the Mercedes through the grey village and down into the fog of the dale.

TWENTY-EIGHT

'I don't think I can go any further.'

It was shock, rather than physical weakness, that was dragging Emmy back as she and Heather clambered the track up from Mosedale. She'd driven, with Heather in the back, and fear at her shoulder. Her misery had been compounded by the knowledge that the gun was behind her and the unpleasant feeling that Heather not only knew how to use it but was quite prepared to.

'Of course you can.' Heather had been walking ahead but she stopped and waved Emmy on. 'You're fit enough. Go on. You know the way.'

Left with no option, Emmy stumbled on. The soft thud of Heather's footsteps behind her in the thick fog was a couple of yards away but she wouldn't be quick enough to make a break for it. If she'd been able to get far enough for the fog to swallow her up, there would be nowhere on the bare hillside for her to hide. At every turn luck had abandoned her. They had passed no other vehicle in the short distance between Blacksty and Bowscale. The parking area at the foot of the lane had been empty, the weather deter-

249

ring even the foolish folk who might have thought there was some pleasure in taking such a short and easy walk. The row of holiday cottages at the bottom of the track had been dark and silent, mocking her with the off-season emptiness.

What will be will be, said Emmy to herself, philosophically forcing one shaking leg in front of the other on the uneven ground. Judgement rested with the Lord, as Rob had once said to her when they'd briefly discussed who might have killed Luke, but now she thought about it his words were sinister and double-edged. Rob had never been a real Christian. He must have intended to take vengeance on her, but not because of Luke; it was because of her feelings for Tino. Now she understood that God was punishing her in a different way, leading her up the long road as if she were Isaac being led to sacrifice by his father, or Christ himself on that long road to Calvary.

'I need to rest,' she pleaded, to delay the moment when Rob and Heather would meet and she'd find out which one would hurt her.

'We can stop here for a moment.'

There was nowhere to sit. The path had become narrow and rutted, and ran with water from overnight rain. Emmy had been wearing light canvas shoes and her feet were soaked and cold. Her legs ached, her fingers were numb and her face stung with the wind and the rain.

Her legs wouldn't hold her any longer. She sank down onto the grass, flecked with bog cotton, and water immediately soaked through the seat of her jeans. Shivering, she drew her knees as close to her chest as she could. Perhaps, after all, what the Lord had in store for her wasn't death at the hand of her husband or her friend, but death by exposure, as she'd so long allowed people to believe had happened to Luke.

Now, of course, she understood what had happened. 'Was it Rob?'

'Was what Rob?'

'Luke. He wanted him out of the way, didn't he? Is that what it is?' It all made sense — how Rob had told her he'd found a gardener but made it quite clear he knew and disliked her from way back. And because Rob wasn't a man to have anything to do with those he disliked, there had to be a reason why he'd allowed this woman into his house. Now both the attempt at blackmail and Heather's determination to become Emmy's friend made sense. Heather had wanted her presence to be a threat to him, a reminder that neither could afford to give the other away.

'He didn't tell you, then?' Heather laughed. 'Anyway, it never happened. At least, not then.'

Rob had allowed her to believe Luke had died. He'd hinted at it without being explicit and when she'd dared to question his meaning he'd turned her interpretation back on her as evidence of her paranoia. It might turn out to be the best thing, he'd said, for all of them. Bit by bit he'd dripped into her mind the understanding that he'd killed her son, or had him killed, and with that knowledge came fear and control.

Oh Rob, she said to herself almost scathingly, *you are so very clever*. 'What are we doing here?'

'I expect your husband wants his money back for the contract I didn't fulfil.' Heather made it sound so commercial, like a delivery of wet fish.

'But what about me?'

'You knew. You'd have talked. That's why I've been keeping an eye on you.'

'But I didn't know! Not for certain.' There must be something in the Bible about false friendship, but Emmy's brain was too overloaded to recall it. 'Did you kill him in the end, then?' Poor Luke, drowning almost within her reach.

'No. He hadn't been in touch with you?'

If only he had been. 'No.' Emmy heard her voice quiver but maybe that was with the cold. Heather sounded disappointed, as though she'd somehow been cheated. 'Is this what all this is about? The police said someone had written *keep quiet* on the pictures? Is that what it was? You wanted me to keep quiet about Luke?' She pressed her fingers to her eyes. If only she'd had the chance. 'Are you sure you didn't kill him?'

'I've never killed anyone, not even in the army. Did you believe me when I said I had? Though they taught me how, so you needn't think I won't, if I have to.'

'I don't believe you're a bad person,' said Emmy, a heroic lie in her own self-interest. Heather might kill her, so she had to do everything in her power to persuade her not to.

'I've done a lot of bad things in my life.'

'But you haven't killed. And you've done good things.' She must have done. Everybody did, even the damned. 'You saved Luke's life.'

'That's what you Christians think, isn't it? That you can be redeemed? But not killing him isn't saving his life. Don't think I won't kill you to save myself and don't think I won't kill your husband if he tries to hurt me.'

Sitting in a pool of mud on the side of the path, with fog and rain seeping into her bones, Emmy understood something else. This moment of rest was, in reality, one of uncertainty. Heather didn't know what to do. She didn't know where Rob was, or what he really wanted. She didn't know how dangerous he was. Heather hadn't killed. She hadn't been able to kill Luke. Why would she bring herself to kill Emmy? 'Heather.'

'What?'

'Can we go back?'

There was no immediate answer. That signalled doubt, and from it sprang hope..

'This is crazy,' persisted Emmy, emboldened. 'You just said yourself. You didn't kill Luke. All you've done is that silly thing with the photos.' A silly thing that had cost her stress and sleepless nights and would do in the future, whether Rob learned of it or not, but it would do her no harm to downplay it. 'I know you took money to kill him but you didn't do it. So it's not so bad, is it? But it will be, if you hurt me.' Or Rob. For all his faults she didn't want him hurt. She didn't want anyone hurt. 'Then you'd be in trouble.'

'It never ends.' Heather sounded unconvinced. 'It's him that wants a confrontation. I'm just protecting myself. That's why you're here. I don't mean anyone any harm.' She shot a look along the narrow path ahead, then all around them, as if something had attracted her attention.

'I think we should go back down.' Emmy levered herself to her feet and took a look around. A shape loomed in the mist and her heart quickened. A sheep, startled, ran along the track, stopped, stared like a dead soul and then ran away in fear, to be swallowed up by the mist. 'I can't make it all the way.'

'We're almost there. If you think you can get back down, you should be able to get up.'

The conviction grew within Emmy that if she went up she'd never come back down. She was collateral damage for both of them. No doubt Rob's intention was to dispose of Heather the way Heather herself was supposed to have disposed of Luke, and in her turn she'd have disappeared and never been found. It was easy enough. There were old mine shafts, or he could tumble her body down the slope and bury her under the sodden turf. Now Heather, understanding the end game, must have decided to take him on, like two gunslingers in the arid west.

But they weren't in the desert of Arizona or the prairies of Wyoming. They were folded in the granite shroud of Mosedale and smothered in a blanket of fog, and whichever one of them emerged triumphant would surely have to kill Emmy, too, in a last, desperate gasp at keeping the secret.

'I'm going home,' she said, and turned back along the path.

Heather stood in front of her and slid the gun out of her pocket. It looked flat and leaden in the heavy atmosphere, but it was pointing downwards and there was doubt on her face.

'Let's go then,' said Emmy again, as crisply as she could. She stepped off the path to pass by and her heart rose as Heather made no attempt to stop her. *Thank you, God.* There was even a spring in her step.

And then Rob rose up, like her conscience, out of the bracken beside the path, his face blazing with fury, and Emmy screamed.

TWENTY-NINE

'I never liked the woman,' said Tino, almost conversationally, as Jude pushed the Mercedes around bend after bend on the switchback road, as fast as the fog allowed, 'but I never had her down as dangerous.'

'The most surprising people are.' Jude slowed as they approached the Mosedale turn. Emmy's silver Renault was parked in the lay-by at an angle, its back wheels perilously close to a short drop into the field below. That spoke volumes about her state of mind. 'How far ahead of us do you reckon they are? Ash, what time did we come past the house?'

'About ten past one, I think.'

'She called me about ten to.' Tino checked his phone. 'They can't have left before that, obviously, and it can't have been long after.'

'Okay. So they've maybe got twenty minutes on us, no more. It might take them...what, forty minutes to walk up there? Is Mrs Leach a good walker?'

'Pretty fit, I'd say, and she knows the route. But I'm

going to guess she wasn't exactly equipped for it.' Tino managed a wry smile.

'Right. So it'll take them longer than that. If we can go up the track at Swineside and park at the end of it, we can get up the hill to the tarn before they do.'

At the next lay-by, they passed Rob's car. Jude took a sideways look at Tino and saw his brows creased together. Even his optimism could only take him so far. 'You can park at the far end of it,' he offered, as if he felt he should earn his keep. There's a wood beyond the farmhouse and a footbridge over the beck. Sometimes folk leave their cars up there for weekends.'

'I know it.' The closeness of Bowscale Tarn to Mosedale Barn might or might not have been a coincidence. The place would look cold and forlorn, now, its once-reinforced door hanging open on a broken hinge. Jude cast his mind back to the night he'd spent staking the place out with his Liverpudlian colleagues. Two cases intersected there. If Luke hadn't been murdered on the night of the raid he might very well have been at the barn and a different story would have unfolded, one with a happy ending.

Or not. Emmy would have been delighted to see her son but it was hard to imagine Rob welcoming him back to the family, and in all likelihood he'd have had a prison sentence to serve before he needed to worry about how he related to his family. And there was Tino, who had an equal stake in Luke's wellbeing. As they passed the barn, Jude found his mind straying from the task in hand. Would he have been pleased to see Luke, or would it have complicated matters even further?

He pulled the car up at the side of the verge, where a plantation of trees curled around it and a wooden footbridge crossed the brimming beck. 'I reckon this is as close as we'll get.'

'This is a good spot.' Tino's nervousness was evident, now, as they got out of the car. He must be one of those people who chattered on endlessly to hide it. 'I park up here to head up to the tarn, normally. I couldn't do it on the day we found Luke. The road was closed. So I had to park down at the main lay-by at the bottom of the track. I imagine that's where I got spotted. I still don't know which busybody saw me.'

Jude tweaked the zip on his Barbour jacket as far up as it would go. There was a rawness to the air that made him glad of his scarf and boots. 'You might want to wait here, Mr Mortimer.'

'Like hell I will. If that woman — or bloody Rob Leach —thinks they're going to hurt Emmy, they'll have to answer to me.'

'I'd much prefer you to stay here.'

'And I won't.' Tino surged off over the bridge. 'I know the way from here. I don't need you.'

Letting him go, Jude checked his watch. Ashleigh was looking at her phone, but it was a waste of time. There was no signal. Unease pulsed within him. 'Great,' he said to her. 'That's all we need. We'd better get after him.'

'He might be some use.' Ashleigh lowered her voice a they strode up the clear path. 'Safety in numbers, and all that.'

'I doubt it. He's an amateur who'll lose his head. And if you want anyone to inflame the situation you'd pick him wouldn't you? Especially if Rob does have some kind of idiocy in mind.'

'Rob isn't the one who wanted Emmy there.'

Jude followed Tino's shape as it solidified slightly in the mist but he held back so as not to lose sight of Ashleigh.

Something niggled at him. Tino had said the road was closed when he'd headed up to the tarn on the day they'd found Luke, but it hadn't been. They'd closed it, briefly, for an hour or so the previous evening when they were setting up the trap, with a closed gate and a warning notice about livestock so as not to alert any passer by.

Tino had had messages from someone claiming to be Luke and the records he'd so helpfully provided had proved that he hadn't replied. But why hadn't he? Surely you'd take any chance to see your much-loved son, especially if there was a realistic prospect that he hadn't died but had run away from his stepfather. He looked at Tino's determined silhouette, pressing on through the rain, with a sense of foreboding.

'Ash.' He dropped back to let her catch up, lowering his voice again, though the mist effectively smothered it. 'Give me your thoughts. What drives Tino Mortimer?'

'What a hell of a question,' she said, 'and what a hell of a time to ask it.' But she picked up on his meaning, or a part of it. 'Is something wrong?'

'Something feels bloody wrong to me about Tino. Yes. But I can't put my finger on it.'

'Right.' She was almost whispering. Jude kept walking, because he didn't dare lose sight of Tino in the mist. Already his sense of the landscape was beginning to blur and at some point the apology for a path might peter out and they could lose him. He frowned.

'If we cut up here,' Tino called back to them, 'we can get up the slope and we'll intersect with the other path a few hundred yards below the tarn.'

'Better not shout,' Jude cautioned him, then turned back to Ashleigh. 'Quick. What do you think?'

'It's Emmy, obviously. He adores her.'

You couldn't dispute that, but throughout the whole

episode, Tino had been reluctant to put himself at any kind of risk to help the woman he claimed to love. He'd abandoned her at the tarn when Luke's body was found. He'd resisted her suggestion that they should call the police about the photographs. Now he was forging ahead, but it was easy to be brave with two police officers at his back and more on the way. 'Not Luke?'

'Well, obviously he adored Luke. Everybody says so.'

'Everybody says so.' Jude was almost whispering now. 'Sure. But there was something my dad said about it.' Although the context hadn't been Luke himself, but Mikey. 'He said every young man needs a male role model and a son never forgives a father for abandoning him. Mikey. Luke.' Even Jude himself, for all his determined even-handedness towards his parents, couldn't shed a nugget of bitterness against his father.

Ashleigh stopped for a moment and motioned him close. Their breath mingled in a swift, whispered conference. 'Wait. What are you saying?'

'We've no actual evidence Tino and Luke got on. He says so. Everybody says so but how do they know? They hardly saw one another and when they did it was down in Manchester or wherever. We only have Tino's word for it. And this is the other thing I can't get my head round. If Tino Mortimer loved his son so much, why didn't he jump at the chance to meet him when he got in touch?'

Ashleigh was silent. If she was thinking what Jude was thinking, neither of them dared say it aloud. 'We'd better not lose sight of him, then.'

Maybe Tino, a charming, positive optimist, was also a liar. And maybe he had, after all, either made contact with his son or had accepted a different form of contact from him that he hadn't revealed.

They scrambled on for a few hundred yards, through

heavy ground and thick, wet bracken. 'Jude. Do you have any idea where we're going?'

'If we keep going uphill we have to hit the path to the tarn.' He frowned, trying to recall the detail of the map. 'This must be the way you came up here on the day they found him.'

'Yes, but it was nothing like as foggy as this.'

'Here's the path!' called Tino, from a little way ahead. He stopped, as if undecided, and waited until they caught up. 'I don't know how far away we are from the tarn. Not far. There's a beck that comes down about half a mile below it. I'd say we're well on the up side of it.'

Would Emmy and Heather have made it to the tarn, and was Rob up there? In the distance the faint wail of sirens indicated that there was help on the way — but how far away? The fog made it impossible to tell.

'Jeez,' said Tino, cheerfully. He rubbed his hands together. 'At least we're not going up to the top. That's a hell of a climb in this kind of weather.'

On the night he'd fallen to his death, Luke had camped on top of Bowscale Fell. It had been the night the track up Mosedale had been closed for a couple of hours to facilitate the police operation at Mosedale Barn. Tino had said he couldn't park there the following morning but by then the road was open. And when Jude cast his mind back, he remembered something else. In the evening before Luke's body was found, he'd driven along the fell-edge road to Mosedale Barn and he'd passed a single car parked up in the layby below the track to Bowscale Tarn. The car had been a dirty old four by four, just like the one that had sat in Tino's shed, overshadowed by his sparkling BMW, and it meant there was every chance that Tino, who had no alibi for the time of Luke's death except a lack of motive and a claim that he'd spent the night in front of the telly, had been up at the tarn that night.

He turned to Ashleigh to whisper his thoughts, but before he could speak, the soft silence of the mist shattered with a woman's scream.

'Emmy!' shouted Tino, and took off down the path towards the sound — and the shot — which followed. 'Em! Are you all right?'

A long wail rose from not far ahead of them. Jude outpaced Tino over even the short distance and skidded to a halt. A figure lay slumped on the path and blood pumped into the slick of mud and water that ran down from the hillside and channelled into the rutted track. Next to it, Emmy was on her knees and Heather Short's body, the front of her coat dark with blood, lay on her back with startled, empty eyes turned upwards.

'He took the gun!' sobbed Emmy. 'It was Rob. She had a gun and he took it and he shot her! Oh God, he's going to kill us all!' She rose to her feet, her body shaking with sobs, and stumbled towards them.

Tino pushed past Jude, gathered her into his arms and held her. 'It's all right, Em. It's all right. I'm here. I'm going to take you away from that evil bastard and I'll look after you. It's all over.'

Ashleigh had dropped to her knees on the path. 'Not a chance, Jude. Not a chance. She's gone.' Her face was pale in the mist.

He hadn't needed to look down at Heather's body to see that much but his priority was the living, those whose lives could be saved. 'Quiet, for God's sake.' The fog had thinned, leaving them exposed and vulnerable. Somewhere close by, Rob Leach must be lingering in the fog and the undergrowth ready, if he chose, to pick them off one by one. 'Ash.' It was a whisper. 'Let's get these folk into some sort of shelter, shall we?' Though shelter was hard to come by on the fellside. 'Right now.'

'Which way did he go?' Ashleigh looked across to Emmy.

'I don't know. There was a shout and a flash. Up the hill. Off the path. Oh God.' She had the sense to keep quiet, her voice reduced to a piteous whimper. Her eyes remained riveted on Heather's corpse.

If they couldn't see Rob, he couldn't see them. That was the only blessing. Jude turned to scan the little he could see of the ground, searching for something that would give them some shelter. 'Mrs Leach. Mr Mortimer. I want you to—'

'Get your hands off my wife!'

The shout came from below the path. Jude turned towards it, instinctively placing himself between Emmy and the shot which followed as he moved.

Rob was no target shooter. The bullet whistled past, harmlessly to the left as Tino hurled Emmy to the ground and flung himself after her. At that moment the sun forced its way out and Rob Leach's crazy, distorted shadow preceded him through the thinning shroud of mist.

Jude threw himself forward. The gun went off once more, again well clear of them. His hand closed on Rob's wrist and the two of them grappled for a second before tumbling face down into the wet heather. With the benefit of the upslope and the aid of gravity, Jude moved swiftly, got the upper hand and ended with a knee in the small of Rob Leach's back. 'Ash. There are handcuffs in the pocket of my jacket.'

'You take handcuffs with you on a day off? Dear God.' She was trying to joke. 'It's funny. I do, too. Just in case.' She passed them over and Jude closed them around Rob's wrists as the man lay struggling in the mud.

'That woman,' Rob spat. 'She cheated me! And she'd have killed me, or my wife.'

'Robert Leach.' Jude cocked his head. He could hear voices, urgent in response to the shouting and the shot. 'By the power vested in me...'

Ashleigh turned towards the path as the first couple of police officers appeared. 'We're over here!'

Jude stood up. 'That's Rob Leach,' he said to them. 'Under arrest. Murder.' Initially. There would be more. 'Up the path — not far — you'll find a body. A woman. Heather Short. And there's a handgun in the heather, over there.' He gestured in the rough direction of where it had fallen when it had gone spinning from Rob's hand. He turned his back on them. 'Are you okay, Ash?'

'Sure.' She was brisk. 'I've seen a lot worse in my time. You can tell he isn't used to guns. He'd never have hit any of us at that distance.'

Rob must have taken out Heather at point blank range. 'We need to get Emmy away from here.'

'I'll take her down the path. I told them to send an ambulance, just in case.'

'Have my coat, Em,' Tino was saying, struggling out of the damp garment and draping it around her quivering shoulders. 'It's going to be all right. He'll be in prison for a long time, and that bitch isn't going to be bullying you ever again. It's all turned out all right. Didn't I always tell you it would?'

Emmy raised her head as he helped her to her feet, and clutched the jacket around her. 'No. It isn't all right. Luke was alive and I never knew. He never tried to get in touch with me. I'm his mother. Why didn't he want to see me? He must know that whatever he did I'd always forgive him. He meant more to me than any other person in the whole wide world. He knew that, and he never got in touch.'

'Don't beat yourself up about it, my darling. It wasn't you. He never got in touch with me, either.'

'But he did.' Jude was beside them on the path, listening. 'That's what you told us. That someone—'

'I didn't think it was him,' he said, swiftly. 'Take no notice, Em. I did have these messages but they weren't real.'

'How did you know they weren't real?' she demanded.

'Come on, Mrs Leach.' Ashleigh offered Emmy a hand to steady her. 'We're going to get you home and get a doctor to look at you.' She scowled at Jude, and he knew why. Tino had been trying to spare Emmy's feelings and Jude's intervention had amplified her distress.

Emmy shook her off. 'Tino. Luke contacted you and you never told me? Why? How could you do this to me?'

'Em, don't get upset. I'll explain later.'

'I'll be very interested in your explanation, Mr Mortimer.' Jude internalised a sigh. The adrenalin of the chase had ebbed and now he saw how it had all fallen out. 'Maybe you'll be able to tell me what you and Luke talked about when he was camped up on top of Tarn Crags on the night he died. And whether what he said might have made you want to kill him.'

Tino stopped in his tracks and turned. His face was a display of complete astonishment. 'How the hell do you know about that?' he asked and then stepped away. 'Shit. Shit. Now I've told you, haven't I? Now you know I did it.'

———

Emmy was still wrapped in Tino's jacket as Ashleigh O'Halloran guided her down the rough track to safety. As they descended the rough track, the fog thinned and a helicopter appeared fleetingly overhead, the rhythmic beat of rotor blades throbbing through the cloud. More police came running up the path and when Ashleigh drew her aside to let them pass, Emmy stopped for a moment and closed her eyes. When she did so she saw, not Heather's body, not Rob rearing up from the fog, not the bulging tent with her son's body, but the look on Tino's face as the chief inspector had carefully turned in his casually-phrased question. In that moment the man she loved had betrayed himself, and her, and their son.

'Are you all right, Mrs Leach?'

God would forgive her, in the end. He forgave everyone. Emmy opened her eyes and gave Sergeant O'Halloran her brightest, most social smile. 'Yes. Thank you.'

'I'm so sorry you've had such a shock.'

Finally, Emmy accepted the offer of support, resting on the sergeant's arm. Her legs were shaking but she'd insisted on making her own way down. If she'd hadn't, she'd have had to wait up there with Heather's body and her two husbands, both of them murderers, both of them destined to spend a long time behind bars. Her own future stretched ahead, a single, childless woman.

'Thank you.' She gave a sideways look and saw that the sergeant's face still bore that open expression of compassion and understanding. If they'd sent her down as the liaison officer instead of bored, judgmental Mandy Phillips she would have found it easier to talk. 'I knew, you know.'

'Did you?'

'Yes. Not exactly. Just that there was something wrong.'

'You don't have to talk about it now. There will be plenty of time later.'

Ashleigh O'Halloran wasn't like the detectives who'd interviewed her when Luke had disappeared. They'd punched hard on every half-thought she'd voiced in her grief and confusion, turning everything inside out and throwing it back at her, never allowing her any time to think until her head was a kaleidoscope of things she wasn't sure whether she'd said or just thought. 'I want to tell you about it.'

'Well, if you want to, that's fine. But you'll be asked for an official statement later on. I can't take notes just now.'

Emmy's water-filled shoes slopped along the path, rubbing her heels raw. 'I need to tell someone.'

'Then I'll listen.'

The sun crept out, a soft touch on her cheek. Even so, she still shivered. 'I think I guessed about Tino. But I didn't know. There was just something in my head, from the moment he ran off and left me up at the tarn that day. Something that made me really uneasy.'

'You were very brave to stay there on your own,' said the sergeant, quickening their pace slightly as the path evened off and became broader. 'Especially with all the memories.'

'But that was why Tino couldn't stay. Don't you see? It puzzled me, because he always said he'd do anything for me, but when it came to it he didn't. There was only one possible reason for that — that he couldn't face it, knowing what he'd done and that Luke was so close.' She forced back a tear. 'I said to him that day, when we were up there laying the flowers. I said I really wanted Luke to come back and he told me to be careful what I wished for.' Luke had already been dead, then, beginning the slow process of decomposition not fifty feet away from her. She was like the woman in *The Monkey's Paw*, who'd wished her long-dead son back and found him at the door in his grave clothes. 'I should have guessed. I know Tino so well.'

'Forgive me if it distresses you to talk about it,' said the sergeant, so carefully that Emmy had forgiven her even before the next words came out, 'but I wondered. We'd always been given to believe that Mr Mortimer got on very well with Luke.'

'I don't know. We didn't see them together. Luke went to Manchester to visit him, but that was it. Tino always said he adored Luke, but when you think about it that was a very Tino kind of thing to say. He was always telling me what a lovely bloke Rob is, and how lucky I was to have him until Tino and I could be together.' Everyone knew that deep down Tino and Rob had loathed one another, but she couldn't quite bring herself to admit it. 'It was the same with my mother. She hated him, but he would always tell people what a charming woman she was. So I don't know why I thought he'd tell the truth about what he felt about Luke.' Unless it was what she'd wanted to hear.

'Do you know why he killed him?'

It was the most gentle of interrogations. 'I don't think he wanted him dead. It was just that he couldn't process the idea of him coming back. That's all.' They were almost at the bottom of the track now, and there was an ambulance parked up against the gate, with two paramedics waiting. Emmy heaved a sigh of relief. 'Will you be the person who takes my statement?'

If only she'd been able to talk to Ashleigh O'Halloran earlier. But it was over now; or the worst of it was.

THIRTY

'Luke had changed,' said Tino Mortimer. He was sitting in the interview room and addressing himself not to Jude or to Ashleigh, or even to his solicitor, but to the recording device in the middle of the table. His arrest for murder seemed to have done nothing to dampen his spirits — if anything the opposite — and even his statement was veined with his natural, bubbly optimism, though underpinned by a melancholy strain. 'Oh, I loved him. Don't get me wrong. You love your children whatever they do. But it's hell when they stop loving you.'

Did they ever? Jude thought, briefly, of Mikey, whose threats to cut himself off from their father for ever never came to anything. Maybe a child who felt rejection merely recast their love into a fixated, toxic rebellion. 'How had he changed? Since when?'

'He was such a sweet toddler. An angel child. He had golden curls, blonde like my mother and the curls that came from my sister — the white sister. I was so proud of him. He was a sunny, smiley little boy. Even after Emmy left me — and God, it was her mother who did that, and the woman's a witch — he was a sweet and loving boy. It was Rob who ruined him.'

Jude was no psychologist but he was an observer of human nature. Everything about Rob Leach suggested this was plausible. In his confession, which had been as clipped as Tino's promised to be rambling, he had been self-right-eous in justification of his every action. 'You didn't see much of Luke after you moved away, though.'

He'd taken care to keep his tone neutral but Tino, lifting his eyes from the table, gave him a reproachful look nonetheless, as if he took that as a criticism. 'You won't believe me but that was for Emmy's sake.'

'Is that right?'

As so many interviewees did, Tino turned away from Jude and towards Ashleigh. 'She liked you. She said you understood. So you might understand what it's like to love someone so much that it consumes you.'

Ashleigh inclined her head to indicate that he should continue, but Jude spotted the rueful smile she couldn't hide. 'Carry on.'

'I love Emmy. I've loved her since the moment I saw her. She isn't just beautiful. She's fundamentally good, the best person I've ever met.' He laughed, out of nowhere. 'I'm not a great Christian myself, if you must know, but I knew she'd never have me if I wasn't so I pretended to begin with, and then it kind of became a habit. As long as I thought there was chance for me with her I kept making the effort, but I was never as devout as she was. And I was never as good at pretending as Rob.'

He picked at his fingernail and frowned. 'Luke was a difficult teenager. I'd expected that. I tried to be patient with him and he wasn't bad with me, but that was because I never spent a lot of time with him and when I did it was easier to spoil him and let Rob pick up the pieces. I wasn't surprised when he disappeared and I didn't think he was dead. I just thought Rob had pushed him too far and he'd come back when he was ready. Emmy would realise Rob was the problem and she'd ditch him, and then she'd find I'd been waiting for her all that time.' A shrug of resignation, a shake of the head in regret. 'It never happened.'

'Were you aware Mr Leach has admitted to taking out a contract on your son when he first disappeared?' asked Jude. Rob's confession, blatant in its coldness, would sting Emmy to the heart when she heard of it.

'No,' said Tino, and put his head in his hands, but only for a second. 'Ha. It's not like Rob to do business without guarantees.'

'He paid Heather Short to do it but she took the money and didn't do the deed. Not, I suspect, out of the goodness of her heart, but because she had alternative ways of making use of him.'

'It was her, was it? That got him in with the bad lot? I don't know if I want to know what happened to him in those years. What I do know is when he came back he wasn't my son any more. He was like an animal.'

'You told us you didn't respond when he contacted you.'

'I didn't reply to his messages. It wasn't that I didn't believe it was him. I knew in my heart it was. But I needed time to think about what it meant, and how it would affect Emmy, and whether it would hurt her or whether it would drive her closer to Rob. I hadn't finished working out what I'd do when he came to see me.'

'At home?'

'No. At work. That was before Christmas. I was delighted to see him but he'd changed.' Tino's expression sagged into regret. 'He wanted money and it was obvious what he wanted it for, but I gave it to him because I didn't know what else to do. In the New Year he was back and he was more aggressive. He wanted more. If I didn't give it to him he said he'd go storming up to Blacksty Farm and tell Emmy lies about me. I couldn't risk that. She'd believe anything he told her. He was her boy.' He shook his head. 'I tried to talk to him but there was nothing in him that I could reach. Drugs do that to you, if they get a hold. However hard I tried, and whatever I did, he was lost to me and he would be to Emmy, too.'

'Is that why you decided to kill him?' asked Ashleigh.

He looked hurt, as though this was an unjust and slanderous allegation. 'It wasn't that I didn't care, but although I'm an optimist I'm a realist, too. After the second meeting I understood. Luke wasn't just a threat to himself. He was a threat to any chance I had with Emmy.'

'You seem to have made pretty good progress with Emmy,' said Ashleigh, dryly, 'judging by the photographs and video.'

'Oh.' He laughed, a self-conscious snigger. 'God will damn me for it, I suppose, in her thinking at least, but I love that woman. I pressurised her into it, I admit it, but she didn't need a lot of tempting. We both knew she'd feel guilty afterwards and I was hoping she'd leave Rob, but she was scared of him. I didn't know why, because she said he was never violent.'

Jude thought back to the team meeting when Ashleigh had put her finger on it. Emmy knew Rob was capable of violence, was sure enough of it to let it determine how she lived her life but not sure enough to do something about it. 'What happened at your last meeting with Luke?'

'Oh, God. Well, that was it. Luke's a smart kid, or he was, but the drugs had got to his brain so he didn't really think things through. He told me what he was going to do.

He knew we go up to the tarn on the anniversary of the day he disappeared. I don't know how, but he knew. He said he'd be waiting for us. I knew I couldn't let him surprise Emmy and I knew I couldn't tell her. I told him I'd make damned sure he didn't distress his mother and he said I couldn't stop him. He'd be up there all night. So, obviously.' He shrugged.

'You went up there in the dark?'

'Yes. I was going to park by the barn and walk up, but the road was closed, so I had to walk from the main road. I went up there in the dark and I couldn't see anything at the tarn itself, but there was a light up at the top, so I scrambled up, and there he was. I asked him, as a father to a son, to leave Emmy alone. He agreed, on condition I gave him more money. I was to bring it and leave it at the tarn the next day, in an agreed spot. If I didn't indicate to him that I'd done that, he'd show himself. And, worse, he had the pictures.'

'Of you and Emmy?'

'Yes. He had the camera with him and showed me. And the look in his eyes. I never for a moment thought he wouldn't do it. I'd have to pay him. I knew how that would end, too.'

Blackmail followed the same track, in every case. A small payment became a demand for a bigger one, ever-increasing amounts at ever-decreasing intervals until the victim cracked. 'Why didn't you just call the police?'

'I didn't think of it. I was up there in the dark with my boy and he was a stranger to me. He was threatening to undermine what I'd been waiting and hoping for for years and was within touching distance — prising Emmy out of the clutches of that sociopath she's married to. He was our son and he'd have stolen our happy ever after. I agreed to everything he asked and I went away and I waited until the light went out and I was sure he was asleep. And then…'

The first signs of remorse. A tear gathered in his eye, but it wasn't clear who it was for. Luke, perhaps, but more likely for Emmy or himself. 'You know what happened,' he said to Jude, reproachfully.

'I'd like your version.'

Tino put his head on his hands again and, when he raised it, addressed himself once more to Ashleigh. 'I crept around and lifted the guy ropes and then I collapsed the tent. He woke up and started shouting and swearing but I managed to get behind it and heaved it over the edge. He went bouncing down and I was going to run but I remembered. The camera. So I went down and the tent was under water. I waited until I was sure he was dead and then I fished it out and took the camera. I thought it might be missed so I took the card and threw the camera away.'

'Do you still have it?'

'Yes, but it was damaged. Maybe your lot can retrieve something from it. I couldn't.' He shrugged. 'And then I went home. And the next morning I parked at the bottom because I knew the road to Mosedale was closed and that was when someone saw me and snitched to the police. I'll have something to say if I ever find out who it was.'

'I saw you.' Jude pushed his chair back. Tino's confession was as complete as Rob's had been, but there was a much greater honesty about it. 'You must have had a hell of a shock when you were sent those pictures.'

'Oh God, yes. I had a mad moment when I thought he wasn't dead, but then I realised. Someone else had a copy of them. I thought it might be Rob but I wasn't sure, and now of course we know it was the woman. If I'd known who it was at the time, I'd have killed her, too. But Rob did the job for me, in the end.'

THIRTY-ONE

We *should go out for a drink tonight,* Jude had said as he and Ashleigh parted in the car park that evening, *to make up for missing lunch.* And she'd said no.

Her excuse had been exhaustion. Emmy's distress had been emotionally draining and the debriefing session which had followed Tino and Rob's confessions had been thorough. Faye, who was as obsessed with the public perception of justice as she was with its execution, had counted Heather's death as a failure and seemed to think they could somehow have prevented it.

It wasn't the real reason. She'd enjoyed that morning's walk too much, just as she'd enjoyed the drink she and Jude had shared at the wine bar. Her experience with Scott had taught her the folly of harking back to the echoes of an old relationship.

'Christ, Ash. I know you have bad days at work, but at least tell me about it and get it off your chest. Or if you can't tell me, tell your bloody tarot cards about it.' Lisa poked a concerned head around the living room door.

Ashleigh had rendered her pack of cards useless in that moment of frustration when she'd set fire to the King of Swords, and there was no image that could do justice to Emmy's pained and total submission to the punishment for her mistakes. 'I can't settle.'

'You need some self care, my lass, that's what you need.' Lisa hesitated. 'Do you want to talk? I've got time.'

Lisa was dressed up to go out, and heading for the pub. Ashleigh shook her head. She was ready to talk, but once she got started she could go on all night and easily end up in tears and Lisa, no matter how handsome the offer, wouldn't understand. 'No. I had a crap day and someone got shot and killed and we didn't get there in time. I hate that there was nothing we could do to stop it.' Faye had made her feel they should have done. 'Don't you worry. Tonight I'll sink a couple of large glasses of something, and tomorrow the psychologists and everyone will be crawling all over me and I'll be looked after to within an inch of my life.'

'You can call me any time, though.' Lisa saw herself out of the house and the clip of her high heels echoed for a few seconds as she headed down the street.

It took less than five minutes for Ashleigh to realise that distraction was a better option than isolation. She regretted having turned Jude down; he must feel as drained by the afternoon's events as she did, and the chance to talk about other things would have done them both good.

On impulse, she scooped up her coat and bag and headed down the hill towards the town and up to Wordsworth Street, where Jude lived. The fog had finally lifted and a flash of late afternoon sunshine had rapidly ceded the countryside to a snap frost that persisted into the darkness. Her feet slithered a little on the icy pavement and she caught at a lamppost to regain her balance. In a flat at the bottom of the street, Adam Fleetwood sat in his living room, watching television with the curtains open.

Jude didn't look in the least surprised when he opened the door. 'Have you changed your mind? You should have called. We could have gone down to town and had fish and chips after all, only with a drink to wash it down.'

'I've already eaten.'

'I can offer you a drink, at least.'

'A G&T would go down nicely.' She followed him into the house, checking her hair and makeup swiftly in the ancient mirror that hung in the hall. It had been several months since they'd stopped dating and she hadn't been in the house since then. He'd moved some of the furniture around but the mirror was reassuringly constant.

'Have a seat.'

She made herself comfortable in the living room, as she used to. Jude's laptop was on the arm of the chair. 'Don't you ever stop working? It's past eight and today of all days, I think you need a break. It's your day off, remember?'

'Yours, too,' he said from the kitchen over the chinking of bottle, glasses and ice. 'After this afternoon's shenanigans I've enough forms to fill in to sink a ship, never mind the actual case notes and so on. Having said that, I'm delighted that you called so I've an excuse not to do it.'

He came back in with a G&T and a beer for himself. 'Are you okay? Struggling?'

'Lisa's away out. But yes, I am a bit down and I wanted someone to talk to. I know you'll understand.'

'Always happy to help.' He raised his glass in salute.

She settled into the comfortable familiarity of his old sofa. 'I know what you'll say, but I can't help myself. It's preying on my mind. I know I could have helped Emmy. She as good as said so.' *If you'd been my FLO I'd have told you everything*, Emmy had said, wearily, *even the things I didn't realise I knew.*

'Yes. I've no doubt about that. If I wanted to put someone into that household who I knew she'd trust, I'd have picked you, without hesitation.'

She swirled the ice in her glass in fury. It hadn't been Emmy's fault, or Mandy's, that the two of them hadn't got on, but Jude should have spotted it. 'Then why didn't you? Faye thought it was a good idea.'

'Up to a point. But we've been here before. You're already more emotionally invested with the woman than you ought to be and in the end that rebounds on you.'

'But Emmy—'

'It's not about Emmy. Rob never hurt her and if she'd reported him there probably wouldn't have been enough evidence to do anything. He'd have had a stern warning at best.'

The merry-go-round would have carried on. Luke was already dead and Emmy and Tino already compromised; Heather had cheated Rob and he knew it. Nothing about the final outcome would have changed. 'I wanted to help. She stayed with him because she was punishing herself.' She sipped, the gin sharp and refreshing on her tongue.

'This is the problem isn't it?' he said. 'It's why I sent Mandy, not you.'

'But—'

'Why does Emmy resonate so much with you? Why do you feel her pain as much as you do?'

The clock on the wall shifted a few seconds forward as Ashleigh thought yet again of Emmy, her goodness downtrodden, her heart always heavy with self-loathing. 'I don't know.'

'Let me put it this way.' He looked beyond her, at the wall behind her shoulder. 'The case echoes for me, too. In my case it's the father-son dynamic that made me think. When I think of Luke I see what might have happened to Mikey if we'd been less lucky. I look at the way Luke fought with his stepfather and I see the way Mikey struggles with Dad.'

'Luke struggled with Tino, too.'

'Yes. And in Mikey's case there's Adam.'

Ashleigh thought of Adam Fleetwood, believing himself wronged, sitting in the rented flat he'd taken just to be a thorn in his former friend's flesh. 'The equivalent of Heather.'

'Yes. Both Luke and Mikey had that older friend who made much of them and supplied them with drugs. I can't help thinking of that. I think it's the same with you and Emmy. Something that rings so true in your own life it hurts.'

'I suppose so.' Ashleigh thought of Scott, a part of her life for so long that the mark he'd left on it would never fade. 'Emmy left the man she loved and it made her unhappy. That made me think. It made me want to help her.'

'Right. But when I stop to think about it, I see the differences as well as the similarities. Mikey didn't get caught up in the really bad stuff. He still loves Dad, and that's why it hurts him so much.'

'I see.' David Satterthwaite hadn't been there when Mikey had needed him and Tino hadn't been there for Luke.

'Yes. Luke took help from someone and the next thing he knew he was hooked on the hard stuff and couldn't get off it. It's no wonder he was reduced to hawking photos of his mum and dad having sex.' He shook his head. 'At least Adam, God help him, never got in so deeply that he was using people to that extent. He went to prison but he came out reformed. He'll never forgive me for it, but it was the best thing that could have happened to him under the circumstances. So yes. Use the similarities to empathise, but don't make parallels where they aren't there. Similar cases don't always end the same way. You and Scott aren't a parallel for Emmy and Rob.'

'Quite the speech,' said Ashleigh, lightly. Her glass was already empty and the gin had gone straight to her head in a pleasantly mellowing way.

'Am I lecturing? I didn't meant to. I was trying to help.'

'You are helping.' She put the glass down. 'Emmy could have left Rob, if she wanted, couldn't she? She chose to stay with him.'

'And why did she leave Tino? Maybe, after all, he wasn't as good for her as he thinks he is, and deep down she knows that. It's not as if he was completely faithful to her after they split up.'

'He wasn't?'

'There were a few girlfriends along the way. It's in the file on the cold case. You should have a read of it.'

She stretched her legs out towards the electric fire and felt her shoulders sag into the comfy old sofa in relaxation. Maybe it was the gin. Maybe it was wise advice. 'I'll always love Scott.'

'Right. But you don't need to let it stop you having any other relationships. Life moves on.'

Scott had already moved on. Lisa, who was an old school friend of both of them, had seen a picture of him on Facebook with a new girlfriend, up a mountain some-where in the French Alps on a skiing holiday. 'It doesn't seem fair to have a new relationship with someone you don't love. That's all. And it's so hard knowing you'll never move on.'

'A new relationship is fair enough if you're honest with a new partner.'

Jude was still in love with Becca. She knew that, had known it even before they started dating. It hadn't stopped her taking him on and in the end the relationship, though it was one she'd ended, wasn't one she thought she'd ever regret. She flashed a grin at him. 'I was honest with you. Wasn't I?'

He smiled back. 'Painfully so. At the beginning and at the end. Does that matter? I know where you stand. You know where I stand.'

She did, but she didn't think he understood his own situation. He thought it was over between Becca and himself, an exact parallel with the final line Ashleigh had drawn under her marriage to Scott. 'What if Becca wants you back?'

'She won't.'

'What if you decide to try again?'

'I asked her and she turned me down flat. I have my pride. I'm not going to risk being humiliated like that again.'

When she looked at him she thought he was being honest with himself, but she also knew he was wrong. If Becca realised what she'd lost, he'd be back with her like a shot. In the meantime, did it matter? Some people might closet themselves away for the rest of their lives just because they lost a lover, but she wasn't one of them. She hated sleeping alone, liked to wake in the night and reach out a hand to find some human warmth behind her. She loved to make love. She'd had all of that when she'd dated Jude, who was more considerate of other people than Scott had ever been, and who was unquestionably good in bed, and yet she'd allowed Scott, a no-hoper, to live rent-free in her head until she'd ended a relationship that worked in a vain attempt to revive one that didn't. 'I think you and I will always be friends. It's just that neither of us will make the mistake of thinking we love each other.' They'd learned their lesson and both of them would be able to live with the knowledge of their unrequited loves.

'Love's overrated,' he said, scratching his head, 'and when it gets toxic it can be pretty destructive. Look at Tino and Emmy. I'm not going to lie. I've missed having you around. You're good company.' He winked. 'You can cook. Sort of. So if you want to stick around a bit longer, that's fine by me.'

'That sounds good to me.'

'Brilliant,' he said, and the smile turned to a broad grin. 'Something good's come out of today, then. Now why don't I go and get us another drink?

ALSO BY JO ALLEN

Death by Dark Waters

DCI Jude Satterthwaite #1

It's high summer, and the Lakes are in the midst of an unrelenting heatwave. Uncontrollable fell fires are breaking out across the moors faster than they can be extinguished. When firefighters uncover the body of a dead child at the heart of the latest blaze, Detective Chief Inspector Jude Satterthwaite's arson investigation turns to one of murder. Jude was born and bred in the Lake District. He knows everyone — and everyone knows him. Except his intriguing new Detective Sergeant, Ashleigh O'Halloran, who is running from a dangerous past and has secrets of her own to hide. Temperatures – and tensions – are increasing, and with the body count rising Jude and his team race against the clock to catch the killer before it's too late...

The first in the gripping, Lake District-set, DCI Jude Satterthwaite series.

Death at Eden's End

DCI Jude Satterthwaite #2

When one-hundred-year-old Violet Ross is found dead at Eden's End, a luxury care home hidden in a secluded nook of Cumbria's Eden Valley, it's not unexpected. Except for the instantly recognisable look in her lifeless eyes — that of pure terror. DCI Jude Satterthwaite heads up the investigation, but as the deaths start to mount up it's clear that he and DS Ashleigh O'Halloran need to uncover a long-buried secret before the killer strikes again...

The second in the unmissable, Lake District-set, DCI Jude Satterthwaite series.

Death on Coffin Lane

DCI Jude Satterthwaite #3

DCI Jude Satterthwaite doesn't get off to a great start with resentful Cody Wilder, who's visiting Grasmere to present her latest research on Wordsworth. With some of the villagers unhappy about her visit, it's up to DCI Satterthwaite to protect her – especially when her assistant is found hanging in the kitchen of their shared cottage.

With a constant flock of tourists and the local hippies welcoming in all who cross their paths, Jude's home in the Lake District isn't short of strangers. But with the ability to make enemies wherever she goes, the violence that follows in Cody's wake leads DCI Satterthwaite's investigation down the hidden paths of those he knows, and those he never knew even existed.

A third mystery for DCI Jude Satterthwaite to solve, in this gripping novel by best-seller Jo Allen.

Death at Rainbow Cottage

DCI Jude Satterthwaite #4

At the end of the rainbow, a man lies dead.

The apparently motiveless murder of a man outside the home of controversial equalities activist Claud Blackwell and his neurotic wife, Natalie, is shocking enough for a peaceful local community. When it's followed by another apparently random killing immediately outside Claud's office, DCI Jude Satterthwaite has his work cut out. Is Claud the killer, or the intended victim?

To add to Jude's problems, the arrival of a hostile new boss causes complications at work, and when a threatening note arrives at the police headquarters, he has real cause to fear for the safety of his friends and colleagues…

A traditional British detective novel set in Cumbria.

Death on the Lake

ACKNOWLEDGMENTS

There are too many people who have helped me with this book for me to name them individually: I hope those I don't mention will forgive me.

I have to thank my lovely beta readers – Amanda, Frances, Julie, Kate, Katey, Liz, Lorraine, Pauline, Sally and Sara – who not only read and commented but also produced support and suggestions throughout the process. I'd also like to thank Graham Bartlett, who kindly advised me on aspects of police procedure. Mary Jayne Baker delivered, as always, a stunning cover.

Finally, as before, I owe a huge debt of gratitude to the eagle-eyed Keith Sutherland, for proofreading.

Printed in Great Britain
by Amazon